Autograph P

Beg For Mercy

A Dark Conclusion

By Lucian Bane

© 2015 by Lucian Bane

All rights reserved. No part of this document may be reproduced or transmitted in any form or by any means, electronic, mechanical, photocopying, recording, or otherwise, without prior written permission of Lucian Bane or his legal representative.

To all the readers, fans, and or reader's clubs. Thank you for supporting my work. I'd also like to ask nicely that you please not Pirate my work. That basically means don't give it away just because you bought it. If you know of anybody that can't afford a copy, just let me know. I'm a nice guy. ☺

Also, if you need a different format, please contact me, the author.

Dedication

This book is dedicated to my beautiful, amazing, gorgeous wife. I love you forever. Thank you so much for putting up with me, for believing in me, for loving me.

Acknowledgements:

KIM POE! THANK YOU. You literally saved my ass in so many ways. I don't know how to thank you enough. It has been quite a ride and I would not have stayed on the pony express had it not been for you. Bottom of my heart thank you.

JAN KINDER. Huge hugs sweetheart. You came in on that white horse, your sword and shield in hand, hacking and whacking at the endless jobs that will never really be done, lol. Nice to have you on board.

SUPER DUPER THANKS To the AWESOME BETA READERS:
KELLY MALLET~ LORAINE CAMBELL~HILLARY SUPPES~TAMMY SINGLETON-BURCH, JAN KINDER and TERRIE MEERSCHAERT!
And now, thank you to my **ENTIRE TEAM!**
LADIES! BOOM BRINGERS! HOLY HELL, YOU ALL ROCK SO HARD!

MERCY DIVISION

FB Groups Team: Cathy Schisel Knuth & Catherine Byerly Coffman
Tsu: Hilary Suppes & Robin Cornelius
Instagram: Louisa Gray
Twitter Team: Kristin Hoard, Nan Lindsay & Michelle Fortress Brown

Google +: Jenny McKinney Shephard & Kathi Goldwyn

DOM WARS DIVISION~ Jan Wade (ROYAL PRINCESS)

FB Groups Team: Captain: Terrie Meerschaert (Sherri Maughan former co-captain)

TSU: Jessie Mora LLewellyn & Tina Eastridge Henry

Instagram: Lianne Heaps : Joy Chapman

Twitter: Katherine DiLauro & Alicia Huckleby

Google +: Mary Forster & Katherine DiLauro

MERGED DIVISIONS

Goodreads Team: Kimmy Johnson, Nathalie Pinette & Jan Kinder

FB Pimping Team: Lorraine Campbell Darcy

FB Contests Team: Lorraine Campbell Darch & Kelly Mallett

Amazon Team: Elaine Kelly & Edith Dubielak

AWESOME PARTY TEAM

Tammy Singleton Burch

Nan Lindsey

Linda Kidwell

Due to space restrictions, the entire list of team members can be found at the end of this great ass book!

Game Winners in Beg For Mercy

Game: What Does Sade's mother look like: Louisa Gray (Picture)

Island Amenities: Emma Jane Marie, Tami Czenkus, Agnese Kohn (Pictures)

Speed Game: When Sade was 3 years old, some of the things he did

Ellie Masters 1. avoid every crack on the sidewalk, just to make sure he didn't break his mother's back. And: 2. He would draw a picture of an angel and put it under his mother's pillow to protect her. 3. He saved his money so his mommy didn't have to sleep with all those bad men. 4. save earth worms

Kim Poe cried at the animals dead on the side of the road

Tammy Singleton Burch 1. Dressed up as a super hero and say he'd save her from all the bad pple 2. Gave her pennies from heaven that he found

Hilary Suppes Tell his momma how good of a mom she was

Mary Carmen Corrao hold his mother's hand when she cried

Game: Pick out their mini mansion in Phillipines: Ruby Hinkleberry (picture)

Game: Make a Playlist

Yvette Grimes~ Muse: Madness

Ruby Hinkleberry~Maryilyn Manson: Killing Strangers

Ruby Hinkleberry~ Rob Bailey & The Hustle Standard: BEAST

Jenny McKinney Shepard~ Imagine Dragons: Demons

Kimmy Johnson~Weekend~Wicked Games

Lyndsey Fairley~ Three Days Grace: Animal I Have Become

Bridget McEvoy~ White Zombie: Blood Milk and Sky

Mary Carmen Corraro~Nine Inch Nails: Closer

Kristen Grammar Lands~30 Seconds to Mars: Hurricane

Louisa Gray~Blake McGrath: Earned it

Mary Forster~Three Days Grace: Chalk Outline

Katherine DiLauro~ Him: You're so Beautiful

Becky Blagola~Ed Sheeran: Make It Rain

Valerie Vital~ Joi: Lick

Elena Cruz~Massive Attack: Tear Drop

Sammie Woods~Khia: My Neck, My Back

Valerie Vital~Marilyn Manson: Sweet Dreams

Chapter One

As per Kane's request, there was a party on the beach with friends from the island to celebrate his mother's return from the dead. But Sade knew better. What it was really for was to take the edge off. Kane saw the edge, felt the edge, brooded over the edge, same as Sade. Same as Bo. Abraham was alive and coming, despite the impossibility of him ever finding them, he was coming. Did they know that as well as Sade did? He wasn't sure. But Sade knew it, smelled it, tasted it, breathed it. For the week since they saw the creepy bastard on TV, karma laughed non-stop like a sick fucking hyena, allowing him no more than thirty minutes of sleep at a time.

And Mercy. Fucking angelic Mercy, trying so hard to accommodate him even while not knowing what was actually going through his head. She knew something was going on and he knew it was only a matter of time before he'd have to come clean. She needed him in every way. Everything she did, every look, move, smile and gesture, begged him for one thing. Make love to me. Please. I'm dying for it, for you.

And therein lay the other major problem.

His body was a wreck along with his mind. His past addictions were spinning in desperation and it was taking everything he had to keep from flying apart. The hunger to hurt and be hurt had never been more volatile and each second he didn't connect with Mercy, it grew worse. But how exactly was a monster cyclone supposed to connect with an angel and not rip her apart in ways that made him feel vile and dirty? Fuck, he never wanted to feel that with her.

Sade tilted his head back and chugged half the bottle of beer while absently turning the meat on the grill and eyeing Mercy. Mercy dancing with that jubilant, lanky, cockroach looking fucker named Ralph. Sade had wondered when she would finally have enough of his distance. When she'd see it as rejection instead of him being so wound tight that one wrong move would snap him.

Well, he had his answer. He really had his answer, and holy fuck the night was not going to end well.

"You need me to take over?"

Kane's sudden voice on his right nearly put him out of his skin.

"Sorry." Kane draped an arm around Sade's shoulder and held him with a grip that said he was measuring his tension. "We need to talk."

Ah, fuck. "About what?" Sade was ready to shake him off as Mercy headed toward the house with ole Ralphy eying her.

"What's in that head of yours. You can't keep holding it all in."

"I can't let it out, either."

"Why not? Mercy is fine, look at me."

"She's not fine." Sade chugged the rest of his beer and set it on the pit.

"Why do you say that?" His wonder was light but Sade felt it, he was holding something back.

He watched Ralphy finally turn in the opposite direction of Mercy before giving Kane his attention. "Because I'm not fine."

Kane met Sade's gaze and locked it with a surprising vicious current. "Well then, you need to get fine."

Sade held that gaze, testing the threat weighing in his words.

"You're thinking correctly, son. Get it together or we're going to take a ride and help you get it together."

Sade's muscles locked in reflex to the odd threat. He held the man's intense blue gaze, his mind at war with the senseless need for blood and pain. But Kane wasn't the enemy. "We're supposed to sit here and wait for that monster to show up at our door?"

Kane held his gaze for endless seconds before finally looking forward. "Well.... what do you think we should do?"

Adrenalin lit up Sade's body at his tone. It wasn't the lethal in his question, it was the intention. Kane intended to do something. And that was exactly what Sade needed. To do something. Anything.

Sade looked around, feeling like the amount of murder suddenly swirling in the air around them would be sensed a mile out. But everybody carried on without a clue, dancing merrily in the island's sultry night. Sade finally looked at Kane, unable to hide his desperate hunger for that something, that anything. The animal inside him surfaced and stared, unable to care who saw it. And then it was suddenly there, right there in the depths of those clear blue eyes. How had he missed it? Maybe it was always there and he only saw it now, looking through his own sick lens. But it was vile and vicious and yet... not.

The contradiction held Sade captivated, making him want to analyze, taste, and discover the difference. Compare the monsters. Maybe see if they could be playmates. Partners. Linked by darkness and sadistic blood.

"I say we hunt the monster," Kane muttered.

Sade's heart hammered in his chest from the sheer excitement. Not just from Kane's words but the hunger carrying them. "How?" Sade whispered.

Kane looked forward again with a slight smile, his tongue sweeping over his lower lip. "Bait it." The calm words came with a direct gaze from those clear, almost innocent blue eyes—same gaze he might wear in church on Sunday. "With something it can't resist."

Ideas exploded in Sade's head like glorious fireworks. "He's into me," Sade whispered. "In a sick way."

Kane drew his head back sharply with a shocked-not-so-shocked look. "Is he." The stated question came with a little grin. But the raw hunger burning bright in his gaze said he'd known that all along. "Imagine that," he whispered, fascinated. "Father Abe, all into you." He chuckled while shaking his head before looking forward again. "Can it get any more perfect than that? I don't think it can."

Fury snaked through Sade, dark and cold as he shot a quick glance around again. "Tell me," he muttered, stepping closer. "Tell me what to do and you can consider it done."

Kane's face had gone unreadable as he studied the ocean. "I'll handle the particulars Son, you don't worry about that. How about you go on and connect with Mercy? Like she needs you to." He swiveled a look at Sade that said he wasn't suggesting nicely. But ordering him. "Preferably before you kill poor Ralph."

The hammering in Sade's heart ricocheted in his dick at the sudden mention of Mercy needing. He realized in that instant just how hungry his body was for her. For his Mercy. To have her in every way for every wretched purpose and illogical reason. To use her perfectly and entirely, to own her with his totalitarian cock and sadistic might.

Heat throbbed in his muscles as he made his way to the house. "Yeah, you're excused," Kane muttered behind him, low laughter in his voice.

With every step toward Mercy, his body tensed with wild urges. Flashes of her naked body accompanied his search on the lower floor. A sheen of sweat covered him as he took the stairs slowly, quietly, two at a time.

Terror set his pulse at a furious thunder as the animal inside got ready to play. But there was something unfamiliar about it. The thing inside wanted to hunt. Wanted to terrify. It wanted to trap and capture. Sade's breath became ragged with the urges burning him.

He fought the devils in his mind with every step he took. But he could feel the new depth he crept around in. The new layer of sick just below the old one. Fuck. Where it came from, what and why, wasn't important in that second. It was what would it ask of him? Demand of him?

Reaching the landing of the second floor, the answer to that question sang with a deadly hum in his blood. It sang irrelevant. It's alllllll irrelevant, Sade. Because there was no turning back now. His body moved stealthily, right through the turmoil in his muscles as he fought to negotiate and beg for a safe balance.

He slowly opened her bedroom door and peeked in. God, fuck. She was naked. Facedown on the bed, inciting a riot in his already unstable body. Unmoving, he waited for his intentions to clue him in. He carefully closed the door and locked it then made his way to her bed. Felt like forever since he'd let himself look at her. And now, that brutal denial was kicking his ass, making him work for his oxygen.

He approached from the left side of the bed and let his eyes get their hungry fill. Slowly. She was splayed out, arms extended at both sides, one leg partially off the bed like she'd nearly missed when collapsing onto it. Why had she gotten naked? Jealousy made his cock ache as he slowly removed his t-shirt. He wanted to savor every second of what he was doing. All night. At least he hoped whatever had a hold insisted he go all night.

He was past the point of caring about how far he might go and what he might do, he just cared that he was doing it. Finally. Finally he'd have his Mercy, he'd have the fuck out of her. And the rest... well, he'd deal with that devil when he reached that fiery crossroad.

Sade removed his pants next, his eyes on her succulent ass. At that moment, his cock jerked with an undeniable need and hunger. To be buried in that tight heat. He let his groan go, not caring about silence.

He walked slowly around to the other side of the bed, waiting for his body to tell him what he'd do first. His heart hammered with too many desires, too many things scrambling for his selection. He wanted everything. He wanted it slow and fast, soft, and so very fucking hard.

He paused next to the bed. What if she didn't cooperate?

The thought brought a slow burning in his muscles, telling him how he'd handle that. He'd have it. That's all he knew, that's all he allowed himself to know. And if it triggered other things... he'd deal with it. Either way, he was going to explore what crawled through his blood.

How did he want her? His gaze scanned her body, making his own burn and tremble. At reaching the lighter skin on her ass where the sun hadn't kissed, his cock jerked. The darker skin surrounding it was like a personal invitation to his cock—ram me, ram me, ram me. Don't stop, God don't stop.

Just like she was, that's how he wanted her. On her stomach. His body pressing hard into hers, fingers tangled in that silky hair. Angling that shocked face to his, feeling her hot breaths and cries as her tight ass clenched his cock, and she fucking begged him. His breath rushed out. He didn't care what she begged for, just so she fucking begged him.

Or did he care?

He stood there, dizzy, gaze roving over her. Come on you monster, tell me what you want. Show me. His muscles remained on lock down right up to the point when she broke his shackles with a tiny whimper—a delicate lick along the head of his cock.

Another wave of euphoric desire rocked him. He climbed on the bed and placed his palms carefully on either side of her. Holding himself above her, that dark hunger tethered his mind, forcing his gaze down at a tormenting pace. He leaned closer and panted quietly, licking along his lips to taste the air. Inhaling her, his eyes locked on her glowing ass right next to his cock that hung inches from her inner thigh. The hammering of his heart throbbed in it, and he clenched his eyes shut, letting the beautiful torment suck at his balls.

She suddenly moaned and turned on her side. Sade held his breath when her hip slid along his cock. Fucking perfect, she was perfect torment. The smell of alcohol intensified as he gasped down at her profile. He'd driven his sweet Mercy to get drunk. To forget what she needed and couldn't get. The need to make restitution brought his lips to her cheek and his cock to rub along her thigh. She moaned softly and turned her head presenting her innocent neck.

The sight shattered the lock-down on his body and in a rush of raging desire, he grabbed her wrists and pinned them above her head, biting and sucking that silk with brutal intensity.

She exploded to life and he growled, bearing his body down on hers. "Don't fucking move," he rasped, his mouth not leaving her neck. "I need you," he shuddered. "I'm going crazy."

Her confused cries turned to desperate moans. "Sade," she whispered, managing to squirm until her legs locked around his waist. The feel of her nakedness gnawed at his control and he growled his way to her mouth until their teeth and tongues clashed. "Do it, please," she begged in his mouth. "I need you, oh God, I need you."

"Hold on to the fucking bed," he growled, "I'm going to eat the fuck out of your pussy."

He made his way down, stopping to bite and suck on her tits. "Sade!" she cried.

Finally between her legs, he stared at her pussy. "God. Open wide for me," he grit. "Fucking show me how bad you want it." He pumped his cock onto the bed, watching as she pulled her knees back until her toes pointed.

Sade growled at the sight and dove on her open pussy, twirling his tongue at the bottom of that perfect slit before dragging the broad side of it up and creating a firestorm on her clit with flicks. When she gave high-pitched moans, he drew back barely, desire pounding through his veins. "Jesus fucking Christ, your pussy," he gasped, plunging his tongue inside with a groan while sliding his nose roughly on her clit.

"Oh my God, Sade," she cried weakly.

"Hold the fucking bed, Mercy, I swear," he ordered when her fingers raked in his hair. "Don't fucking disobey again." She held the bed and he shoved a finger inside her, then another, feeling every inch of her. "Do you fucking know what you do to me? Do you? Do you fucking know? Jesus Christ tell me you know what you do to me, fucking tell me," he gasped, his lips on her again as her hot silk spasmed around his fingers and those sounds she made drove him to need things he should never need, could never need.

"So very fucking good," he whispered, opening his mouth wide and sucking on her inner thigh with a deep groan, pulling with the same intensity that he stroked her core with.

"Please, don't stop, don't stop!" She bowed off the bed and he pulled his fingers out and shoved them in his mouth. "Fucking pussy," he moaned eating her off him with lusty grunts. "Fuck, I'm going to make you scream," he gasped, grabbing her hips roughly and yanking that hot silk onto his open mouth.

"Oh Jesus," she strained, shuddering.

Holding her ass in a brutal grip he sucked and nibbled all over, growling with her every shudder and tremble in his hands and under his mouth. He delivered chaotic flicks of his tongue on the tip of her clit until his name was a constant plea, and she was right at orgasm.

He pulled away, his breaths quaking as he thrust his cock onto the bed, ready to fucking come, but even more ready to deny himself. But not her, though. Mercy needed to take whatever he wanted to give her.

Chapter Two

Mercy had gone from drunk to nearly sober in five minutes. God, she needed him. And it was as barbaric as it was pathetic. And yet it wasn't just for her that she needed, it was for him. Seven days she'd been feeling his need and pain. She knew he was dealing with some dark issues. She wanted to help him process because she remembered things. A lot of things. She remembered the techniques her dad taught for overcoming her own abuse. And she wanted to show him how, but he never gave her one opening, not one. And a week of that hell turned her into somebody she'd never remembered being. Angry. Livid. Because she felt so useless and fucking helpless.

And now, a half-starved man lay between her half-starved legs and all she could think was don't stop. Her body had its own needs that had nothing to do with therapy. Fuck Sade. That was all the therapy she could think of, that was the only therapy there was, only therapy they really needed, she was sure.

But it was his hunger that served as a very thin tether to her common sense. The fact that his needs were overwhelming, reminded her of what lurked inside. She could hear it in his voice, feel it in his body. He was on the verge of snapping and she didn't know what might break free and take control of him. And God help them both, she couldn't forget what was at the end of his rope—his demons. His insatiable, cruel demons. They wanted pain and suffering—for their host and anyone they could reach through him. Her in this case.

All she had to remember in the throes of ecstasy was to not become his demon's chew toy. He'd hate himself, and eventually resent her for allowing him.

Not to mention, that darkness inside would gain more hold of him. There was no bottom to the stomachs of those kinds of monsters. You were only hungry, never satisfied. Always eating, never getting full, taking what you think you needed, only to find that the boundaries of your appetite had expanded. Again.

But in that second, he was bent on her pleasure. God was he ever bent on her pleasure. It took everything she had not to let go of the bed and latch her fingers in his hair and grind his face onto her clit until she had that explosion he dangled just out of her reach.

He thrust his tongue in her again and she bucked her hips, bringing her clit in perfect contact with his nose. So close. "Don't stop, please Sade." She wanted to scream and demand it, but he wanted her begging. She'd give him that much for now, because she'd damn well have her turn with him. He needed to learn how to suffer properly. At the command of her hands, her lips and tongue. And she couldn't wait to force the issue.

He gave a long groan and let her have it. His finger plunged deep and flicked hard and fast as she rotated between the jolts of pleasure and her bones melting from it. Before she could recover, he flipped her on her stomach and shoved her legs open with his knees.

God, he was fast. His brutal hold gripped her with fear at what he might do. She fought to turn her upper body only to have his hand slam down between her shoulders, shoving her to the bed.

"Don't fight me," he growled at her ear now.

The vicious threat in his tone brought more panic. He was too desperate. "I won't fight you," she barely managed under his full weight. "Let me… hold on right."

He lifted just enough. Counting on reflex and sweaty bodies, she flipped over and won his forearm shoved in her neck. Thrashing under his body weight while staring up into his brutal face, she held her breath and yanked on his forearm. Jesus, fuck. She dug her claws in and he grit his teeth, adding more pressure on her windpipe.

Panic fought against her training. He wouldn't choke her out. She'd be no good for his game, then. She kept her gaze locked on his and sent out the order for her body to stop fighting. She finally let her eyes slowly close.

Seconds passed, and she focused on the heat of his breath trembling on her face. He finally released the pressure on her neck but the weight of his body remained unforgiving, not allowing her any leverage. Except one.

She snapped her head forward with all her might, bringing her forehead slamming into his face. He roared and instinct said to brace for sudden impact, but training said strike again. Another head snap forward and she shoved both hands under his forearm once again pushing into her neck.

"Be still, Mercy. I need you!"

She clenched her teeth, eyeing him while working enough of her hand under his arm to keep from being choked. Still unable to talk and barely able to breathe, she managed to get one of her legs between his. He growled and pushed his hips harder onto her. Blood dripped onto her mouth from his busted lip and fury made her spit in his face. He leaned down, maybe to kiss her, and again she snapped her head forward. This time he jerked back before she could hit him.

"I'm getting off of you," he growled between gasps. "Before I fucking kill you. God I want to hurt you so bad, I can taste it, I want to hurt you," he rasped.

Pain stole her breath at his words, not that he'd said them but that he was so imprisoned by them. Tears blurred her vision and he jumped off of her to pace next to the bed. Holding his head, he heaved in the silence then whispered,

"I'm a fucking animal, I'm a fucking animal."

The bewildered sound in his broken voice gave her back some courage.

"You're not an animal." She ended up coughing the words out, her neck throbbing still.

He looked at her, still pacing as though he were barely hanging on. "I need you but you need to leave," he gasped shaking his head. "I should be restrained, you need to leave, you need to tie me up. Oh my God, don't fucking try to leave this room, Mercy."

She watched him pace, trapped in his own body. "I'm not leaving. And I'm not restraining you."

He paused and stared at her until her heart raced, and run instincts bit like a million ants at her muscles. Everything about him said he was ready to fight again. Make her.

"If you try anything," she gasped when he took his first lethal step toward her.

"You'll what? Fight me? What if I fucking want that!"

"I mean it, this won't end well, Sade. Stop."

"I haven't even started," he whispered, coming closer.

Mercy walked in reverse until her legs hit the bed.

"You want to fight?" he asked. "You want me to make you, is that it?" His tone had gone too controlled, his steps too sure as he gave a slow one-sided smile. "You like being made. Deep down, you like me to fucking make you take whatever I fucking give you."

Her privates tingled with the truth of his words but her heart hammered with fear at hearing the monster from his past force him to its will. He gradually advanced and she held a hand toward him while climbing on the bed. "I like you… in control of you."

When he got in lunging distance, she made her way off the other side. Her chest ached to know that when he was a young boy, he'd felt the same terror she did now. She knew that terror. But all the monsters in her life had been strangers. What was it like to have somebody who was supposed to love you, become your worst nightmare?

The sadistic look on his face said her words hadn't touched the sane part of him. "I like me in control too. Of you. You taking my cock however I want to give it, whenever, why-ever, for whatever." He held both arms at his sides. "Right in this second, I want the head of my cock hitting the back of your throat, your teeth tearing at me," he growled. "Then I want it buried in that tight. Fucking. Ass."

His words created a tug-of-war between desire and fear. She darted a gaze to the right, seeking a clear route of escape. God, she wanted him. But not while he was being played by that animal he hated. "You can have all that," she whispered. "But not like this, I won't let you."

"You won't let me?" He stepped up on the bed now, his chest heaving. "You really think you have a choice, Baby?"

The bedroom door leading out, pulled on every muscle. Run. Now. "I always have a choice, and so do you."

"I do yes. I choose to take it. It's not like it isn't mine to take. It's not like you don't belong—to me." He slammed his hands on his chest, taking another step, making the bed creak loudly under his weight.

"Let's talk about it," she gasped, fighting for casual while working her way to safety.

"Talk…" He stepped one foot off the bed and stared at her. "About what?"

"About us. How I can help you."

He stood poised there, one foot on the bed, gaze burning down her body. "I don't think you can handle that while I fuck you." His eyes rolled back up to hers and locked hard. "Soul meshing? When my cock is driving into your ass?"

Oh Jesus. The thought of having his angry dick in her ass wasn't something she'd let him do. Not quickly. But the sadistic tilt of his lips said he was two seconds away from losing any form of control she needed him to have in the matter.

Self-defense measures began presenting themselves as she kept her reverse steps undetectable. She could scream. The fear of her father getting involved should wake his ass up. She could fight him too but there was no telling how that might end. God, she needed some distance between them. A lot.

He stepped off the bed and terror sent her racing for the exit out of the nightmare. She jerked on the knob and his growl came with his naked body slamming into hers, shoving her into the door.

Survival instincts engaged and she slithered right out of his hold and ran for the balcony doors, his feet pounding behind her. She was in flight mode and couldn't even scream as she fought with the lock. Her head snapped back, his fingers biting into her hair as he held her to his body, one arm locked around her neck, the other across her front.

She shot a hand behind her and grabbed his balls and squeezed. He growled in her ear, the arm at her neck, choking her.

"Fucking do it," he barely managed, agony and pleasure in the shaky words.

Darkness slowly swam in her mind as he increased the pressure, maybe not even realizing he was. Kill and maim maneuvers rapidly flashed in her mind. She fought each one, refusing to lose hope in him. He'd catch himself. He'd... catch his... head. "I... love you." The words barely made it out as she slowly released and went limp. He suddenly shoved her away from him and she hit the floor in a sprawl.

"What the fuck are you doing, Mercy?" he gasped, sounding confused.

She turned on the floor, coughing again, struggling to get enough air. "You're not an animal," she sputtered. "That's not… who you are, Sade. You have to fight this." He froze and just stared at her until she got nervous again. "You can fight it," she pleaded, sitting up.

He gasped several times then hurried to the far side of the room, and paced. "I fucking want to do things Mercy. I want your pleasure, but God, I want your fucking pain," he seethed, sounding as terrified as he was hungry. "I don't want to be this person, I fucking don't!" he roared at her.

Mercy climbed to her feet and made her way to him, carefully.

"Get away from me." He put his hands up and stepped back. "I can't touch you right now, I can't."

"I'm not leaving, I won't. You're going to stop," she whispered calmly. "You're going to sit on that bed, right fucking now, Sade. And you're going to calm. The fuck. Down."

He stared at her, appearing bewildered. Like a scared little boy that was being made to do things he dreaded. And yet craved.

Sensing a break in the fiery wall around his mind, she pointed to the bed and ordered the trembling command, "Sit. Down." When he continued to only stare at her, seeming unable, she whispered, "You won't win the fight with me, Sade. You'll have to kill me. I won't give in to your devils, do you hear me?" Tears filled her eyes and she gasped, "I… will fucking never give in to your devils, so you had better… sit down."

His body was suddenly heaving as his head shook and his face contorted with brutal emotions, none she could name. It was all like a dream, she was standing there watching him one moment, then he was on her the next, his mouth crushing hers, hand pulling brutally in her hair. Mercy grasped his shoulders to keep from falling when a sob tore out of him. He cupped her face now in a trembling carefulness, kissing as though salvation could be found in the worship of her mouth and tongue. "Fucking help me!" he gasped. "Please!" The desperate word wrenched from deep inside him, a lost man, horribly desperate to be free. "Don't leave me, please don't give up, I need you."

Mercy gasped when he enveloped her in a full body embrace. "I'm here," she sobbed back, "I'm not leaving, I'm not leaving you."

"I don't fucking want to go, I don't want to go." The terrified words trembled out between heaving breaths.

She managed to stroke his head pressing in her shoulder. "Go where baby, where do you have to go?" she whispered, scared for him.

"To that fucking place," he choked. "That place, Mercy."

"You don't have to go, you don't have to. I'm here, I'm here."

"I don't want to go there, Mercy," he gasped again. "I hate that place, I hate it so fucking bad."

"Then you'll never go again, that's all there is to it," she cried hotly in his ear. "You'll never ever have to go again baby, I won't let you. I'm here, I have you. Do you understand me? You're not going back there. You and me, we're walking the fuck out of there."

She gripped him hard and a deep sob tore from him like he fought a thousand more ten times worse. "I don't want to go," he demanded before whispering over and over, "I don't want to go, I don't want to fucking go, I don't want to hurt you, please don't let me."

Chapter Three

Sade made his way quietly downstairs, hoping to make it to the coffee pot and out the door without getting caught. He needed to breathe air not saturated with Mercy. Needed to think about what was happening with her and him. Mostly him. He didn't remember ever feeling like he did now, the things he was dealing with were new. At least his old shit was familiar but this… this was different and he needed to figure what and why before he did something he'd eternally regret. As it was, he skirted disaster no matter which way he turned. He was in quicksand and any move he made sucked him a little bit further under. And when she was near him, his mind stepped into a blender set to puree. A look, a kiss, a smell from her—it all ate away the cement holding his mosaic life together, the broken pieces that had been glued together into a halfway usable something by which he existed if you could call it that. He knew one thing. She didn't deserve this. Him and his sickness.

Entering the kitchen, he nearly sighed in relief until his mother spun from the far end. "Gooood morning my precious baby," she gasped, hurrying over with both arms open and a bright smile on her face.

"Hey Mom," he said, embracing her.

"Oh my God, I can't get used to hugging you, you're so huge! I've been dying to have a cup of coffee with my son one of these fine mornings!" He smiled at how she hugged him, rocking side to side like they used to when he was small enough to stand on her feet. "I'll make you some toast! Would you like me to make you some coffee milk with it?"

The sheer hopefulness in her tone took care of that answer. "That would be great."

"Awwww, thank you for indulging me, baby." She reached up and stroked a thumb along his cheek and ruffled his hair before spinning to the counter. "But if you want regular coffee, I won't be offended you know. How do you take your coffee normally?"

He grinned, glancing all around. "I take it black." She gasped and looked over her shoulder. "Black! Of course you do, you're such a strong man!" she bragged, making him grin and shake his head. "Don't tell me you're shy!"

"Nah, just not used to all this attention." More like not used to having a mom caring. Or just having a mom.

She sucked in a breath, putting bread in the toaster. "I don't know, that Mercy of ours seems to show you plenty, hmmm?"

He gave a light shrug and pulled the island barstool out and straddled it, the mention of that making him feel like shit. "Yeah."

His mom suddenly stood across from him, forearms on the counter, leaning toward him with an inquisitive look. "What's wrong with you?" she asked quietly, her tone soft.

He shook his head, not meeting her all-knowing gaze.

"Don't bullshit me, young man," she whispered firmer. "I may have missed a lot of years with you but I know when you're fibbing. Now, talk to me," she finished with a soft beg, "you know you can, look at me. Look at me." Sade looked at her, hating how hard that was. It was close to looking in a mirror for him. "Who are you looking at?" she continued, opening both arms with a beautiful smile. "I'm your mother," she hissed, sounding thrilled and amazed. "Now, come on. Fess up. Talk to me."

Sade regarded her secretive look and took a deep breath before glancing around for an escape.

The toaster popped and she went in reverse, pointing at him it. "Organize your thoughts while I get your toast. Then we'll take this outside, the morning is gorgeous!" she squealed, hurrying to the fridge, sky blue silk robe flowing behind her. "Don't tell," she whispered, mischief in her voice, "but I'm up to surprise Kane with breakfast in bed."

"Aw Mom, don't let me stop you."

"Shut uuuup!" she cried, tossing him an incredulous gaze while loading a wooden tray with their morning goodies. She picked it up and headed toward the door. "Now come on, follow meeeee," she sang, kicking open the screen door and hurrying through it.

Sade ran and caught it before it could slam and wake up the house. But what did it matter? Having a heart to heart with his mom about this shit was the last thing he wanted. Ever.

She placed the tray on a small table before a pair of white rocking chairs then sat in one and patted the other. Sade took another breath as he sat, dreading what she might manage to drag out of him. She handed him his toast and coffee with a smile, like she'd dreamed of doing that, then drew her feet up, getting comfortable. "Mmmm," she said, embracing her cup in both hands while sipping. "Look at this place. What a view, baby, right?"

He gazed out at the ocean that had called to him this morning. Like it had secrets to share with him. "It is. Very." He slid his gaze along the softly breathing giant, the blanket of diamonds on its surface nearly blinding in the first sunlight.

"Okay spill it, what's bothering you?"

God, he didn't want to do this with her. Not his mother. He just wanted to have nice moments with her. Hadn't they had enough shit together? Sade set his toast down.

"Ohh," she muttered. "So bad you lose your appetite? That's no good!"

He stared into his cup of coffee now, still debating on escape tactics.

"You think everybody doesn't see it?"

He looked at her, panic hitting his stomach.

"All the stress you're under? Come on, what's wrong, we're at this island, everything is beautiful, you have the woman you love?"

Sade slid his jaw to the right at that, nodding absently in the deafening silence that ensued.

"Oh come on, you're not going to sit there and act like you don't love Mercy, are you?"

He snorted a little and shrugged, looking out. "Love," he muttered.

"Yes, love," she repeated, sounding concerned. "I know you probably didn't think you'd ever experience it, but I always knew you would, sweetie."

He scanned the empty beach again.

"What?" she pried.

"I don't know," he muttered. "I just…" he shook his head and slid his finger over the rim of his cup. "How would I even know what that is?"

She set her coffee down and leaned over, grabbing his wrist firmly. "You listen to me young man. Look at me."

Sade couldn't deny her that much and met her clear, silver gaze.

"I am your mother and I know some things. I know some things about you, young man. You do know what love is. Oh my God," she wailed softly then. "You, mister, have a very big heart."

The absurdity of that nearly made him laugh, but the longing for her to be the slightest bit right, stole his voice. He wasn't sure what fantasy drug she was taking, but that wasn't the reality.

"Don't shake your head at me, I'm not crazy here. You listen to me, you know what love is, you have a huge heart. Oh my God, stop snorting!" she shrilled lightly. "Do you remember how you used to rescue those nasty little earthworms? In your pocket?" She giggled. "And those pennies you'd find on the ground and say it had fallen from Heaven? You'd always put them in your little jar," she said dreamily.

He did remember that. "To buy you that stairway to heaven." That never existed. He wasn't happy that she let him believe in such a thing when she knew it didn't really exist. Not something he'd held nearly sacred at the time. But he allowed for the fact that she probably needed to have something nice to pretend about.

And yet she gasped, "Yes!" sounding so happy about it still. "And what about how you used to cry over dead animals on the side of the road, or-or avoid every crack not to break your mother's back!" She gave in to silent giggles.

A sudden sadness hit him, adding to the other bullshit inside. His childhood ignorance had fought so valiantly against the cruel realities of life, and lost.

"And those angel pictures you drew for me and put under my pillow to protect me. And how you dressed in a superhero costume to fight the bad guys?"

Sade's stomach knotted with the other stuff that came with those memories. There had been too many bad guys. But how did she still not get the punch line? The joke was on them, on him. All his trying to protect, believe and overcome… all blown to hell. And yet she sat there and talked like they'd escaped it and lived happily ever fucking after.

"And how you held my hand when I cried? Remember that day I was going to work? You tried to stop me, you gave me all your saved pennies so that I didn't have to…"

Sade's chest tightened with fury at hearing her on the verge of crying. Just what he fucking couldn't take right now. Why was she doing this?

She shook her head roughly and wiped her eyes. "Oh honey, you—are a very good boy, Johnny, do you hear me? Look at me." He cringed at the name, wishing she wouldn't call him that ever again. He hated that he didn't like his own mother using it. If anybody deserved to call him that name, it was her. He took her hand when she reached for him, unable to resist kissing it. "Only people who love, do those things. That was all you. You did all that because that's who you are inside."

He pulled his hand away now. "Was, maybe."

"No, are!"

Growing more annoyed, he raked all his fingers through his hair. "Things changed Mom," he muttered, hoping she'd realize the outcome of that story and end their trip down nightmare lane, littered with blood, suffering and cute angel pictures drawn by a little boy who cried himself to sleep every fucking night. Just like her.

"Listen, we endured a lot of shit baby, I give you that. But we didn't let it change us."

Jesus fucking Christ. "How can you even say that, you know what happened, you know what I do for the man."

"Did, Johnny! And you did what you had to until you could do something else, you were planning a way out." She shot a finger at him. "You hadn't given him everything, you hadn't and you know it."

He stood and faced the ocean, ready to jump out of his skin. "I don't want to talk about this. Not with you."

"Then talk to Mercy, but talk to somebody!"

"Especially not her. Not about this."

"Why not!" she gasped.

Why not? Why not? He searched himself for that answer, realizing he didn't really have an answer to that. But he would. He'd have that answer and he'd give it to Mercy. And she'd leave him. She'd leave him like all good things did. Like he fucking deserved because that's the product, the sum, the quotient, the difference in his life. Good always equaled gone.

Because you're scared, that's why," his mother helped. "And baby, that's okay, it's normal."

"There is nothing fucking normal about me, Mom," he barely muttered.

"Don't you say that, there are tons of things normal about you. Sure you fought and fucked all your life, so have I. You don't think I was scared?"

She stood next to him now, sharing the view with him. "I was terrified. For you, for me. For us. I know terror, I know fear, trust me."

That, he knew was truth. "She's… she's different."

"Of course she is," his mom hissed. "That's why you love her."

"I mean she doesn't… understand the things…" No, he knew that wasn't true. He knew she understood. Too much maybe. "I don't want her in my shit, Mom."

"Oh honey, that's too fucking bad," she said matter-of-factly. "She's not going anywhere, you can hang that up. And that woman loves you. I see it and I thank God for that! And do you know why?"

"No, I don't know why. It's a mystery to me why—a fucking… oxymoron."

"Because she sees the good man in you, baby!" she squealed.

"There is no good man in me," he argued, his frustration mounting.

"You're stupid if you think you'll convince her or me of that."

He looked at her. "I'm not going to stand here and pretend that I'm somebody I'm not. I may have been good once upon a time but that's gone, trust me. I'm not just saying it. You think I want to be this person? Am making this up?" He slapped his chest. "I'm a sadist who loves getting and giving pain of any kind. You think that's something she needs? In any capacity? An animal that wants to hurt her?"

She shook her head, but the denial kind, making him want to growl. "I get it but that's not all of you and you know it. You've got to reach deeper than that and become the man you are deeper inside."

"You sound like her now."

"Then she's right!" his mom cried.

"Yeah?" He looked at her. "You think I haven't tried to do that all these years? Tried to not be that motherfucker? Try still to this fucking day not to be him? You would think that having somebody like her in my life would help, but it's worse than fucking ever," he hissed.

She stared at him, sympathy in her silver gaze. "I know it's not easy, sweetheart, I know what it's like to battle demons." She gave a sad smile and stroked his face and he realized how true that had to be for her. He didn't even want to imagine what kind of demons she battled. No doubt, the same kind Mercy had to. But where they'd fought the monster, he'd embraced it. The can't beat 'em, join 'em mentality. He could almost remember the day it happened, when he thought 'I'll just pretend, I'll play the game'. But somewhere along the way, the game played him.

"It's too late," he muttered.

"No." She shook her head emphatically, looking out again. "It's not, it's not too late."

"I don't…" he looked away from her, closing his eyes, fighting the anger taking him. "I don't know… how to come back from it. The wires are fried."

"You just need help with it, Mercy can do that, she's your soul mate, I see that."

He snorted full out now. "What a fucking joke for her. An angel lives a life of fucking ruin and ends up with the monster. It's a good thing I don't believe in God," he muttered, "because that right there would be a problem for me." She gasped the second he said it and he shook his head. "You're shocked? Yeah, that's old news. I lost that a long time ago."

She gave another incredulous sound, more than the first. "That's it!? Sorry Ma? Sorry, I lost my faith!?"

"Add it to the fucking list of faults I have. Sade couldn't hang, he joined the crowd, he gave in, he embraced the monster." He pinned her with a furious gaze. "You think I wanted that? You think I fucking wanted that? Wanted to begin to wonder why? Why didn't you love me, God? Why did you give me a father that hated me, hated my mom? A dad that was only nice after he had his way with me? Yeah, I fucking took it," he seethed as she covered her mouth. "I took what I could, whatever good feelings I could get, how's that for a good boy? Every good boy just looooves to be fucked by their father to feel one—ounce—of fucking—love!" he roared. "Don't tell me I'm good! Don't you fucking tell me God is good! Because if He's good, then that means I'm one, unworthy bastard! And yeah," he nodded, gasping for air at his mom now on her knees, hiding behind both hands. "I can go with that. Little Johnny's not… worthy enough," Sade gasped a laugh, gripping the porch rail. "… for even God to…. fucking…" He grit his teeth and slammed his fist into the post. "Fuck this! This is fucking bullshit!"

"When?" she wailed on her knees. "When did he, Johnny. I didn't know, I didn't know." She suddenly shot up to her feet and grabbed his t-shirt in her fists. "I'll kill him, I'll kill that motherfucker," she growled, shaking her head rapidly. "Not that, not that." Her face crimped and she sobbed, "Not! That, not that, not that," she wailed. "I didn't know, I didn't know, I would've killed him! I'm going to kill that motherfucker!" She struggled to get free, like she'd leave that second. "Oh my God, I thought I could forgive him," she wailed again, collapsing into him. "But not that, not that!"

Sade was trembling and fighting to breathe as he held her head to his chest, stifling her screaming sobs as she repeated, "No, not that."

Sade held her head to his chest, stifling her screaming sobs as she repeated not that. "Shhh, shhhhh," he whispered, holding her with eyes closed. He'd not meant to say all of that. But really, deep down, he figured she'd known. How would she not?

She suddenly pushed him away and pointed in his face, "You listen to me! You... listen... to me!" she gasped. "God loves you! God has always loved you." She shook her head again. "He's not the one that chose your father, He didn't choose that life," she patted her chest rapidly. "That was me, that was me. God never wanted that, I promise you, baby. God loves you," she cried, bitterly. "Who do you think helped me escape? It was Kane, and who do you think told him to help me?" She pointed up and nodded, her teary eyes wide and hopeful. "That's right, the Man upstairs, He told Kane to help me. And he listened." She gasped several times, face crimping in agony again. "But I didn't. I knew better than that life, I knew it was wrong but I was young and stupid. Don't you fucking listen to those lies in your head," she hissed. "All lies. The truth is in here," she pressed her palm firmly to his chest. "It's all in here."

A deep sadness clutched Sade as he reached up and put his hand over hers, holding it there. Holding it to that dark, shattered mess she called his heart. There was no point in telling her he was broken and beyond fixing. That he was not the son she remembered or envisioned in her lovely, sweet mind and heart. He wished so badly that he was. He wished so much that he could go back in time to that day when he embraced it all, and just found a way to die. While he was innocent. "I love you Mom," he gasped, kissing the top of her head, over and over. "That will never change. Ever."

The sound of the ocean surf kissing the beach, reached out to him. He closed his eyes as the cold fingers stroked over that cavern in his chest to finally impart its secret. Love. It's what Mercy desperately needed from him. And it's what he didn't have to give. Not the kind she deserved. All he had was a mind and body twisted and tangled with the cruelty of his life. A man he hated and was deeply ashamed of in the light of her pureness. But the worst part... the part he loathed the most about himself... was how much he loved the filth within.

Chapter Four

Mercy woke abruptly, sitting up in bed, feeling like she'd forgotten something important. Like she wasn't supposed to have fallen asleep maybe.

Sade.

Panic shot her out of the bed and to her closet, looking for a robe to throw on. Where was he? Oh God, he'd broken down with her. As good as it was for that to happen, she knew what came after that. A new level of isolation and distance. She couldn't let that happen. She'd give him time and space but only so much. He'd broken with her in such a way that was dangerous. The kind of break that leaves you open to very bad things. She needed to be there to protect him, help guide him through that place he wanted to keep her out of, to protect her from, so she didn't get hurt, didn't get infected by his disease. As amazing and perfect as that was coming from a sadist, it wasn't fucking happening. She was here for him for a reason. She was in his life for a reason. His life. And this was it. To help him see that he deserved this. Love, life. Mercy.

Flying downstairs she nearly ran over Sade's mom.

"He's on the beach. Go to him."

Mercy didn't wait to ask what was wrong, she just hurried out, trying not to panic. What did his mother know? What happened? Why did she sound so distraught? Mercy had managed to get him to lay in bed with her after his meltdown and he'd fallen asleep. Everything seemed fine.

Opening the screen door, she blocked the sun with a hand, hurrying down the steps while searching the beach for signs of him. She spotted a black dot and looked both ways before heading toward it. Had to be him. She forced herself to walk, but allowed herself a brisk pace. The air was warm already, promising a blistering day. Took her a while to realize the person was walking away from her, not towards.

"Sade!" Three yells later, the form stopped and seemed to turn. She waved at him and held her breath, waiting. A hand raised and she gasped out a laugh of relief, her eyes flooding with tears. She couldn't bear him not wanting to be around her even if it wasn't his or her fault.

She hurried towards him and when only ten feet separated them, he stopped and faced the ocean. She slowed her steps and crossed her arms over her chest, suddenly feeling like a desperate lover, running after him in a night robe. She gazed out at the ocean. "Beautiful morning for a walk," she gasped, trying not to sound as winded as she was.

He nodded. "Sure is."

She came to stand a few feet from him, respecting his unspoken need for space.

"You sleep okay? Man, I slept like a log."

An awkward silence followed with Mercy struggling for something to lighten the mood with. She remembered about their trip to the neighboring island they were supposed to take, they were scheduled to leave at noon and return in a few days. They were going to make a little fun vacation out of it—swim, fish, scuba-dive maybe. Just the idea of being with Sade in one spot gave her butterflies. He'd been very evasive with her, always seeming to need to do something else the second she came around. Something that involved being away from her. "Ready to hook a shark?"

He continued studying the horizon to the right. "I'm not going," he said.

Pain slammed her and she fought to think around it. Wait…. She didn't have to go either. "Oh, okay. I'm honestly not that keen about deep sea fishing, either," she admitted truthfully.

"You should go," he said.

That pain returned, worse than before at hearing he wanted her to, wanted to not be with her. "Ralph might go," she said, grasping for something that would incite his possessive side. Where had that gone? But even angry jealousy was better than this, this cold distance.

"The more reason for you to go, he seems like a nice guy."

Oh my God. Agony from his words hit her like a sledgehammer, making her gasp. She fought to swallow but the rock in her throat strangled the oxygen from her. This was... so fucking ridiculous, was he really going to pass her off to another man? Like she was just disposable to him? Like what they shared meant nothing to him?

She fought to get a hold of her emotions—to think logically. Maybe he was testing her. Well in that case, maybe she'd teach him not to fucking test her in such a way. "He's very nice, yes. A good fisherman from what I hear." When he didn't respond, her stomach burned. "And cook. He's supposed to teach me how to fillet."

Her heart shot into her throat when he turned to her, his silver eyes pensive for a very missed soul mesh. "I'm sure you'll do great. In anything you ever choose to do."

She gasped a laugh, mostly to hide her sob. What the fuck was that supposed to mean, anything she does, like in the future as well? "I'm sure," she nodded, swallowing. "Well, I'm gonna go get ready. Pick out what I'm wearing. I'll see you around."

She spun and left, holding her breath long enough to not allow that sob to burst out. She broke out in a jog, wanting to get as far from him as she could, ignoring the therapist in her that screamed she was failing her patient. But what about her? Fuck him! He was failing her, she didn't deserve this!

Mercy made a beeline to the back entrance of the beach house and hurried up the outside flight of stairs that led to their bedroom. A bedroom he'd not slept in, except last night.

In a blind fury, she went through her drawers and found that sexy white bikini and matching sheer shawl. Yanking it out, she stormed to the bathroom and got in the shower. Turning it as hot as she could stand, she washed her hair and scrubbed at her body, feeling like ants were all over her.

"Ralph's a nice guy... I'm sure you'll do great... in anything you ever do."

Mercy clutched her chest and gasped in pain, a sick sob wrenching out of her. Her stomach heaved, threatening to empty. She braced a trembling hand on the wall and clenched her eyes tight then her jaw.

Fuck him! Fuck that bastard.

Just who did he think he was, who did he think she was? One of his sluts to fuck and throw away?

That was not happening, motherfucker! She finished her shower, then ripped the brush through her hair. You want to play with me, Mr. Sade?

You want to fuck with me? I can play, I'll show you play.

Mercy finished dressing, her makeup and hair done to slutty perfection. She made her way down stairs, hearing loud chatter mixed with the kind of laughter she longed to experience. How had things turned so bad so suddenly between them? What had she done? Was she not the same woman he remembered even though she remembered everything, she was pretty sure? Was she missing pieces of herself she wasn't aware of, but he was?

She paused on the stairs making out Bo, Liberty, her dad, his mom... she listened for Sade then heard Ralph.

Jesus, fuck, not him. She didn't like him one bit. He was sweet, and cute, and would make a nice friend, but that was it. Sure, he'd probably like more but with Sade giving him the death stare, he didn't even attempt any semblance of going there with her. Why did Sade act like he cared but didn't care? Obviously he was torn about something with her, but what? If she were to think logically and positively about the situation, she would say he was suffering from the shame and guilt of what he wanted and couldn't have with her and therefore sought to remove her from his life… to protect her.

If she were thinking emotionally, she would say it was something she was doing wrong, or different than she used to and he just wasn't that into her anymore and didn't know how to exit the relationship now. The way he'd broken down in front her, she was leaning toward the shame part. Now he was pushing her away in hopes that she would do the job for him.

Well, on both those fronts—Fuck. That. He'd have to work to get rid of her and she wouldn't let him go easy. She'd go with the logical reasons for now and if her emotions got in the way, she'd deal with it then. She had feelings too. Needs. Hurts. He didn't get to call all the shots, especially when he wasn't thinking straight.

Her stomach got sick at thinking about the other option—the he wasn't that into her anymore because she changed option. If that was the case… oh God, please let that not be it.

Bracing for a joyful act, she breezed into the kitchen where the action was. They were packing, she realized at a glance.

"Look who decided to wake up," her father called.

Mercy let out a jovial laugh and sashayed to her dad's open embrace, hoping Sade was hanging around in some corner.

She briefly flashed her peripheral at exiting the hug. "And I wasn't sleeping, I was getting ready."

He hugged her again and whispered in her ear, "I'm glad to hear you're coming even though Sade is staying behind."

"Yeah," Bo said, peeking his head into their conversation space, "no Sade or Liberty, looks like we're the party."

"Liberty's not going?" Mercy's heart raced, along with instant negative thoughts.

"She's not feeling good," Bo whispered. "But if you ask me, she's scared of the deep blue and is too proud to admit it." He winked and leaned further in, kissing her on the cheek.

"How's my precious girl," Sade's mom cooed, coming in with a kiss on Mercy's forehead. "I'm glad you're still coming, I need a girl to keep me company."

Fuck, shit.

"Don't worry," Ralph called out, "I brought my lighter gear for the women."

"Lighter," Sade's mom balked, "You can keep it, I want the tough stuff. I plan on catching the biggest fish! I'm apparently very good at catching nice, strong, fish." She wiggled her brows at Kane who pulled her into his embrace with a chuckle.

"You're likely to catch Godzilla with your beginners luck." Her dad pecked her forehead and intimate kissing bloomed from there with sounds that belonged in a bedroom.

"Get a room, geez," Bo muttered, passing them.

Mercy finally allowed herself to look for Sade all around. "Anybody see Sade?" she asked.

"He mentioned getting a few groceries in the village. Liberty took him."

Panic stabbed her. "I thought she was sick?" Mercy said before she could catch herself.

"Exxxactly what I said," Bo raised his brows. "Like I said… she's just chicken of the sea." He burst out laughing at his own joke while Mercy's gut churned with fear and fury.

Mercy laughed and smacked his shoulder while barely hanging on to her act. By some miracle, she managed to help with the packing, all the while plotting in unhealthy fury. What the fuck was going on? Something was. Going into town for groceries, my fucking ass. Mercy thought back to the events of the previous week with Liberty in the scenario. Mercy hadn't been great company with Sade being distant with her and now that she thought about it, Liberty seemed just fine with that. At the time, Mercy was relieved to not have to deal with talking when she was miserable, so she never thought twice about it.

Mercy froze at recalling an incident. She'd walked out and found Sade and Liberty chatting on the porch outside. She hadn't thought anything of it once Bo had come out and they began their love play. Then Sade had made excuses to be somewhere else as usual, and that was all Mercy could think about. Him leaving her presence. Again.

But now…. Now she couldn't help but wonder if he left for other reasons. The thought made her need to vomit.

An hour passed and Sade and Liberty still didn't return. Was she the only one that found that odd? She wanted to ask questions, like when did they leave and how long was it supposed to take to get a few groceries in a village supposedly close enough to ride a bike to? If it hadn't been for Ralph coming over, she wasn't even sure there was a village with the exclusion of the beach house.

Mercy opened the fridge, fighting panic. "You ready sweetheart?" her dad asked behind her, making her jump. "We're all loaded up."

She turned and took a deep breath. "Dad…"

He pulled her into his embrace. "Oh honey," he murmured. "Are you feeling sick too?" he half joked.

"Yes, actually."

"I know you are, I'm not blind. He needs a little space is all, he's dealing with a lot of things. He's a special kid, but he's a very good kid, okay?"

Hearing her father defend him gave her conflicting feelings. "I know," she whispered, keeping her voice low. But she didn't know, that was the problem. She didn't know anything anymore. "Dad?" she asked, looking up at him, fighting down the sob in her throat. "Am I... much different than before the accident? I mean I feel like I remember everything but then maybe I'm not, maybe I'm acting weird and different and I don't realize it?" she gasped, swiping the stupid tears.

"Oh honey," he said, pulling her back into a hug. "You're the same beautiful Mercy you've always been. Maybe even more so."

"You're not the right person to ask," she mumbled.

"I most certainly am," he assured. "I wouldn't poo poo around about that."

She smiled against his chest at the poo poo term. "I know you wouldn't." He'd always gone out of his way not to use harsh language in front of her. It used to offend her because she felt like he was saying she wasn't mature enough to handle it. But now... now she realized he did it because he respected her.

"So you won't be mad if I don't go?"

"Not at all. I wasn't that keen on you coming anyway." She pulled away and looked at him.

"Paranoid father syndrome sweetie, but I won't apologize for it." She smiled.

"Faith wanted me to go."

"She's fine. She only said all that so you felt welcomed."

Mercy snorted. "Now I feel really special."

"She would've loved for you to come but you must know that we hate sharing each other."

Mercy smiled at hearing that. "I'm so glad you two have each other Dad. Really."

"I'm sorry I couldn't tell you before. It was hard."

"Like winning the lottery and not being able to tell anybody?"

He laughed and the sound warmed her at how genuine it was. "Exactly that. You take care of that boy. He needs you."

"You may need to tell him that," she muttered.

"He knows, trust me."

"Well I'm getting a little sick of him not showing it."

"Coming," her dad yelled when Bo warned the ship was sailing.

He kissed her forehead again. "Remember who you are," he said. "Remember everything I taught you. All the things you've had to overcome?"

She nodded.

"Don't let him push you around. You got this," he said. "You get on the bull, and you ride until he sees who the master is. Relentless. Unforgiving. Merciless. You know the drill. The only place the broken past has in our present, is the place we give it. So, don't give it, and don't let him give it."

Mercy embraced him tight, his words giving her courage and hope. "Oh God, thank you Dad. Pray for me?"

"I never stop."

She believed that. Once again he'd walked right into her life and casually slayed the giants. She didn't know what she'd ever done to deserve that kind of saving, but she was so grateful to have it. "I love you."

"Just do me one favor," he said, setting her in front of him while pinning her with that familiar stern stare. "Stay put while we're gone, no sightseeing till I get back. No swimming in the ocean, either."

Sightseeing? Was he joking? "How long does it take to go into town?" she finally asked, biting back her sarcasm. "And why the hell is Liberty with him?"

"Oh no you don't," he said, chucking her chin. "Liberty's fine, she would never do anything to come between the two of you. That, I'm sure of."

Shame warmed her cheeks at hearing the way she sounded. "Ok. You better go. I'll… find something to read until they get back."

"I want you to lock up and stay in until he gets back. Once he does, if you want to swim, use the pool. I don't want you in the ocean while I'm not here."

"I know, you just said that. No ocean, no sightseeing."

"And if you need anything, the radio in the basement reaches the boat. There's a manual pinned to the wall next to the radio telling you exactly how to use it. Okay?" He stroked the back of his fingers over her cheek. "Try to relax and enjoy some private time with him."

She rolled her eyes. "I'm not making him. He either wants me or he doesn't."

He leaned in and kissed her cheek. "He wants you," he muttered as he pulled away and walked off.

The matter-of-fact tone in his voice made her heart skip a beat. She needed so bad to believe that. "Catch me a whale, I haven't eaten whale before," she called when he was at the door.

"It's a deal." He winked as he reached inside and locked the door then closed it. The deadbolt engaged next as he locked her in.

Chapter Five

Five minutes later, Mercy paced around the house trying to figure out what to do, peeking out every window she passed. She went around making sure all the doors and windows were locked, but really it was so she could see which gave her the best view of the long driveway leading to the beach house. And also to make sure he'd have to knock to get in, at which point he'd see she was there.

Would he be pissed? Glad?

What the fuck was taking them so long? Didn't matter that her dad thought Liberty was a saint, it still burned her damn ass that she was with Sade. That he was with her. After ignoring her for a week straight, then trying to rape her. In the ass!

Mercy was fuming four hours later when they still hadn't returned. She almost radioed her dad four times just to ask what the hell could he be doing? Did he go to get food or go plant it and watch it grow, stupid fucker!

There was no way to radio him without sounding like a jealous idiot. Oh she was going to have words with him. Was she ever going to have words with him. Many. Many, many harsh ones. She should kick his ass, literally.

She headed upstairs to the window with the best view then froze at hearing something. Shit. She thought quick, wondering where to hide. Part of her wanted to bust him doing something bad, and another said don't give him the chance, or she'd die if he did. The two desperate forces pulled her left and right in indecision before she hurried back upstairs to the hall closet. If he was the kind of person to do what she most feared, then she needed to know it. And hopefully, the huge closet that serviced the four upstairs bedrooms put her in the location that would allow her to discover whatever needed discovering.

Closing herself inside the large closet with the half-slatted door, she crouched on the floor, listening. What if they didn't go upstairs? She reached up and felt around on the door handle for a lock, realizing it was stupid that they wouldn't have one in a closet.

Her heart hammered in her ears, making it hard to hear. They were definitely inside. Mumbling and low laughter reached her itching ears. Female. When she heard his laughter, a fire exploded in her stomach, making her nauseous. What the fuck was he laughing about, how dare he laugh, Mr. depressed twenty-four seven around her. God, that laughing lying bastard.

She waited in the closet, fighting the pain by feeding her fury. Sweat soon dripped off of her in the hot box. Did they plan to stay downstairs? Shit. She hoped they did but that meant she wouldn't know what they were doing. She realized it had gotten quiet. Had they gone outside? To the pool? To the patio swing? To visit like best friends?

The idea that he was with another woman in any capacity had her trembling with so many emotions, none healthy for her or anybody else. This was bullshit. She opened the door and stuck her head out, gasping on fresh air. She crept her way down the stairs, head leading first, trying to see what she could see. She finally spied something that made her heart leap in her throat. Flying down the stairs, she raced to Sade, face down on the floor.

"Shh!"

Mercy jerked her head up to find Liberty in the corner with her finger on her lips and shaking her head.

"Don't disturb the sleeping giant," she whispered.

Mercy looked down at him, hearing him snoring.

"It wasn't easy to get him to drink that last drink with the Ambien but I finally did. Wondering where you were and when you'd get down here. Your father is the one who asked me to stay behind," she whispered at seeing Mercy's confusion. "He was worried Sade might try something stupid. And don't worry," Liberty said, hands up in innocence, "your dad decided that before he thought you were staying behind. Not that he'd have changed the plans since you seem to be gasoline to Mr. Sade's fire."

Mercy leaned back on her haunches in utter relief. Thank you, God, thank you. It wasn't what she'd feared.

"Where the hell did you guys go?"

"To the local tavern where he drank himself to shit," she hissed, not happy.

"Barely got him in the house, had help getting him into the car but getting him out was another matter. And then…" she shrugged with wide amazed eyes, "he got out and actually walked. The next thing I know he's wanting to swim in the goddamn ocean, so I helped put him out of his misery before he found a way to conveniently kill himself."

Fear gripped her at how accurate that likely was with him. Once his self-destruct missions hit, they were nearly unstoppable, shy of tying him up. She looked up at Liberty then, sick that she'd misread everything. Sick that Sade was this bad off, and she'd been busy with jealousy.

"What?" Liberty wondered, cautiously.

"Can you help me get him to my bed? And then help me secure him?"

"Secure him?"

"As in tie him up," Mercy whispered, worried he might hear. "When he wakes up and sees me here, he'll leave."

The look on Liberty's face said she knew that was true. "Jesus," she muttered, flopping back in the chair like she was tired at just the idea of the task. "You realize how heavy he's going to be dead weight? And he may wake up!"

Mercy chewed her lower lip and looked around. "Maybe we can rig something up."

"Like an elevator?"

"Like an elevator, yes," Mercy said, undeterred with her sarcasm.

"You're serious," she said, fascinated.

"You just said he's a threat to himself. You know he'll try to leave when he wakes up."

"So you're going to tie him up," she said, as though making sure she was understanding Mercy's exact intentions.

"Restrain him." Medical procedure, dummy. "Like they do in psych wards when people are a threat to themselves?" Where did you get your training, she wanted to ask.

She eyed Sade, head slowly shaking. "How are we supposed to get him up the stairs, why not take one of the spare bedroom downstairs?"

"Yes!" Mercy realized. "That would work." Quickly standing, Mercy looked around. "We could… roll him onto a blanket and drag him?"

Liberty thought a moment before her mouth turned down with an impressed smirk. "We could manage that."

Fifteen minutes of huffing and puffing later, they had Sade at the bedside in one of the spare rooms, both of them sweating. "Let's take a moment," Mercy said, sitting on the bed. Liberty did the same, not arguing. They sat in the silence catching their breath and Mercy thought about how they were going to get him onto the bed. Maybe they didn't need to. They could secure his one arm and leg to the bed frame and she would… find other things to secure the other side. "We have any kind of chain?"

Still breathing hard, Liberty shot her thumb behind her. "There's a supply room. I can dig around."

"Look for something we can anchor into the floor, something he can't pull out."

Liberty went in search while Mercy inspected the bed. It wasn't sound enough, he could probably break it. She found a spacious spot on the floor. They would have to just put four anchors into it. Like a bed only... not. She yanked all the covers off the bed and made a pallet on the floor where she'd roll him. She'd put the anchors first so she could secure him immediately after she rolled him there. In case he woke up... sober.

She didn't let herself think about what he'd say or do when he did finally wake and find himself restrained. It was doctoring time for him. And she'd just deal with the angry patient syndrome later.

****

Vomit burned Sade's throat just as he fought to turn on his side and puke. His hands and ankles were held by something and he only managed to turn his head. "Hey!" he yelled, his throat feeling swollen.

"Oh my God, I'm coming, I'm coming."

Sade fought to focus his eyes and clear his mind. Mercy. Mercy and those words, *oh my God, I'm coming I'm coming* translated to one thing for him, but it was said from far, in some place where he wasn't and it lit an insane fury in him.

Where was he? When was he? What the fuck, why was he tied?

She flew into the room and the first thing his mind saw was that she was fully clothed—blue jeaned shorts and white tank. "I got you, I got you." She knelt next to him and lifted his head. "Just turn if you need to vomit. Damn, I was worried this might happen."

"What… the fuck are you doing? I can't turn, why am I tied?"

"I'm sorry," she whispered. "But you made me." He struggled to make sense of the sincere words. "And this shouldn't surprise you," she said with light flippancy. "You should know if you become a threat to yourself that I'll do this. You should damn well know it."

"Th…" He shook his head out of her hold. "The fuck do you mean?" He remembered shit now. She was supposed to be on the boat, with her father. Safe. What are you doing here?"

"I decided to stay behind."

"No fucking shit," he gasped. "Un-fucking tie me, Mercy."

"Be right back." She ran off and entered a door in the room and he heard water running. "And I'm sorry," she called from inside it, "I can't untie you, not happening." She returned with a washcloth and wiped his mouth and dabbed it along his body.

She'd fucking stayed behind? And now she'd fucking tied him up? He yanked on the restraints and growled, looking around now. "Where the fuck am I? Where's Liberty!"

She looked at him, her green eyes flashing with anger. "What the fuck does that matter!"

She shot up and went back to what had to be the bathroom. He looked all around. He was on the floor, on blankets. His arms were at his side, nearly immovable except for maybe four inches. His ankles the same. "How'd you… holy fuck you installed shit in the floor?" He stared at her when she came back into the room. "I need to fucking *piss* Mercy."

She knelt at his feet and adjusted what looked like washcloths between the chain and his skin before standing and heading back to the bathroom. "Got you covered, there," she said.

She returned, unscrewing a small mason jar. "Fucking Christ," he said, "you're serious?"

"Dead," she sang, kneeling next to him with the jar. "Not like I've not seen you before."

He needed it too fucking bad to fight at that second. He looked down and groaned as she worked his pants open. "Fucking hurry, Jesus!"

"I'm trying," she cried, "lift your ass, it's not tied to the floor," she grit, fighting to yank his pants down.

He raised up and then she lowered his underwear, making his breath gush out from the pain. "Oh fuck," he said, when she quickly put the jar over his cock. He angled his hips a little and let his bladder go with a groan at the sweet agony.

"Oh shit," she whispered alarmed, his bladder releasing with the force of fire hose. "Are you almost done?"

"Fuck no!" he hissed, looking down at the near full jar.

"Angle your hips more, oh my God!" she squealed, "it's going to overflow!"

"God you're fucking getting it," he promised, struggling to turn more. When he was finally done, he moaned in relief, eying her as she very carefully removed the full jar. "Untie me," he muttered. "I mean it."

"No can do. Dad thinks you need watching."

The flippant answer infuriated him. "Fuck your fucking dad!"

She snapped her green gaze at him. "KANE, said to watch you."

"He told *you* to watch me?" That was a flat out lie.

"Doesn't matter, does it?"

"Yes, it does, I don't want to be around you, he knows that."

"Oh?" she regarded him with an arrogant look. "Not what he told me."

"You're what's wrong with me and he knows that, there is no way in *fucking* hell he asked you to watch me. He asked Liberty to, if anything. Didn't he," he called to her slow walking form as she navigated his urine to the toilet. She didn't answer him and he waited for her to return with his dick hanging out of his pants. She took her sweet time and he yelled, "So what the fuck are you doing here? Why aren't you with Ralph? In your slutty white bikini?"

The toilet flushed and she stormed back in, stopping a few feet before his feet, hands on her hips. But it was that *fight* in her eyes that made his cock jerk awake. It was almost enough to distract her from her rant as she pointed at him. "You asked for that one, mister."

Mister? Sade seethed at how fucking angelic she was even after he'd hurt her in hopes of getting her to leave him alone. He yanked on his chains and growled at her. And always, always it managed to bring the worst out in him. Everything about her screamed *crush me* and his dick was tall and eager to take part in that sick affair.

"And I'll tell you something else," she said, stepping closer with that finger aimed at him. "You... are not going to treat me like this."

His attention went to her heaving tits beneath the tight white tank. Fucking tease, that's what she was to his body. And she'd been going far out of her way to tempt him, he knew that's what she was doing, that was her way of fighting it. But he couldn't give in, he couldn't lose the ground he'd gained with her, then he'd have to start over. Do the dirty deeds again, better, harder, worse. "Treat you like what? Not jumping when you shake your ass at me twenty-four seven?"

She gasped. "Shake my ass?"

He recalled in fury how she'd tried to make him jealous with *Ralph* now. "Did I fucking stutter? And then when you don't get your pussy's desire, you shook your ass for whoever the fuck would look. *Ralph*," he spelled it out for her, drawling the stupid name. "You two deserve each other."

Her bare foot slammed in his ribs and blasted the wind from him.

"You fucking bastard," she grit. "You ignore me for weeks? What have I done to deserve that? Love you? Take care of you? Try to fucking protect you?" she screamed, kicking him again. "Which of those things are you hurting me for?" Another slam of her foot in his side made his cock harder. Especially because she was holding back. Even in her fury, she didn't want to hurt him. But the physical pain taunted other things in him, things he couldn't stop once they started.

"Mercy, Mercy, Mercy," he said with lethal intention, glaring up at her. "How about you untie me and we sort this out?"

"You can sort it right where you are, you lying bastard."

"What the *fuck* do you want from me," he roared. "Unfucking tie me!"

"I want the man I love back, that's what I want," she yelled. "Where is he?"

"Here I fucking am, Mercy. What you see is what you get," he grit at her, seething with anger. "Don't fucking like it? Huh? Well, get the fuck over it, because that's what you get when you fall in love with a sadistic motherfucker like me," he said with growls. "But you knew that, right? Miss Mercy?" He licked his lower lip, winded. "Miss help the bad man? Did you really fucking think you could just stare into these eyes and fix everything? Huh baby?" he mocked.

She knelt next to him and gripped his jaw in her hand and made him face her. "Listen up. You listening tough guy? You need help. And I am the crazy bitch that plans to get it for you. You feel me? Mr. Sade?" she mocked back. "Don't be fooled or intimidated by my name, Mr. Meanie pants, because I sure as hell am not fooled or intimidated with yours. You're getting help. End. Of. Discussion."

Her determination set off every sadistic devil inside him and he yanked at the chains and roared in her face. "You can't fix this, Mercy, I don't want to be fixed, I don't want you. Do you hear me? You and me? We don't mix, we don't fucking match. I love pain, getting and giving it! You can't *handle* that!"

"You're such a coward," she muttered.

"Fuck you," he muttered back.

"Oh I will," she calmly said, standing. "I will most certainly fuck you, Mr. Sade. But on *my* terms. *My* way. The *right* way."

He glared at her, his body in chaotic confusion with her threat and all the needs he'd denied. It was ready to take whatever it could get. "Fine baby, take it. Take it, give your pretty pussy what it needs. Right here, right now."

"You want it?"

He tried to read what that quirked brow meant. He didn't really care, either way. "I so fucking do."

"Well if you want it, you'll have to work for it."

"I should've known," he muttered. "I guess we're back to reading romance books? Soul meshing?"

As pissed as he was, his heart broke in his fucking chest at the thought of it and how it was the road to a heaven that ended in a dead end. And she would force him down it and he would go. He would fucking have to go, just so he could *show* her. See Mercy? See the brick fucking wall, here? See those words there, Angel? They say *damned* beyond this point. You cannot pass. You're not allowed in. You've reached the bottom, the end, the place where anything remotely normal stops and darkness begins.

"You'll get no details until you agree to let me help you."

He stared at her, his head shaking a little. "Back to square fucking one. Unbelievable," he muttered. She was blind. She was so fucking stubborn. She was the kind of person who had to get burned, had to feel it down to their fucking soul before they understood.

"Not square one at all," she said, oh so confidently. "I've come a long way baby. Paid close attention. Took notes. And what you need is something no therapist could ever give you. But I can."

His jaw slid slowly left as he studied her, back to battling his crazy urges for her. Battling those demons now plotting how to have what he fought to deny. How to hurt her. "Keep talking, baby."

She seemed taken aback by his cooperation but recovered almost immediately. Sade groaned when she reached for his groin and tugged his underwear back on. "You'll need to sign a contract," she said firmly, jerking at his pants next. "Lift your ass, you're not an invalid. And you'll agree that you'll allow me to perform sessions with you every night. For four hours."

Holy fuck. She was like Mercy only... more so. Mercy high octane. The notion that he was dealing with a new-ish personality, brought on a burning hot eagerness, followed by dread. He finally busted out in low chuckles. "You're dead serious."

She zipped his pants, not giving him a glance. "You have no idea."

God, the threat in that tone. So fucking irresistible. "And what do I get if I cooperate?" he asked, the monster in him calm now that it knew it would get a chance. That's all it ever needed or wanted. One tiny chance.

She suddenly soul meshed with him and his heart hammered with what burned in those gorgeous green eyes. Sheer strength. Sheer power. "You get fucking *well*, you get *help*. If you want more, I can give little gold stars too."

Fucking. Priceless. "And what if you fail?"

She shrugged her shoulders. "Then we can say we tried."

"Ohhhh, so you're asking me to sign my body over to you for you to experiment on and I'm just supposed to go with that? Did it occur to that lovely mind of yours that I don't want your fucking therapy?" Judging by the look on her face, it had definitely occurred that he might not want it, and she didn't care one bit. "If I'm going all in, I want something in return."

She stared at him and crossed her arms, the look on her face stirring some of his nastiest demons until he yanked on his restraints, hungry to crush her to smithereens and make her a slave to his every devious desire. "Fine, what? What do you want?"

His body answered first and his tongue slid out and licked hungrily over his lips as he thought about his answer. This was it. The turn of the table he'd been looking for. She'd gain his cooperation in her efforts and he'd gain hers in his. "If you fail… we're done."

She stared at him and his heart hammered fiercely with too many fears to name. "Done? You'll need to be more specific."

Pain sledge-hammered him at seeing the first peek of the devastation he was about to deliver to her. Seeing her unable to hide it confirmed what he knew. But the choice was break her heart or break her spirit, and he would not leave this world with that sin on his hands. Not that. She could recover from the first, but not from the second. She could not recover from having her spirit broken by somebody she loved. He would fucking know. "Done, me and you. Break up, divorce, whatever you want to call it. No more me and you doing whatever the fuck it is you call what we do together."

She continued to stare at him, an open book of raw emotion that stole his breath. He let out a bored sigh and stared at the ceiling to get away from the power in that gaze. "How long?"

"How long what?"

"How long do I have? To try?"

He shrugged, fighting not to feel what her tone did to him. The desperation to fix him. The desperation to have him normal. "You tell me."

She stared absently between them, her pretty brows drawn hard in careful thought.

"Yes, think carefully. Because I mean it. You fail, we're done." His entire chest felt crushed under the weight of knowing she would fail. Because he'd make sure of it. He'd make so fucking sure that she'd quit after two days. Three tops. Clean cut. Precision. Him out of her life and his sweet Mercy safe from all the monsters that had eaten his soul and left nothing but a shell of bones.

She swallowed and finally turned that innocent gaze to him. But there was something in it that intimidated even the cruelest of his demons. He wasn't sure what it was, but he felt the quake inside. "Five days," she whispered.

He barked out a laugh, mostly to hide his fury at the ridiculous amount of time and the impossibility of what she was attempting. It was like he couldn't help wanting her to win while knowing she couldn't. At finding her dead serious and those green eyes on fire with more of what he'd just seen a second before, he realized what that shit was in her stare. A whole lot of fucking fight. Again the weight in his chest became nearly unbearable until he growled and yanked on the chains, bearing his teeth at her. She'd fucking fight and make this hard. Make him crush her quick. Without mercy.

"You laugh…" She set her jaw and stood tall, looking down at him for several seconds, her chest heaving. "But you won't for long."

Sade's heart thundered as she turned and walked out in a boldness that made him roar and yank at the chains. The door shut hard, and the sound was a final nail in her coffin, his coffin, their coffin, slamming home. He gasped and strained on the agony, clenching his eyes tight until his body trembled with it. He wouldn't laugh. God, no, he wouldn't, not even for a fucking second, Angel.

Why? Why her, anybody but that mother*fucking* angel, *anybody but his Angel.*

Sade roared again. And again. Until his throat was on fire with the agony, until he tore the flesh at his wrists and ankles. But she didn't return. No matter how much he yelled, cursed, threatened. She didn't return. Panting in the silence, he prayed to whatever fucking God she believed in. *Please don't help her, don't you dare fucking help her!*

Chapter Six

Mercy paced in her room, hands over her ears to block out his screams, her stomach a quiver of nerves. She focused on the plan. Five days? What was she thinking? She'd panicked. Then when he laughed, her pride kicked in and she couldn't bring herself to change it. She'd have to work up a contract. A real one. She could hinge something to the five days, like if there was any sort of progress, she could add another five days. And she needed rules for him. Strict ones. If he broke them, more time was added. At that rate she'd have his stubborn ass in therapy for the rest of his life.

She raced to the vanity table that served more like a desk, and dug out a pen then something to write on. After finding a journal looking tablet with seashells on the front, she sat and tapped her pen on the table, thinking of what should be first. Her emotions raced and she closed her eyes, focusing her energy into that place inside her where she conducted self-discipline. She let out a slow breath and took another one slowly in. Sade. What did he need? God, he needed to quit fucking screaming like that.

She pressed her fingers into her eyeballs for a minute. At hearing him coughing up his guts only to begin roaring again, she slammed the pen down and stalked to her drawer. Digging out a pair of pantyhose, she headed to his room.

Mercy threw open the door, letting it bang on the wall as she stormed over and knelt next to his head with the pantyhose.

"What the fuck is that?" he barked.

"I can't concentrate with all this racket," she muttered, stretching the leg of the pantyhose long and heading for his mouth with it.

He jerked his head all over—left, up, down, right—evading her. Next he snapped at her with his teeth and Mercy finally gave him a good whack across the face. The very brief second of shock allowed her to slam the pantyhose in between his lips. "There we go," she cooed, quickly placing a knee on the side of his head so he couldn't thrash while she tried to secure the damn thing. "The more you fight, the harder I press," she grit, fighting the strength of his neck as he pushed with all his might. She finally got it tied and backed quickly away. "There." she gasped, winded. "Much better."

She got up and left, not even giving him one more look. She couldn't stand to see that hate for her contorting in his face, anyway.

Back at her desk, she went through another five minute calming procedure before she could focus again. What did he need? He needed retraining. Re-shaping. What was she reshaping? His body responses to intimacy. His body responses to pain. Pleasure. His mental process with all that.

But where did she start?

His mind. No, his body in this case.

She took another breath and let it out, praying for clarity. Help me, God. Special case. Show me what he needs. Do I work from his mind, body, or heart?

They were synced but with the wrong things. Her eyes popped open and she wrote on the paper.

All three.

Of course all three, she knew this. Okay, so she'd work from all three. Engage all three at once. That was the key. Her father's training began to pour back into her mind. Yes, the mind, heart, and body should always be engaged in that way. Mind… where logic and reason took place. Heart… where feelings and emotions resided. Body… the expression of the one or combined two. But it was matter over mind starting out. Pleasure is good. Pain is bad. Those are the messages the body is first hard-wired to give when receiving pleasure and pain. But when the two are forced at once, over and over while sexuality is still being shaped and formed, it can wire the brain that way—pain is pleasure. Pleasure is good. Pain is good.

She wrote that into her notes furiously.

His mind formed pain/pleasure connections and even when the mind reached the stage of logic and reasoning, where he knew that the pain and pleasure being perpetrated on him was unjust and wrong, there was no escaping the clutches of the hard wiring already formed. And his heart.

Tears burned her eyes and fell on the paper. His heart was still good. But he couldn't see it. The self-loathing and shame over the truth of what happened and who he now was brought more anger and rage. And the fighting… oh God, not just the fighting. It was all the pain he engaged in, the sexual, mental and physical… he focused everything there because he couldn't take the pain in his shattered heart.

She let out a sob and put her head on the desk. *He used this pain to punish himself. For never being good enough. For trying so hard and never being good enough. He always got pain for his efforts. Always pain.*

Oh God, was she crazy? To play therapist with him? What if she screwed him up even more somehow? Could he be more screwed up? God, she hoped not. *Please don't let me hurt him more than he already is.*

She wiped her eyes and got back to writing. Time to come up with the contract. She worked on it and images of Sade's torn flesh kept flashing. He'd yanked it right off at his wrists and ankles. Worried about him, she decided to finish up in his room. She needed to see him, make sure he was as okay as he could be, considering. Why was he suddenly so furious? What had he wanted that he didn't get? All that to be untied? Didn't seem likely. It was something way more.

He mumbled something that sounded like "What's that?" followed by a clearly mumbled, "When do I eat," then it sounded like "do I get to fucking eat in your little homemade google triage?"

She sighed and went over to him. Kneeling, she set the notebook down and ungagged him. "What answer do you want first?"

He turned his head and spit several times before eying her. "You are so going to pay for this, just letting you know now," he said too calmly before his eyes darted to the notebook. "What are you writing? A love poem?"

"You could call it that," she said lightly, picking it up, determined not to let his scathing words and tone bother her. "A love poem in the form of a contract."

"Fucking lovely," he said dryly. "Do you plan on getting my input, doc, or are you going to just take care of your needs in it?"

"My needs are not the issue here, this is all for you." She got up, turned to the desk and sat, tapping her pen to re-focus.

"Sure it is. So what are we doing for these twenty hours of fix-your-fuck? Or do you need more time to make shit up as you go? How are you going to even manage this without google?"

"Verrrrry cute. For one, you'll need to agree to be nice."

He barked a dry laugh. "Because you can't take the truth?"

"The truth doesn't bother me when it's true."

"So is it the sarcasm you hate or the truth of what I'm saying?"

"It's the sarcasm. Because it's not true what you're saying."

"What if it's true to me, don't I get to have my thoughts on things? Pretty sure that's standard even in the google-therapy spectrum. Doc."

She turned from the desk where she sat about ten feet away and faced him. "You are surely free to think what you want."

"But just not voice it."

"Sarcastically," she corrected.

He laid his head back down and stared at the ceiling. "So I can say it, I just have to candy coat it for the delicate doc."

She pursed her lips, thinking more carefully about it. He should be free to speak his mind as long as he did it kindly. "That's right."

"Put that into the contract on my side of the deal then. I'm allowed to say what the fuck I want as long as I say it delicately."

At hearing he planned to exploit that privilege, she squinted her eyes at him, ready to change her mind. Then he lifted his head and looked at her with that hard, daring gaze. "That's correct," she answered in her most motherly tone and gentle nod.

That earned her a quirked brow before he dropped his head back down. "What about eating."

"During therapy?"

"During fucking now! I'm starving. And when the fuck are you letting me out of my cage? Doc?"

She thought about that. Once he signed the contract, she supposed. She couldn't keep him locked up for a week. If he were going to leave then… she was done. "When you sign the contract."

He stared at her again. "So I get my freedom when I sign your contract. I like that. Nothing like coercion to ensure the success of therapy."

"No, nothing like doing whatever it takes to ensure you don't self-harm. And this love poem contract is that very means of protection."

"How about I need to take a shit."

She turned back to her paper. "You'll need to hold it until I'm done."

"And if I can't?' he spat.

"Then shit." She waited for his response to determine if he were in dire need.

"Suit yourself."

She rolled her eyes at the unspoken threat. "You are such a fucking brat," she muttered, "I'm almost done here. I don't think we'll reach that extreme. If you would shut up for half a minute I could go a lot faster."

"Whatever, hurry up."

She went back to focusing while he somehow remained quiet. Five days. From 7-11 at night. Longer if he wanted. But not less. She didn't put any details of the therapy other than as per her discretion. He'd have to accept, that's all there was to it. Mostly because she didn't have a plan yet. She did have some basic things down that allowed her to alter the contract.

    1.   He would allow her to call him Johnathon, the birth name given by his mother.

    2.   He would need to be kind and respectful.

    3.   He would be on time.

4. He would do as he was told.

5. He would perform homework.

6. He would keep all of it confidential. As would she.

She stared at the final product feeling like she was leaving out major things. Oh, she almost forgot the allowance for extension.

She wrote that if there were obvious signs of improvement—to be determined honestly by her—then she got another week of therapy added.

Standing while looking over it one last time, she walked the contract over to him and held it above his face to read.

He read out loud, freaking out at the first. "Fucking no to number one."

"Why?"

He glared at her for many seconds. "Fucking. No. Is enough answer for you."

The amount of venom in his gaze said it wasn't worth the fight. Not today.

She scratched it off the list. "Fine." She put the contract before his face again and he read for several seconds, head shaking. "So I have no idea what you have in mind for therapy—could be shock treatments for all I know—and I'm just supposed to sign this. And homework?" He gave her a hateful glare. "That's way more than four hours if there's therapy after therapy."

"That's how therapy works. You get the teaching then you go home and apply it. You know this," she said.

"Stop using a fucking mommy tone with me."

"Then stop acting like a belligerent child."

"And what about my conditions?"

"What about them?"

"Where the fuck are they?"

"I can put them."

"You can put them, fucking right you can, and yet you didn't. Not even started, and already you prove to me you have no fucking integrity."

"I forgot!" she yelled, jerking the paper away and staring at him with wide eyes. "Jesus Christ! Cut me some slack, I'm not your damn enemy, Sade."

He stared at her, no, glared at her. "Slack? *You* want slack?" He gave a derisive snort. "Candy coated words, slack. What else does the good doc need? Gentle pussy eating? Gentle fucking? Gentle ass licking?"

She stormed back to the desk and sat, reading loudly as she wrote his demands. *"If the therapy doesn't work, then Sade and Mercy are DONE. DONE.'* There, I wrote it twice and capped them. And you can be so fucking sure that we will be done if I'm unable to help you. You can be so fucking sure," she muttered, walking the contract back to him.

"Goooood," he sang, like she were finally seeing his dark light. "So very good."

She pulled the key from her pocket and took hold of the lock on his left hand.

"Fucking priceless," he muttered. She looked at him and he wagged his other hand. "Right handed, doc. I can see this is going to be a quick week of therapy before you and I are done."

She went to his other wrist, not allowing his anger to shake her resolve. She would definitely need to prepare hard to endure therapy with him. He was so pissed. Pissed she was forcing this, that's all. He didn't like being forced, not by her, not in this. If she were forcing him to bleed and hurt physically, that would be fine, but not this. As long as he cooperated and as long as he was nice—starting during sessions—it didn't matter.

She unlocked his hand and braced for possible retaliation. He stared at her while rotating his blood-crusted wrist. She held the notebook before him at signature distance and handed him the pen, her heart hammering with the sudden threat pulsating in the air between them. He slowly took the pen from her hand and it took all she had to demonstrate she trusted him, pointing at the line where he needed to sign.

Never letting his gaze drift from hers, he slowly reached for the pen and apparently used his peripheral to sign. Then handed it back to her. She took the pen and his iron fingers latched around her throat, pulling her right to his face. She stared into his gaze, not fighting him, not physically anyway. She didn't blink as she meshed her soul to his, letting her heart say it for her. *I'm not your enemy. But I am here to fight your enemy. I am not backing down. I'm not afraid. Do what you want, just so you know that.*

He shoved her away and she coughed and snatched the tablet back, standing to her feet.

"Where the fuck are you going," he asked as she headed out the door.

"For a swim. You just earned a time out."

She pulled the door softly shut, ignoring his laughter with all its unspoken threats of retaliation. She took a deep breath and headed to her room to change. He could bring his best fight. He was clearly under the false impression that she was incapable of standing against him. But she didn't plan to stand against him. Just stand for him. Until he realized that change was possible. That's all she needed to get him to see. The possibility was there. There for him to grab hold of. There for him to use. With or without her.

Chapter Seven

Sade fought his body. It was beyond burning for her. His sadistic fury was going to be a huge problem because he'd need it to head off his sexual perversions he craved worse than ever with her. The double-edged sword pressed relentlessly into his throat at every turn, flooding his muscles with reflexes he couldn't seem to stop. He'd wanted to crush her esophagus in that second. But that fucking look in her gaze. That fucking look had encased his heart like a hot silk, caressing, promising, calling him out in ways that confused his mind. The contradiction was enough to break his fury long enough for him to let go.

For a swim. You just earned a time out. Fucking beautiful.

This was going to be hard. Maybe harder than he imagined. He'd have to fucking prepare for therapy with her. Just to keep from killing her.

He wondered how long she'd planned to leave him. How long would tell him a lot about her strength. If she left him too short of a time, she was easy. If she left him too long, she was pissed and that too made her easy. She had great self-control, he gave her that much. But he knew there was a hurricane beneath that façade. Again, points for having the ability to suppress it.

The door opened right at the exact moment he was thinking it would be a bad time for her to return. In she walked, lighting his body up with that white bikini and sheer cover, hair and skin still wet like she'd just stepped out of the water.

She knelt next to his feet, key in hand, brows raised at his groin. "You know, your cock makes a great meter for reading you."

"I agree," he said, energy rushing through him at the prospect of freedom. "When I want to hurt you, it gets hard. When I want to be hurt by you, it gets hard. The meter ends there."

She angled her head with pursed lips, eyes still on his cock, making him harder. "I wonder if…" She crawled along his side until she knelt next to the cock-o-meter now reading extremely hard. She stroked her finger over his length beneath the denim. "…maybe you're wrong about your arousal with me?"

Fuck. His chest heaved now.

"Do you mind if I try something?"

"Pre-cum therapy?" His hips rolled on their own, wanting anything. Desperate.

"You could call it that."

"Suit yourself, doc."

He barely kept the desire from the words as she opened his pants and he lifted to help get them lowered. "Can I free your legs so you can open them for me?"

Her casual question made his cock jerk. "You're the doc."

"You kick me and you'll be tied up for no telling how long."

"If I kicked you, I'd crush your chest, so, your dare, doc."

She eyed him for several seconds. "I'm going to trust you to be smarter than that. Now, put your free wrist where it belongs so I can re-secure it."

He did and she stooped to lock it back. He was so very glad she was trusting because while he couldn't be trusted in the ordinary sense of the word, he had to have her touch. And who, what, why, when, or where, was irrelevant now. Not to mention his curiosity was burning up with the rest of him.

"I'm going to remove your pants and underwear for this."

He accommodated her casual tone, raising his hips. He watched in amused fascination as she folded his pants and underwear and set them neatly next to her. Then she stood and removed her bikini bottom, slowly. Desire zapped through him and he yanked hard at the chains still holding his wrists. He wanted to take that. That right there.

"What I'd like to see is how your body responds to gentle pleasure."

The gentle word translated to torture and made him harder. She quirked her brow at his cock and knelt between his legs.

"What about your top?" he asked, breathless.

She shook her head. "I'd rather not. Open your legs."

He grunted and pulled his knees up and let them fall open, rolling his hips and making his cock reach for her. "Why just your bottom?"

"Shhh," she said, placing her finger under his balls and slowly running it up until she reached the tip where she tickled his pulsing head with his pre-cum.

He gasped and pushed his hips up for more.

"You like this, see?" she whispered, her tone soft like her touch.

"Because of what I want, not what I'm getting," he gasped.

"Are you sure?" she wondered, sliding her wet finger all along the ridge, making him burn. "I'm going to suck you slowly. Gently," she warned, her fingers gliding along his inner thighs now. "Would you like that?"

"You're the doc," he barely managed.

She eyed him. "I need your permission."

"You do? I'm tied up."

"It doesn't matter. I always want your consent. Just as you should always want mine."

Oh he wanted her consent alright. But for what, was the problem. "Be my guest."

"Would you like me to?"

He cocked his jaw slowly. "I'd like you to try, yes." Fucking suck it already.

"Okay." She positioned herself between his legs, semi laying on his left one, her right hand propping her head up as she used her other to toy gently with him. "Have I ever told you how beautiful your cock is?"

"Talking or sucking?" he said, desperate.

"Both, I think are important. Your cock is very beautiful," she whispered, leaning in to lick along the ridge.

Sade stared at her lips and tongue, transfixed and hungry. "Fucking suck it," he finally gasped.

She took the head into her mouth and sucked him like fucking delicate silk. He pulled at his wrist restraints, clenching his eyes tight. She licked slowly then, from his balls up his entire length. "Did I ever tell you how good your cum tastes?" Her words were sultry satin as she flicked her torment over the slit of his cock.

He was beyond words as he strained to get more.

"Do you want to know the best part of making love to you?"

He wanted to know if it made her suck harder. He answered with a gasp and thrust of his hips.

"Is seeing how much you want me. Need me. Open your eyes and watch what I'm doing," she said, sucking the head softly.

He yanked on the chains.

"Stop," she said sharply, looking at him, his cum making her lips shine. "Don't pull on the restraints. Control yourself. Take what I'm giving you the way I want to give it."

"Fucking tormenting me, Mercy."

"While loving on your cock," she whispered, taking his entire length into her mouth, making Sade's head come forward to see and buck his hips. She pressed a hand on his lower stomach and shoved him back down. "Be still," she gasped after his cock popped from her wet lips. "Take it the way I give it," she ordered, flicking her tongue all over the ridge again.

Her firm hand pressing down on his pelvis sent shock waves of bondage heat into his cock. His body shifted gears and suddenly wanted whatever torment she gave. "Yes," he gasped, when his cock hit the back of her throat and she moaned, pulling up slowly, the suction impossibly tight.

"Ffffuuuuck," he moaned, thrusting his hips, only to encounter the sharp press of her hand again.

"I'm going to tell you when you can come," she whispered, raining fire on the head of his cock with the tip of her tongue. "And when I tell you, I expect you to do it."

Jesus Christ. He gave his body to her little therapeutic game.

"Does it feel good like this?" she gasped, going down slowly on his length again.

"Fuck yes. Your fucking mouth is so tight and hot," he grit, thrusting against the press of her palm. He yanked at his wrist restraints again and she pulled up abruptly and stood. Not looking at him, she stepped out from between his legs and picked up her bikini bottom and began to put it on.

His pride didn't allow him to ask questions.

"I asked you nicely to not pull on your restraints, and you did it. This will help you learn to control yourself. Therapy is over."

She walked out leaving him with *holy fucking Christ, did she just leave?*

He dropped his head back and clenched his eyes and jaw together, ready to scream. "Mercy! Unfucking shackle me goddammit!"

The door opened and she strolled back in with wide eyes and a guilty grimace. "Sorry about that, I forgot." He eyed her as she unlocked his right wrist then stood and strolled to the left. His cock-o-meter had gone flat at her unusual behavior, body and mind unsure of how to exactly misfire. After she undid the left one, it took all Sade's strength not to wrestle her to the same submission she'd just forced him in. But instead he watched her stand and walk to the door, captivated by her succulent ass hanging out of her bikini as she went in the most sexy confidence he'd ever seen her in.

He sat there for several seconds, going over everything that had happened, feeling the need to keep notes before he got lost. Lost in her little games. Or before his demons tricked him into something very bad. He finally got up and examined his ankles and wrists. He was sure he smelled like a fucking sponge soaked in alcohol as he made his way to the room's bathroom. He locked the door and turned on the shower, wondering how she'd stood sucking him. He wasn't dirty but… he felt it. He stepped into the glass enclosure, debating on hot or cold. Hot would hurt like fuck. Hot it was.

He showered, thinking of Mercy the entire time. What he needed to do to ensure her failing. Because he surely needed to with the way things were going. She had no idea how close he was to hurting her. To not caring if he did. It's like whatever wall that used to be there, protecting her from his monsters, was gone. He wasn't sure how or why, just that they were.

He put his head against the shower wall, closing his eyes and gasping around the pain in his chest. Felt like a fucking death waiting to happen. He was giving her up. He was setting her free. That's all. It was right. It was right and for once he'd do whatever it took to protect her. Even if it meant removing himself from the equation.

He stepped out of the shower and froze at finding Mercy there. "I wanted to take care of your wrists and ankles." She wagged a first aid kit at him with a bright smile, eyes glued to his. He yanked a towel off the bar on his right and wrapped it around his waist, thinking of the best way to proceed. He needed to knock her off her game. "This more of your therapy?" He walked to the vanity and turned, leaning his ass against it and crossing his arms over his chest, meeting her bright innocent gaze.

"Just first aid," she muttered, nodding but not moving.

He stared at her, his mind giving up a full blown bathroom fantasy. There needed to be none of that. And having her this close was too dangerous. "Leave it, I'll do it." He turned to the mirror and grabbed a hand towel. "You think privacy is too much to ask for? Doc?"

"No, of course not." She cleared her throat lightly and set it on the counter next to him. "I was thinking we could start therapy tonight. Six o'clock."

He turned on the water and wet a washcloth. "Whatever you say, doc. The sooner we start, the sooner we finish."

"Okay then. Was thinking we'd do the sessions in my room."

He only nodded.

"Just… bring yourself. For the first session."

He didn't answer her as he put the hot washcloth over his face.

"Alright then. See you at six. In my room. I made breakfast by the way. In the kitchen."

He let her ramble and pretended she'd given him the privacy he'd asked for. When he didn't hear anything for a few seconds, he removed the washcloth and found her gone. Her absence was so much more painful than her presence when thinking of what he was doing. Fuck, but he needed to. She was kryptonite and he needed to figure out how to stay in the game but stay out of her. In all ways. But something told him her little display of therapy earlier said more of that was coming. He was just going to have to learn how to drown without dying.

Sade made his way to his own room in only a towel and got dressed then headed downstairs, hoping he didn't run into her. He located the breakfast she mentioned and eyed the empty beach themed kitchen and dining, listening for signs of where anybody was. By the time he fed his gut, he casually strolled around, scoping things out. Nobody was at the pool, or downstairs except Liberty who was in her room. He went upstairs and peeked around. Where the fuck was she? She knew better than to be on the beach alone. He hurried downstairs and out the patio door leading to the beach path. He scanned the beach, not seeing anything but blinding white sand kissing diamond studded sapphire. Pissed, he raced around the house and found the jeep still there.

By the time he was back inside, he was out of breath and ready to radio the fucking boat. The basement. He hadn't checked there. There was a gym, God she better be fucking there.

At reaching the bottom of the stairs he heard muffled music. Pausing at the outside of the door, he recognized hardcore dance music. He slowly cracked it open and his breath rushed out in relief at finding her there only to freeze back just as quickly at seeing what she was doing. Shadow fighting. Blindfolded. Wearing skintight black shorts and matching sports bra, using one of them Wing Chun looking wooden dummies. Judging by the sweat flying off her body with every rapid punch and kick, she'd been at it a while.

Desire gripped Sade as he watched all those tan muscles rippling with sexy perfection. And God that fucking ass. If anything brought him down, it would be that forbidden perfection.

He slipped inside and carefully shut the door as she put to shame an invisible mini-army surrounding her. Sade forgot all about therapy and games as he watched her. She was fucking epic, her body graceful and strong, begging to be fucked so very perfectly and properly. His dick was like a rock as he leaned against the wall, taking the torture. Fucking formidable. He studied her fighting style, spotting so many in one. He didn't remember ever being so fixated on anything. So hungry. She was sadistic violence wrapped in succulent silk and he wanted to devour that with every part of him. He realized something that stirred his anger. She'd never once unleashed this kind of fighting on him. Not once. She'd been taking it easy on him. His demons didn't like that one bit. He wasn't sure why, but they didn't.

But he liked it.

It suddenly seemed frugal to not be found there when she was done and as hard as it was to leave, he did so, very quietly, wondering as he made his way to his room, what fight or war she was practicing or preparing for.

Chapter Eight

Mercy dug through her closet, still dripping wet from her shower. She'd called in backup, and radioed her father with suppositional questions that he indulged her in, even though she was pretty sure he knew what she was asking for. "Suppose you have a man who is a sadomasochist who thinks pain is pleasure? How would you go about reversing that?"

Basically her father said what she was thinking, confirmed her thoughts. She just wanted to make sure, this was Sade's life she was messing with. But she had her first day's therapy in mind. Actually it would be mostly the same for all five days. Utter sensuality, sensitivity, love, tenderness—all the things he never had, that's what she'd give him. Give him in ways he couldn't resist. In ways he'd not had them if ever he did. She would create new desires in him to help give him a fighting chance to change. Out with the old, in with the new. Sounded so simple but she knew it would be anything but with him. He was being extra stubborn. She got that he was afraid of hurting her, she got that he hated that part of him with her. But geez he needed to give himself some credit and cut himself some slack.

She pulled out a light pink, flimsy dress. The material was thin enough to need a slip. Perfect. She'd not wear one. She had three hours till therapy and she wanted to be ready. She'd be a vision of delicacy, a wet dream of feminine sensuality. She put on a tiny bit of perfume, and just enough makeup. She wanted to be beautiful. Not sexy, beautiful. A sensual, beautiful woman. She'd never really been that before, so this was new ground for her too.

And to keep control of the situation, she was going to lay ground rules starting out. She'd had the brilliant idea of creating the classic, therapist-patient fantasy—only she wouldn't tell him. The excitement of the things she could teach him and help him with made her giddy. He would learn a new desire for new things. And God, her privates were the happiest of all about that. But there was no time for guilt about it. She needed to find things around the beach house to serve her purpose. Soft items, sensual items. She froze, thinking. *I should blindfold him. So the senses were heightened.* Maybe not the entire time, just… some of the time. She needed him to make visual connections too. Or maybe she should just require him to close his eyes. And then open them. Whenever she felt it needed.

She needed to be prepared for his snarky attitude, though. He'd be trying to break her. Clobbering her with candy coated sarcasm.

She was ready for that.

****

Sade stared at the contract in his hands, reading. He'd found it in a neat envelope on the bed—his copy. He brought the envelope to his nose. Perfume? His cock twitched at the delicate floral scent, his mind trying to define the flower. Lavender maybe. With… vanilla. The combination made him hungry. He looked over the list, checking to make sure everything was the way it was when he signed it. He tossed it on the bed when finding it in order, wanting to vomit after reading over his conditions. He took a deep breath and sat on the bed. In thirty minutes he'd start the disconnect process with her. Count down to imminent and dire desolation.

Unlike her, he didn't work out in the gym. He needed to be worked up, not relaxed. He would count on his violent anger in this to keep from needing other things. He just hoped if she pushed the sexual issue that he'd be able to pull off what he needed to. He was not fucking looking forward to using candy coated brutality with her. The only reason he could do it was how fucking bad it hurt him to do that. He'd aimed that pain at himself, he deserved that. Deserved all the pain he had to cause to protect her, even the pain he inflicted on her to accomplish it.

Therapy in her room. His heart hammered his chest when the time came to go.

He raised his hand to knock on the door then gave five rough knocks, hoping to throw her off her game from jump. And what was that game? Part of him was beyond curious and couldn't wait to see what she pulled out of her hat of tricks. His sweet fucking magician, always wanting to do magic on him.

"Come in," she called. More like sang. Score—Mercy 1, Sade 0.

He opened the door and walked in, shutting it behind him. His eyes locked on her—the fuck was she wearing? She faced away from him, before the desk that she seemed to have turned for an office type scenario. Or classroom. The dress she had on was nothing he'd ever seen her in, the clear thin material showed her perfect ass plain as day while she leaned over the desk doing who cares what. His eyes lowered over her muscular legs exposed from the upper thigh. If she bent a little more, he'd have a shot of her fucking ass and he was pretty damn sure she knew that.

He made his way to the chair before her desk and sat, hoping the view improved. His gaze dropped to those sexy ass pussy pink heels she wore. Fuck, she smelled good. His eyes went back up her legs, noticing the shine on them. His mouth watered, wanting to lick and taste and bite, and just fucking eat.

"So," she said lightly, finally turning.

Sade averted his gaze and held back a laugh at the obvious show she'd just put on. After scanning the room, he finally made eye contact. Oh fuck. She was so fucking beautiful he had to look away. "Clock's ticking, what's the plan?"

"I want to talk to you."

He forced himself to look at her again, putting plenty of cocky in his gaze. "About?"

"About your condition."

"What about it?"

"I just…" she had her palms on the desk and when she lifted her shoulders, his eyes lowered to her tits for another sledgehammer to the stomach. There they were, fucking perky handfuls, staring at him through the paper-thin, pussy pink fabric. "I mean are you aware how you became a sadomasochist?"

Score—Mercy 2. Sade 0.

He lowered his gaze, not wanting her to see the heat burning in it. "Yes," was the only answer to give.

"And are you aware that—"

"It's not normal, no fucking shit, yes. I'm aware." He looked right, stretching out his left leg to make room for his dick.

"Okay," she said softly. "Just want to make sure we're on the same page. So the plan of therapy I'd like to begin with you is introducing elements that you're not normally aroused by, and see if we can create new arousals."

The only thing Sade's cock heard was create new arousal. And being the dick that it was, it jerked with eager attentiveness. He needed to calm down. He quickly threw in a couple thoughts of his father and in seconds, he put that fire right the fuck out.

"You okay with that? With me trying this?"

"You're the doc," he said, forcing the dry in his tone.

"Fantastic." Her eagerness tickled his balls and he shifted in his seat. "I'd like you naked for this, please."

She faced her desk now and presented that fucking ass for her little slam dunk. "No way."

She turned, the look on her face saying she might have been expecting trouble there. "As your therapist Sade, I will need you to cooperate with me or this will not work. I'd like to keep this as professional as we can to ensure its success."

He couldn't stop the laugh from barking out.

"I mean it, I'm taking this very seriously," she said, sounding oh so sincere.

"Are you getting naked?" he challenged. There was no way in hell he could manage under those conditions.

"No, I'm not. And the thing is, I need your entire body available for influence."

He cocked his head, eying her now.

"And I won't touch you." She raised her hands up before him.

The strange conditions had him oh so fucking curious. He slowly stood. "No touching?"

"No touching."

He reached for the hem of his shirt and pulled it over his head, tossing it on the floor next to his chair. When he went to undo his pants, she turned and cleared her throat, and of course his eyes zeroed in on that ass. He removed his pants and underwear and noticed she was tying a blindfold on herself. "I'm blindfolding myself until you tell me I can take it off. I don't want to rush you though. Tell me when I can turn."

"You didn't have to," Sade said. But he was kind of glad she did, he could look at her now in that dress. Definitely hadn't seen her in any such thing before. And the fact that she wasn't wearing bra and panties said she was trying really hard to arouse him. And it was working like a fucking charm. "I'm ready."

She carefully turned back around and then sat partially on the desk, keeping one pink high heel on the floor. "So, how are you feeling?" His head angled on its own when the position gave a promising view to what was beneath. Oh fuck. Matching pink sheer. So she had on a thong.

"Fine."

"I mean what are you feeling? What emotions. Are you afraid? Angry? Aroused?"

He studied her tits, deciding that he liked this set up of her not seeing him but him seeing her. "Maybe all three."

"Oh," she said, curious. "Let's explore those three. Starting with angry, why are you angry?"

"Because I think this is stupid," he half lied.

She smiled and he studied her lips. "Fair enough." The soft tone of her voice licked the tip of his cock. "What about afraid?"

She sat fully on the desk, crossing her legs, exposing a generous portion of her outer thigh nearly all the way to her ass. "Afraid of…" He was going to say of falling asleep but decided he wanted to play just a little. "Of you."

"Of me?" she asked surprised and maybe disappointed. Maybe.

"Of what you might do."

"Do you trust me?"

"Not at all."

She actually gave him the sweetest smile. Fuck she was pretty blindfolded in that matching material. Maybe an accessory for the dress in some capacity. Surely not that one. "I don't believe you," she whispered.

"Why not?"

"Okay, then tell me what I've done to make you distrust me?"

"Our fun little relationship was founded on lies." He licked his lower lip, noticing her toenails matched the dress. And her nails.

She actually grimaced, making his cock ache. "You're right. Okay, can you not count that since I didn't really know you yet? How about after, what have I done to make you not trust me?"

He opened his legs a little. "I would have to go with the whole tying me up without my permission bit."

"Ugh, ok, ok, fine. But I did that with the best intentions. In fact, my reasons should actually prove I'm trust worthy with the things that really matter."

"To you." He realized her lips held the same tint of pink then.

"Yes," she said softly. "To me. You matter to me."

Score: Mercy—winning, Sade—losing.

He had no good words for that. Even the bad ones didn't work in his favor.

"Okay fine," she said, her voice still silky. "Maybe I have done a few things to make you not trust me." She held up both hands. "I'm sorry, baby. Sade, I mean," she corrected, biting her lip.

Jesus Christ, his cock was about to explode if she got any more sexy.

"Okay, so next thing."

Yes, that.

This time when she bit her lower lip, she let it slide slowly out of her mouth before licking it. "Why... are you aroused?"

"Is that a trick question?"

"No," she said quickly, her soft tone genuine. "I... really want to know."

"I'm pretty much always aroused. Part of my condition."

"But what part of this situation is painful that you would be aroused?"

"My guess is because I'm denying urges and it's nearly painful."

"Oh," she said, the word a soft gasp. "Makes sense. Are you... ready for me to begin?"

His cock jerked. "Begin what?"

"My therapy."

"I thought you were."

"Well, I was just wanting to break the ice. What I'd like to do is give you something new."

"Like what?" he couldn't stop from saying.

"Like a new pleasure? Remember?"

Jesus, fuck. "New, how?"

"New as in you've never had it before?"

Officially fucking interested. He was pretty sure he'd had all manner of pleasure he was able to have. "I thought you said no touching."

"I'm not going to touch you." She giggled and the sound fascinated him. Excited him. He wanted to explore her little secret angle now.

"What are you going to do?"

"You're going to touch yourself. But I won't look. Will you do that for me?"

"Masturbation?"

"Yes."

He slowly licked his lips, his heart hammering. "I can only orgasm if I'm fantasizing about things you wouldn't approve, doc."

"Oh, not orgasm. Just masturbate."

He quirked his brow. Why else did a person masturbate if not to orgasm? "It's your show. Doc."

The fucking smile she gave. This was going all wrong.

Chapter Nine

"Okay, first, I'd like you to open your legs for me."

He spread his knees wide, the position making his cock stand up. "Open."

"Very good." Her soft tone made it jerk. She angled her head slightly away from him. "I want you to hold yourself at the base of your cock. Use your left hand, even though you're right-handed."

He did as she said, his gaze on her mouth and the flush in her cheeks. "Done." It was the first soft word he'd used with her. It really needed to be the last.

"Thank you," she nearly whispered. Then she stood and knelt on the floor, several feet from him. "Your legs are open?"

Fuck, what was she planning? "Yes."

"Use your right hand to cup your balls for me. Tell me when you're doing it."

Her breathy tone got him even harder. She was fucking aroused and he bet her pussy was dripping.

"Cupping my balls, doc," he said, his voice gruff.

She licked her lips with a nod and small smile. "Ok, squeeze them very softly for me, gently. A caress."

It usually did nothing for him but with her kneeling there, telling him while blindfolded and turned on in her see through, pussy pink dress, made all the difference.

"Are you… doing it?"

"Squeezing very softly. Gently. A caress."

She swallowed and licked her lips. "Okay. Very good. Now, I want you to slide your left hand up your cock now. When you get to the head, tell me."

Fuck. "My hand is at the head," he said, stifling a groan.

"Slide your middle finger over the slit for me."

His lips parted for constant intake of more air now as he watched her, the way her own lips remained parted.

"Are you wet?" she whispered.

Fucking God. "Very," he said, gritting his teeth.

"Softly," she whispered, "don't forget. I want you to caress your balls very softly. Tell me you are."

"I am," he gasped.

"Open your legs wider for me," she said.

"Very wide now," he whispered, getting more winded by the second.

"I want you to run your wet finger along the ridge of your cock, where it's very thick." Her words were extremely breathy and hungry sounding. "Make sure you only do what I say. When I say."

"Yes," he said. "I'm rubbing the ridge where it's very thick."

She paused a few seconds and he could see her chest heaving. "Is it very hot?"

"God, yes."

She bit her lower lip. "Good. That's so very good," she whispered. "I want you to continue caressing your balls that way and slowly slide your finger over your slit again."

He locked his gaze on her tits, wishing he could see them as he rubbed pre-cum over his slit.

"Does it feel good?"

"Yes," he whispered, hissing.

"Mmm, very good, you're doing so very good. Now I want you to take your hands off of your balls and cock and clasp them behind your head. Tell me when you're done."

The odd request while he wanted to continue, threw him. But he didn't dare interrupt her little show. "Done."

"Okay. Now, I'm going to change this up a little." She stood before him and he looked up. "Are you okay with me taking this blindfold off and putting it on you now? But don't worry, I'll stay right behind you. And still no touching."

"I like being blindfolded it's what I do when—"

"I know," she whispered at his ear now. "Please trust me." The warmth of her breath shot into his cock as she finished securing the blindfold on him.

"Hands back in position," she said at his ear. "Left one on the base of your big cock. Right one softly caressing your balls."

He did as she said.

"Very good," she whispered hotly, making him realize she was watching now. Fuck.

"Finger back on your wet slit now. Make it hot for me." The words trembled next to his ear. "Very good baby," she said as he stroked the slit. "Yes, push into your fist for me. So very good, you're doing so good with this." The arousal in her voice was off the charts and he grunted. "Oh God, is it hot in your cock?"

"Fuck yes."

"Stroke the length now. With a tight grip. Let me see your cock sliding in and out of your fist. Oh God, yes," she whispered, her breath fanning his neck. "Open your legs wider for me. Gently caressing your balls are you obeying that?"

"Jesus, yes."

"You're doing so amazing." Her breath shuddered out and he turned toward it. "Keep stroking baby. When you get to that pretty thick head, make it wet with your cum."

"Mercy," he whispered.

"Call me Doc during therapy. Do you understand?"

"Yes," he gushed, hearing wet sounds behind him. "What are you doing?" he gasped.

"I have my middle finger in my pussy. I'm so wet, so hot. I'm touching my clit and it's very hard," she said with a light whimper. Do you like me to finger my pussy like this?"

"Fuck yes, God, fuck," he said harshly. "Finger it deep baby."

"You're going to fuck your fist while I finger myself. Are you still gently squeezing your balls?"

"Yes, I want to squeeze harder."

"No," she whispered sharply. "Do as I say. Do you understand?"

"Yes," he whispered. "I do." He was beyond lying now.

"Would you like me to stick two fingers in my pussy?"

"Yes. Fucking deep."

"My cum is dripping down my hand. I'm going to put my fingers by your mouth but don't move." Her sultry, naughty tone sent heat waves through him. "I just want you to smell me. Don't stop stroking your sexy cock. Do it quicker now," she whispered urgently, like her own pleasure hinged on it.

The smell of her pussy flooded his nostrils and all the air left him in one breath. "Fuck, yes."

"You like the smell of my pussy?"

"So much," he said, his breaths ragged.

"Taste me."

Her fingers slipped into his mouth and he sucked and growled with vigor, his tongue sliding all over them until he was dizzy.

"Stroke your cock while you suck my pussy off my fingers. Stroke it so fast now. But don't come. I'm not done with your therapy yet. Make it so very hot in your balls for me." Her voice quaked. "God my clit is begging for it. Tell me when you feel it coming baby, that fire."

"I feel it," he gasped.

"Stop," she said, her tone firm and sharp. "Put your hands behind your head."

Sade bit down on those urges getting stronger and did as she said, his eyes clenched tight.

"Final phase. I'm going to remove your blindfold."

She slid it off and walked to the desk, her stride sexy as fuck as he fought to catch his breath.

She sat on the desk. "Look at me."

Sade had to tear his desperate gaze from between her legs to obey, still in shock from her little magic trick. More. That's all he could think of in that second. Give me so much fucking more.

She slowly opened her legs then pulled her knees up and back. Fucking God, he was gone. His legs opened in response. "I want you to watch now, but don't touch yourself yet. Open your legs wide for me and get ready for my command."

His heart thundered at her commanding words. His body was very familiar with the concept, but coming from her, there was something potent about it.

"Fuck, do it," he said, when she slipped her middle finger in her pussy until it was buried. She gave a sexy moan, one that delicately asked *do you like it?* His hands locked harder behind his head as he watched her, his cock pounding with desire, throbbing to be touched in anyway.

"Look at me," she whispered.

Sade locked his gaze to her semi-closed, his breaths coming faster at seeing her feeling so fucking good.

"No talking for you," she said. "Just watch me... Mmmm." She gave a slow, heated hiss then bit her lip while lifting her ass off the desk to flick her hips. "My pussy is tight on my finger," she whimpered, adding another finger, making him groan. "I'm going to teach you how to feel good," she said. "Keep looking at my fingers. Look how wet they are." She pulled them from her pussy and swirled them slowly over her clit. "Oh God, it's so hot," she gasped. "Is your cock ready?"

"Fuck yes," he gushed. "Tell me. Tell me what to do."

"You like that? Me making you?"

"Yes." More than he ever imagined he could.

"I like making you, I really like it. Open your legs wider for me. Use your left hand to hold your cock and get it nice and wet for me again, with your middle finger."

He gripped the base of his cock with a grunt and pushed into the tight hold while stroking his finger over the tip, spreading his cum.

"Oh yes, swirl it all over. Gently on those pretty balls baby, do you understand? Don't disobey me."

Fuck. He clenched his eyes tight at the sexy fucking command wrapped in silk.

"Stay with me baby, look at me."

He opened his eyes and locked them onto hers.

"I want you to pump your cock into your fist but watch my fingers and follow my pace."

He let out a hiss, watching her two fingers slide in and out slowly. When she pulled out to rub her clit, he rubbed the slit of his cock and ridge, gasping for air.

"That's it, you're doing so fucking good," she said.

The curse words brought him to old places and he grit his teeth on a surge of masochistic desires.

"Sade," she commanded, her voice sharp.

He gasped, looking at her again.

She got off the desk and turned, facing it. Laying her top half on it, she walked her legs apart just enough. The desk was low so that it put her perfect ass high. She turned her upper body enough to see him behind her and began fingering herself again. "Stroke your cock Sade. Do it. I want to hear your cock moving in and out of your tight fist."

Sade grunted hard, flicking his hips as he watched her fingers pump in and out.

"Oh," she whimpered. "My clit is so hot."

The delicate sound snapped him in half and in one step, he was on her, hand pressing her down onto the desk, his cock slamming inside her.

Her sharp cry and gasp finished him off, and Sade grabbed a handful of her hair, stealing her leverage as he rammed in and out of her. His other hand bit into her shoulder and she gave a short roar as she grabbed hold of the desk, sending things crashing to the floor while he pounded into that soft pussy the way he fucking needed-- hard and fast. "Take my fucking cock," he grit. "Make your pussy come, make it come all over me." His fingers pulled harder in her hair until she gave a stifled half scream. "Are you rubbing your clit? I want your fucking fingers on it, fucking make yourself come." He made the demand without slowing his strokes. "Come all over me while I hammer your perfect pussy Mercy, fucking do it!" he growled.

She let out her first orgasmic shriek and Sade grabbed her hips in both hands, yanking her faster onto him. He clenched his eyes tight as she spasmed and quivered on his raging hard on.

He pressed his hand between her shoulders, holding her down as he pulled his cock out of her and stroked the wet head on her tight ass.

"Sade," she whimpered. "I can't, I can't, I'm scared, please."

The begging brought his rage full throttle and he growled, biting into her hips with his fingers as he fought the urge to shove in and tear her.

"Go slow Sade, please."

"Don't… beg me," he barked, straining.

"Okay, okay," she gasped. "I'm trying, I want to do this for you, I do but I swear if you fucking hurt me, it's over, do you fucking hear me?" she cried bitterly, looking over her shoulder. "I will kill you and then I will leave," she gasped, the words shaking with her body now.

It was too late. "Be so fucking still, Mercy. And breathe, do you fucking hear me? Breathe while I fuck your perfect ass."

"Okay, okay," she gasped.

Sade gasped at feeling the pressure on his head and grabbed a hand full of her hair again, pulling hard to keep from ramming. He let out a low growling hiss as he worked the tip of his head into that tight opening. "Fucking perfect," he seethed, looking down at it.

"Oh God, oh God," she whimpered.

"Fucking breathe," he ordered, raking his fingers down the center of her back. "You're taking my cock, Angel. You're taking all of my bad cock, that's what you want, isn't it?"

"Yes," she gasped. "I want it."

He felt her muscles quivering in attempt to accommodate him. "I want your fingers in your pussy while you rub that pretty clit. And I want you to do it until you're coming again, do you understand?"

"Yes," she cried sharply when his cock slid in a few more inches.

"Are you fucking yourself?" He slid in even deeper.

"Oh, God, yes. Sade, slower."

He slammed his palm down on her ass, making her scream. "Are you fucking yourself!" he growled.

"I'm fucking myself!"

He slid all the way in and both her hands shot out and gripped the desk with a sharp cry. The disobedience flooded him with desire and he fell forward, pinning her with his weight. "You didn't listen," he shuddered, rolling his hips and turning her face to his. "You never listen to me. Now you get to be fucked like an animal, that's what you wanted?"

"Sade," she gasped. "Please. Wait."

The beg drove him to his edge. "Your fucking ass… so fucking tight on me." Dizziness hit him as he pumped his cock in and out. "So fucking tight, so fucking perfect, always begging for me to *fuck,* fast and hard!" he grit, sucking on her shoulder then biting down when his thrusts turned faster.

She screamed *stop* but to his mind, it was don't stop, don't ever stop. And he fucking didn't, not until his pounding cock shot its evil seed in her, that's all that mattered, that's all he knew. That's all he heard until she let out a loud shriek.

The sound was different and startled him. Sade suddenly realized he was on top of Mercy on the desk and she was sobbing under him.

Terror gripped him and he flew off of her, making her scream. The sight of blood on her legs, stole his strength and he stumbled back.

She turned, her face crimped and streaked with tears. "Oh fuck," he gasped, shaking his head. "No, no, no."

Mercy suddenly flew off the desk and stormed to him. He saw the look on her face, the lethal look in her eyes, but he'd never seen it aimed at him. He didn't try to stop her. The first round of fists and feet told him she'd been pushed over the edge. He'd turned her into something he'd never seen.

"Come on!" she screamed, kicking and hitting. "You want to hurt, you want to hurt me? Let's do it! Let's fucking fight, you and me, let's fucking bleed! We can bleed, one on one!"

Her furious shrieks of pain, agony and regret pierced him so fucking hard, it put him in that place inside where his sanity hid out during monster time.

"Let's fight!" she roared between shrieking sobs. "Let's fight! You love me! You don't fucking hate me, you love me!" she screamed, not letting up.

I don't hate you baby. I do love you. So fucking much, he wanted to tell her. *I just want to protect you. From this. From me.* He said the words so hard inside him, praying she would somehow hear him from that quiet place where there was no talking allowed. There was only crouching in a corner, arms over his head while he waited for the outside pain to rescue him from the inside pain.

"You're killing meeeee," she screamed. "Why won't you help me, help you! Please, help me!"

She continued to beat on him in her own insane oblivion, and in his mind he held her in a tight embrace. He held her so tight and kissed her on the top of her head, whispering promises he couldn't keep. *Stop crying baby. I'll help you, I promise. I promise to be good. I promise to do good, I'll do better.* It was the same words he'd always said after he failed. He'd always failed. Always.

Sade focused on the words in Mercy's screams—like a broken love song. *"I'll teach you! I'll fucking teach you, you can learn! You can learn to never fucking do that!"* It went on and on, soothing him. Don't stop. Don't stop, baby. Don't you stop.

And she didn't.

He wasn't sure how long it took before he actually hit that floor. He tried to stay on his feet as long as he could, tried to take it. Because once he hit the floor, he knew it was a countdown till darkness. He didn't want it to come. Not unless it was coming for good. Maybe this time it would. Maybe his Mercy would succeed where so many before had failed. Yes, she could. She could bring the darkness for good, she was his angel.

Another voice mixed with Mercy's and Sade barely recognized it was Liberty. Mild panic hit him as he fought to speak. *Don't stop her, please. Let her finish. Let her fucking finish what she started. Let her finish me.*

"Don't fight me, Mercy!" Liberty yelled.

"I have to teach him!" she screamed. "He doesn't want to be that! I need to teach him!"

Mercy escaped Liberty and he welcomed her foot flying at his head.

"Mercy! You're going to kill him, you're going to kill Sade!"

"He has to learn!"

The sound of a body hit the floor followed by only gasps. "I really didn't want to fucking do that."

Sadness hit Sade at hearing it was Liberty. Whatever she'd done... had silenced his sweet angel of Mercy.

Chapter Ten

Mercy stood in the shower, holding her body, trying to stop the violent trembling. Felt like she'd been in a car wreck and her limbs were still in shock, her mind numb. She reached out with a trembling hand and turned the hot water off, gasping in the sudden cold, praying it reset her system. She stood there, just feeling the spray, focusing on getting her breathing in line.

Flashes of memory shot through her veins, Sade's cock pounding into her. Her beating him. Him letting her. She gasped on pain, holding her stomach again, leaning into the shower wall as her strength left. Tiny groans of agony accompanied her every breath as her body processed the memories scarring her. She'd woken up in her bed, remembering all of it. Dreaming about it, that's what had woke her. Liberty was there at her bed telling her everything was okay. Sade was resting and would be fine, that he was just a little banged up. Few bruises is all.

God, she knew that wasn't true, she remembered how she hadn't held back like she usually did. She remembered how he didn't fight back. A sob gushed out of her and she covered her mouth with a trembling hand. And all for what? For fucking her in her stupid ass? It was just a fucking ass! And the lessons? She had loved it so much. It had awakened something in her, a desire to command his desires, to be in control of them. For him. And the ass part… she'd just panicked. She knew it would hurt like hell and she'd panicked. And then he got to that unstable point and before she could stop him, he'd lost himself to it. And she'd taken it. She'd let him fuck her in the ass when she'd wanted him to stop and Jesus, it hurt. It hurt still, but it didn't justify what she did. This was her fault. He'd warned her. He'd tried to warn her but no. Mercy knew better.

She was going to shower, she would shower and go see him, make sure he was okay. Sade's swollen face flashed in her mind and stole her strength again. Tears poured down her face and she let out a loud sob, stifling the avalanche of them. And she'd planned on letting him do it, she did. Just when he was sane and sober, in control. Somewhat even. She loved more than anything, no craved, the feel of power in his hands, his body, his voice. His *need,* his desire for *her*. But she never wanted to be scared of him, and when he got like that, she very much was. But why? Why should she be scared? It's not like she couldn't defend herself or stop him. The problem was, she froze up. Froze up in fear. And then other triggers hit from the really bad memories and just like him, she'd lost herself to that darkness that once had control of her and her entire life. She was just like him still. He just hadn't hit her buttons like she hit his.

Thank God Liberty had stopped her. The idea that she'd hurt him like that, broke her so badly inside, the pain was suffocating. She hurt somebody precious to her. After she practically forced him into a situation that would tempt him. She practically begged him for it, waving her ass in the air. Good job, doc. You drove your patient over the edge, the man you love and now he'll hate himself for it. Good fucking job.

And now what? Now that session one was a fucking nightmare disaster, now what? How were they supposed to come back from that?

Mercy quickly dressed and made her way to Sade's room, looking around for Liberty as she did. She looked at the closed door, her stomach suddenly sick. She hurried downstairs and found Liberty, sleeping in the recliner. She touched her on her arm and she nearly leapt out of the recliner, scaring the shit out of Mercy.

"Damn it, Mercy! Don't ever wake me up like that!"

"I'm sorry, I didn't know."

Liberty slid her good hand across her face and looked around. "What time is it?"

"Nearly dawn. I was going to check on Sade."

Liberty flopped back into the chair. "Good, save me the trouble."

"How is he?"

"He's fine," she mumbled. "I told you, few bruises."

"Few bruises," Mercy said, swallowing, wanting better details. "Few is three to fifty, can you be more specific?"

She shrugged with a yawn, "Bout' forty eight maybe."

"Oh God," Mercy gasped.

"Stop, he's had much worse from one of his thrown weekend fights."

Mercy nodded, walking in erratic circles. "I'm going to see him."

"You said that, yes. Let me know if you need any help with anything," she mumbled, putting the recliner all the way back and turning on her side.

Mercy made her way back to his room and stared at the door again. She turned the knob so very slowly, not wanting to make any noise if he were sleeping. She didn't let herself look as she slipped in and closed the door, facing away from the bed, her eyes closed.

"You lost?"

She spun around and at seeing his deformed face, she covered her eyes with both hands, gasping for air.

"Baby," he croaked after a moment. "You'll hyperventilate. Come here."

"Oh God," she whispered. "I can't."

"Yes you can," he said softly.

She shook her head. "I can't, I can't," she barely whispered.

"Please?"

"Sade," she cried, still holding her hands before her eyes.

"Come here, Angel," he muttered, his voice deep. "I need you."

The broken sound in his voice drew her to his bed but she kept her eyes on the floor as she went. She sat next to him, facing so that he was barely in her peripheral.

"Angel," he whispered, stroking a finger over her arm. She cringed and he drew it back with a heavy sigh. She clenched her eyes in the silence, wanting to see him but terrified to. "I'm so fucking sorry," he whispered.

"You?" she gasped. "I can't bear to look at you."

"I don't blame you."

She realized what he was saying and gasped. "Not because of what you did, because of what I did to you!"

"Oh God, Angel," he whispered. "There's only one monster here."

"Yes, me!" she choked out. "I hurt you! Look at you!"

"Holy fuck, stop. Look at me. Mercy, look! At me!"

"No, I can't." She shook her head. "I can't stand to see what I did."

He went quiet for a few seconds before whispering in baffled shock, "Wow."

"Whatever," she cried.

"I've gotten so much worse."

"Yeah, by other animals!" she wailed, wiping her tears.

"Motherfuck," he mumbled.

"Motherfuck?"

"Yes, motherfuck."

"Why motherfuck, why are you saying that?"

"Because after all this, nothing has changed."

She chanced a look at him. "Oh my God," she jerked away, "I'm going to be sick."

"Just stop!" he said, his voice hard. "You are not doing this, you are not going to turn this around and act like you're the criminal and I'm the goddamn *victim!*"

She jerked to him again. "How can you lay there, beat half to death and *say* that?" The shocked words came in a shrill hiss.

"Mercy!" he yelled now. "I raped your ass! You were sobbing and bleeding, what the *fuck?* I guess you asked for it, begged for it? Is that it, is that what you're going with, doc?"

"Oh my God." She covered her mouth nodding. "Sade, if you think about it—"

"Holy shit!" he said, furious.

"Not holy shit! Not holy shit, I mean it!" she demanded back, hardly able to stand looking at him. "You told me no, no Mercy, don't do it, you warned me over and over not to push you, that you were unstable, and there I was, wagging my ass right in your face!" she shrilled.

"Oh my God, don't fucking do this Mercy, don't. Don't make it something it's not."

"No!" she stood up and faced him, jabbing a finger. "You don't make it something it's not. It's not your fault you have these issues, it's not your fault. I knew you did! I even knew how to stop you so why didn't I? Huh? No, I let you do it then cried like a little bitch, and then tried to kill you," she wailed, covering her mouth with a hand, stifling a sob. "I'm the animal here."

"Jesus fucking Christ," he muttered, shaking his lowered head. "So I basically got my ass beat for nothing." He looked at her with his barely one good eye. "Am I to assume we'll be resuming classes tomorrow evening from my wheelchair?"

She gasped. "Sade, that's not fucking funny! I'm sorry, okay?"

"I don't want your apology, godammit, I want your common fucking sense!"

"And I'd like your common fucking sense," she argued back. "Why didn't I *listen?* Maybe I'm the real sadist or masochist here and wanted this to happen! Think about it," she said over his mumblings and head shakings. "I'm not stupid, I know this shit," she said.

"You know this shit," he mumbled, looking up. "She knows this shit, did you hear that? Are you listening to this? Are you? I hope you fucking are and you need to have a little chat with your girl before she doesn't return from this. You feel me? Do you feel me!" he yelled at the ceiling.

"I am just saying," she plead, "that I'm no better in this."

"I'm not doing this," he shook his head emphatically. "Not doing this at all."

"Okay, fine, then let's not do this."

"Are we done then?" he asked her.

She regarded him, not sure what that meant.

"Look at me, Mercy," he said softer, his head angled. "What the fuck are we doing here, baby? What is this? Junkyard therapy? The patient rapes, the doctor brutalizes? I mean what? The fuck? Are we doing, baby? You seeing it, you seeing in this mirror?"

"I messed up, okay?" she wailed. "I freaked out, the assplay triggered me."

"Ass *rape,*" he yelled, "don't fucking down play it. Fucking right it triggered you, do you know why it triggered you, Mercy? Because it reminded you of those motherfucking bastards that hurt you, that was *me!* Mercy!" he pounded his chest with a fist, making her sick.

Sorrow strangled her throat, making her choke the words out, "I could've stopped you. I knew how, I knew what to do, I just... I panicked. I just won't panic again."

"You could've stopped it? Are you so sure of that, baby?"

She sat there nodding emphatically, trying to get her shit together. "*Very* sure," she said in firm sincerity. "Very, very, very sure." She turned more to him. "That's my point, Sade. The reason I didn't do what I needed to is *not* your fault—that fault lies with me. And it's not your fault that you have your issues. Nor," she said louder, pointing at him when he looked ready to interrupt, "is it my fault I have my issues, but *how* we handle them is where we have to lay blame. How we handle what has happened to us is where we become responsible."

"So I'm guilty, then," he said as though she proved his point.

"As. Am. I. No, don't shake your head, you know this is true, if you're willing to be reasonable."

"Un. Fucking. Believable," he said in soft amazement, looking just to the right. He finally turned to her. "This can't happen again."

"I agree," she said. "And it doesn't have to."

"Oh it won't. Because we're done."

She stared at him, her stomach roiling and tight. She got up and began to pace next to the bed. "So… you're just going to throw it away."

"No," he said, quietly, "I'm going to save what precious few memories we have left."

She snorted, still pacing. "Precious few memories," she muttered, eying him as she went. "It's an ass Sade, it barely hurt."

"You fucking lie!" he yelled, making her jump inside.

"It hurt, fine," she yelled back, but look at you!" she threw her hand at him. "Why Sade?" she stopped and stared at him, tears filling her eyes. "Why are you so damn stubborn, I'm riding a goddamn bull that keeps throwing me off, how about you let me help you, how about *you* fucking help me help you?"

"Because I'm *sick* Mercy, okay? You want me to use the medical terms, you want to play a real doctor, I'm. Fucking. Sick! And there is *no* cure!"

"I can help and you know it, you know damn well what I'm trying to do can work if you'd give it a chance! But you won't, you will not, you are fighting me and you're right!" she grit while pointing at him, "it will *never* work without *your* cooperation!"

"Wow," he said, shaking his head in wide-eyed wonder. "You're the bull, not me."

"Oh I'm a bull alright," she mumbled, back to pacing. "And this bull says we are *not* done."

"We're done."

"Fucking no, we're not," she sang lightly, shaking her head. "We are not done. We are going to regroup. We are going to refocus," she ticked the items off on her fingers with each step she took toward him, "and we are going to re-plan. We're getting back in the game, baby, you and me," she wagged a finger between them. "It's not over yet. This show is just beginning. And you *knew* there would be a few rough spots, I mean you *know* this, anything worth fighting for has them."

He busted out laughing. "Rough spots? Raping your ass is just a little rough spot now? Beating your patient half to death is a little *rough spot?*"

"Stop it," she said, hating how he rubbed it in. "The assplay is nothing," she said, "once I get used to it, it won't be like that, it'll be smooth sailing.

He stared at her for endless seconds. "Smooth sailing," he mocked.

She spun to him. "It's just an ass! A muscle that feels good gripping your cock, I'm very much in favor of offering you this pleasure. This is not some... sacred tunnel to the third heaven that you've trespassed. And you've done worse," she aimed her finger at him, "at that other hideout we were at?"

"Oh, I've done worse! Well fuck me gently, what was I thinking?" He started clapping slowly. "Bravo, Sade. Growing by leaps and bounds."

She stared at him, exhaustion and depression slowly covering her until her head lowered and shoulders sagged with it. Everything was suddenly beyond her. Too big. Too much. Too heavy. Why did it have to be so complicated for him? Why couldn't he just work with her a little more? "I just…" she barely whispered, sobs pushing at the door of her heart. "I just need you, Sade," She shook her head, wiping the tears from her face. "Broken or whole, remember? You said that."

The silence that spanned between them felt bottomless and endless. "Why?" he asked.

The eternal agony in his one word, eternal, self-hatred, choked her. Why would you ever want me for anything? She swallowed and gasped for air, not really knowing the answer, not caring if she did. "I… I just do, okay?" She swiped the tears from her face. "I do and I don't really know why, I don't have answers for everything, I just know… that I need you. All my life, I've needed you."

"What do you want from me?"

He sounded so confused and she suddenly felt like a dirty criminal with needs he couldn't meet, demands he couldn't perform. She felt like a loser, a desperate, lonely, stupid loser. "I… don't want anything, I just…" She swallowed and fresh tears stung her eyes. "Never mind," she barely whispered, hurrying to leave.

"Don't you fucking walk out," he gasped now.

She froze in her steps at hearing such a deep and broken sorrow in his voice. Turning, she faced him and he looked away from her, shaking his head a little. "Do you want to know the one question I have? That... really baffles me?" he whispered, still not looking at her.

She made her way back to the bed and sat next to him, sobbing softly at the sight of a tear rolling down his beat up face.

"Why would God..." his voice trembled out with several gasps, "send me... an angel?" He turned to her, so confused, his bloodshot eyes, pleading for answers. "Do you think..." his voice barely whispered now, "that maybe... He made a mistake?"

Her sobs burst out and she threw herself on his chest. "God doesn't make mistakes baby," she wept, her heart shattered for him. "Humans do, humans make mistakes!"

She hugged him tight, unable to keep back the pent up sorrow for him and he embraced her back so tight, like a man hanging on for dear life. He pressed his mouth onto her head and silently cried with her.

"Please, Sade, tell me you'll help me, please, please, I'm begging. I'm fucking begging goddammit! Please," she wailed.

"Shhhh," he whispered, stroking her head. "Don't cry, sweet Angel. Don't cry.

"Help meeeeee," she cried.

He stroked her head and shhhh'd over and over before giving her the words she desperately needed. "I'll help you."

Chapter Eleven

Sade held Mercy while they slept. He told himself it was to comfort her. That he needed to be what she deserved when he could. That he owed her that. But that didn't erase the stain of guilt. Of having something that should never have been his. He wished he could stop the feelings but he couldn't they were just there, like ants biting him. Felt like he was stealing from God's tabernacle, desecrating something just being near her. And to touch her? Smell her? Taste her? The feeling that gave, said there could be no greater sin.

When the day stretched out and she was still asleep, he left. He couldn't wake up with her. What if she wanted something from him that he was even more terrified to give. He'd had a long time to think as he laid with her all morning and half the day. He needed help, more than what Mercy could offer. And it hit him who might be able to. Kane.

Tomorrow night they were due back, he hoped they were on time. Sade planned to talk to Mercy about discontinuing therapy for obvious reasons. He'd let her know his plan to talk to her father and that should be enough, that should make her feel better. He was getting the help she wanted without putting herself at risk. Everybody could be happy about that.

Sade hated to, but he avoided her all afternoon. Or maybe she was avoiding him. God, he could hardly face her, and yet needed to. Always that war inside him to hurt and be hurt, he was so fucking sick of it. Tired of dancing with those devils, so very tired. And even still, one thought of what he'd done and his cock was hard. Burning with ache. To do it again. And again. Longer. So much longer.

Sade groaned as he took the steps down to the basement. His body hurt like a motherfucker and the masochistic idea to work out had popped into his head. He was hoping for a two hour work out but an hour in, and his angel showed up dressed in that same cock hardening outfit from before, only white this time. So utterly perfect for her.

"Oh, sorry," she said at spotting him.

"I was just done," he gasped, dropping the two dumbbells he'd used to crucify his arms with.

"You can stay, I'll be using the uh, shadow boxing area."

She didn't look at him and he wasn't sure why. His own guilt said it was because of what he'd done but knowing her, it was her guilt over what she'd done. "I'm nearly healed," he joked, his body screaming in agony at him.

She shot a furious glance his way. "You look horrible," she gasped.

So it was her guilt that kept her gaze away. Figured. "Thanks."

"You know what I mean," she said, still not looking at him.

"Yeah," he muttered, snatching the towel from the weight bar. "I was... headed for a swim. I'll see you later?"

"Can we meet in my room at six?"

He froze. "For what?"

"Therapy."

Her confused tone said she'd expected the show to just go on. "Of course just to talk," she added, maybe thinking he was worried she might make him do things. And he was. Not that he would but he didn't want to be alone with her, both of them were too unpredictable. But then maybe that would be the perfect time to bring up his idea.

"Yeah," he said, rubbing his hand on his head. "Six. I'll be there." He hurried out before she could say or do anything he'd be helpless to say no to.

"Bye," she called, sounding offended with his quick escape.

He felt like shit that he couldn't stick around and be normal. Really, what the fuck was wrong with him? Why did it seem like everything was getting worse? Was it his mother back in his life? Was it because he was so close to happiness? Was it fear of losing that? Causing a war inside him with his devils?

If he asked Mercy, she'd have some sunshine and rainbow answer for him. She always had her eyes set on the light. But Sade couldn't take his off of the darkness, because the second he did, it would devour him, and then her.

After power swimming for an hour, he walked out to the beach, hoping that maybe the ocean would have something useful to impart to him. An omen maybe, confirming what he knew inside. He would ruin her. Sure as the sun rose and set everyday in the sky, he would ruin his sweet angel beyond repair. Just like he was. And she'd make excuses for him while letting him.

I'll help you, shhh, I'll help you.

Fucking dumbass. He was stupid coming and going with her, there was no winning. He grabbed his head with both hands, thinking about therapy that night. They weren't doing anything, just talking, he reminded his fears. But he could feel his animals salivating, pushing his pussy-ass Romeo toward a corner. He needed to get his fucking head back in the game, get his shit on track. He'd done it all these years, he needed to get that fight back.

Worst case scenario, all he had to do was last five mother fucking days with no improvement to show for shit. Then it was done. Problem was, at the rate everything was deteriorating, there wouldn't be shit left.

He should just leave. Right now. He scanned the beach, his heart hammering with the urge to run, run as fast and as far away from her as he could. She'd get over it. She'd have to.

His mother. That would mean leaving her. Fuck, he needed a plan to protect Mercy better. The only thing going for him at the moment was her losing. Fair and square. Fuck, he'd come full circle. Back to throwing the fight. His devils stirred, back to loving that idea. They'd get to play their dark game one last time. Their prize? Him. Utterly broken and useless. It would be the greatest masochistic pleasure he'd ever felt since his mother's supposed death.

Sade finally headed back and spotted purple color at the grassy bank near the wood pier leading to the beach house. He walked over to inspect, finding flowers. He stared down at them, feeling like he should pick them.

Back at the house, he found a glass to put the bouquet of soft purple flowers in then snuck them into her room. He spotted her desk and walked them over. As he stared down at it, pain stole his breath at feeling like the flowers were for their grave.

His ears picked up the sound of her shower and before he could act on any stupid urges, he hurried to his own bathroom to get ready. Therapy was in forty-five minutes. He'd eat after, to avoid throwing up. He was a fucking wreck inside. He knew they weren't attempting anything sexual, but that didn't stop him from craving it. The things she'd done before he'd lost his mind were….wow… fucking phenomenal.

And he wanted it again. More.

****

Mercy sat *behind* the desk this time. It had taken her longer to figure out what to wear than what to do. Pathetic. She went back and forth between regular Mercy attire to, no, she needed to get back in the game, attire. Not to mention why waste the closet full of gorgeous clothes Sade's mother had stocked for her?

After round ten in the clothing debate, she settled for *back in the game,* wearing an elegant, cream colored pants suit with a light purple silk blouse. It matched the flowers she suspected—hoped rather—that Sade had gotten her. She leaned and smelled them for the tenth time. Who else would put them there? There was a slim possibility that Liberty *might* have, despite it being a very *anti-Liberty* thing, so she wouldn't assume openly.

And dear God, another point of huge debate was what to talk about? The emotional side of therapy seemed a prudent way to help him maintain that anti-physical position. Not that she needed him to, but she could see he needed it. The debate ended up being settled at *play it by ear.*

She rapped her pen lightly on the desk, looking at the small jeweled watch on her wrist. Five more minutes. Should she be waiting or be busy?

A soft knock sounded on the door and the violent jerk in her stomach made her gasp. Jesus. "It's open," she called firmly.

He walked in, dressed in raggedy jeans and a tattered black t-shirt. Despite the shabby appearance, he looked delicious, as long as she didn't look at his face and get nauseated. The swelling was down, and all that was left was the black, blue and purple. "Have a seat," she said stupidly as he sat. "Nice shirt," she went on. "Is that like your lucky shirt from that one gunfight?" She laughed too loud at her own joke while he slid a thumb along his nose without a reply or even looking at her.

Okay, awkward. She took a breath, moving along. "I feel overdressed now, but really I do it because I'm very serious about this." The second it came out, she realized the insult.

She waited for him to defend himself and say he did care but it didn't happen. Moving along again.

Her pulse beat like a snare drum when he finally looked at her. "Your dad is supposed to come back tomorrow night."

"Right," she said, nervous about what he was getting at.

"So, I was thinking."

Uh oh. She swallowed, trying to maintain a confident look.

"I need all the help I can get and your father… he helped you, right?"

Excitement roared through her at what he seemed to be suggesting. "Right, yes, he did." She didn't want to jump the gun, she'd make sure that's where he was headed.

"And…" he shrugged, looking out the balcony doors that she'd left open, "was thinking of asking if he could help me."

"Oh my God, yes! Of course he would, I know he would. Between him and I, imagine the progress!" The lines on his lowered forehead furrowed, slowly stealing her joy. "Unless you had other ideas," she said.

He rubbed his hand over his lowered head. "Actually, I was thinking of one on one. Me and him for a while."

Keep a positive attitude. Smile. "Okay," she said softly. "Do you mind if I at least finish my five days?"

He looked at her and her heart fell a little more. "I was thinking it would be a good idea to do them separately."

"Okay," she said. Final test. "So we'll renegotiate the contract. Move the date up? How long would you like?" At his long hesitation, she said, "So you would prefer to not do therapy with me at all if I'm reading between the lines correctly?

"No, we can renegotiate the contract," he said. "I just don't have a time."

She sat there, scribbling on the paper blindly, trying to get at his real angle. To get out of therapy with her. But why? She suddenly realized tonight might be their last session unless she convinced him she could do him any good.

"Thank you for the flowers by the way. Assuming you gave them."

"You're welcome."

She waited for more, particularly why he did it. "It's my favorite color," she said.

He nodded a little. "I didn't know."

"You just… felt in the mood to pick me flowers? I'm just wondering why you did, no big deal."

He shrugged, leaning back with one leg out. "I guess to say thank you," he looked around the room.

"Well, it was sweet."

She scanned through the dozen ideas in her head that she'd contemplated to help connect him with his emotions. "I want you to know that I'm so glad you'll talk to dad." She made sure to leave out the *my* part. How great it would be if he would make new emotional ties to her father. He was the perfect man for that.

"Me too. Figured if anybody could help me, he could." His gaze flitted over her again. He wasn't into looking at her tonight. Probably scared to scare her. Felt more like he was scared *of* her.

"He's such an amazing father. I think you will both get along, I hope you and he get some father son time together," she joked, laughing a little.

"Nah, don't need a father."

Pain stabbed her at hearing that. "No harm in having a father figure in your life."

He shook his head. "Never had a father," he said casually, eying her now. "Learned to live without one." He shrugged, glancing toward the balcony again.

She got curious then. "Did your father have a relationship with his father?"

Another shrug. "No idea. If he did, he never talked about it."

"Makes me wonder what kind of life leads a man to become what he did."

"The selfish bastard kind," he muttered.

"Usually it's either taught directly or picked up indirectly."

"Or forced."

Her stomach knotted at hearing the massive amount of issues hiding behind those words. "I have to believe that… somewhere in the minds of sick parents… there exists a bond or connection, even if it's buried way deep."

He rolled his eyes up to her. "If there is, it's a sick one."

She leaned back, looking at him. "Some people have a hard time expressing love, they express it in ways—"

"My father was an animal," he cut in, his words hard.

"I know, I know," she said. "And animals begat animals." She realized she was categorizing him into that but she'd meant his father's father.

"Living proof of that one, doc."

Shit. "Do you think your dad has any good in him? The way you have in you, despite what he's taught you?"

He gave a soft dry laugh. "What are you doing, doc?" he gazed right at her. "You want to talk about my father? You can. But I'm not going to stick around for it."

"Okay, I'm sorry." She cleared her throat, feeling like her chance to gain ground was slowly slipping away. She thought of his mother and the guilt she dealt with over leaving him to fend for himself. She wondered why he only let her call him by his Christian name. "Can I ask you a question?"

He put both elbows on his legs and leaned forward, raking his fingers through his short dark hair. "Shoot, doc."

"Why can't I call you Johnathon?"

His fingers stopped midway in his hair. "Rather not say," he said lightly.

"Can I call you Johnathon outside of therapy?"

"No," he said.

"Well, just an fyi, I really like the name."

"Well, just an fyi,I don't give a fuck if you do like it. Don't use it. Not now, not ever, and especially not in clever passing therapeutic questioning, are we clear?"

At hitting the ugly snake pit, she considered her words carefully. "Very clear," she said, nodding. "I'm sorry, I was just trying to help."

He squinted his gaze at her. "Help what, doc? What are you helping? You want me to love my dad? You think me loving my dad is going to help me? Or me pretending he loved me?"

She shook her head, "Not that, no."

"Then what, why would you bring that filthy fucker into this room, into my head space?"

Mercy took a deep breath, hating the disgusted look he aimed at her, the accusing look. "Not for the reasons you seem to think," she said.

"Then enlighten me," he said. "You're just playing therapist? Digging around in the holes to see what bloody pieces you can get at and examine? Just tell me what you want doc, and I'll hand it to you on a silver platter, no need to trick it out of me, or fish it out. I'm open," he said spreading his arms. "No dissecting needed."

Her heart raced. "Okay," she said softly. "If you're open, then tell me about last night."

He stared at her, slowly sitting back. "A lot happened last night, doc. Care to be a little more specific?"

"What were you feeling while you were doing it?"

He squinted his eyes at her again, like she baffled him. "A lot of bad things, doc. Mostly that I wanted it and *nobody*, not even you, would stop me."

Her stomach quivered at his words and she focused on where she was headed with her questions. "How did you feel after?"

"Right after?"

"Yes."

He shrugged. "Furious."

"Why?"

"Furious that I did it. You having fun yet, doc?"

The insult hit home and she moved on. "Okay, fine," she conceded, "you were furious. What else did you feel after?"

"That's it."

"No guilt?"

He glared at her. "What the fuck do you think?"

"I want to hear you say it, I don't want to guess or assume."

"You want to hear it," he mused, like she were an idiot playing a little game. But as hard as it was, they needed to get accustomed to talking about the hard stuff. It was key with dealing, her father would be the first one to tell him that. And would, too. "Yes, doc. I felt guilty. Just like I always feel after giving in to the urge to rape any woman in the ass."

She ignored the *any woman* part. "So you've done this before?"

He stared at her, his jaw sliding barely right. "Maybe. But it was consensual."

"How do you consensually rape a woman in the ass?" she asked, her stomach churning.

He shrugged. "She asks for it."

"She asks to be raped in the ass," she repeated, hoping he heard how that sounded.

"Raped in the ass, the mouth, the pussy," he said, seeming to enjoy telling her. He was just pissed. Hurting over the Johnathon and father probing.

"I get it now," she said lightly.

"So thrilled to hear that."

"So, did you feel joy or any other similar feelings during?"

"Of fucking course," he said lightly. "Fucking you when you didn't want it gave me great pleasure if you want to call that, joy."

"I wouldn't say I didn't want it," she admitted, hoping to steer him back to the nice side of his honesty.

He gave another stupid shrug. "I was only going by your word, doc. Not going by if you lied about it."

She held his gaze for several seconds, holding tight to her control. "Fair enough."

"If you say so."

Wow. This was so not going any kind of good. "So what about after?"

"After what, doc?" His tone was soft and patient now, condescending.

"How did you feel about what you did after therapy?" She was ready to hurry and finish with him so she could turn the tables and go through the same questions about herself in regards to the abuse she'd inflicted on him.

He held both hands up. "Guilty. Which is why I slept with you. You didn't deserve any of that and you wanted comfort. I gave that. I agreed to try and help you. That doesn't mean I believe you can, that just means I won't fight you," he finished calmly.

Okay, that was a lie, or some serious denial. "Do you often tell women you love them when you feel guilty?"

Again he shrugged. "I did what I felt you needed."

"So that was all for me, not you." Pain crowded her throat even though she was ready to wager he was lying his ass off. But why? All over the Johnathon bit?

"Why would it be for me?" Disgust crimped his face as he eyed her. "Do I look like the type to want love and affection after I rape a woman in the *ass*?"

The generic *woman* term stung, and Mercy forced it aside, determined not to let him win this. "Even sadomasochists want love and affection," she said softly.

"Not this one, not last night."

"Do you ever remember a time when you wanted affection and love?"

"Sure. With my mother. And when I thought she died, that need died with her."

"And… now that you realize she's alive? Has the need for love and affection returned?"

"With her, of course. It never went away."

Illogical jealousy stabbed Mercy and she doodled on her tablet, not looking at him. "Of course with her," she said lightly. "As it should be."

"But with women that I can fuck, the need for affection and love is never realized. I guess it's crowded out by my need to hurt them or be hurt by them, sexually."

"Just hurt them sexually?"

"So far, yes."

The pen drummed lightly on the desk as she contemplated how to pull the rug out from under his cocky feet. "So you're saying there's nobody at any point that you wanted love and affection from besides your mom?"

"It's all about pain and fucking for me, doc. Sorry."

"No need to be sorry, Johnathon."

Chapter Twelve

Time slowed to a crawl as Sade stared at Mercy. Mercy and that pensive green gaze, always wanting to doctor him. Her gaze held his, *testing,* and his fury slowly mounted. He knew what was coming, he knew there would be no controlling it or stopping it.

"Why can't I use that name," she whispered. "Your name given by your mother. You allow your mother to use it."

He fought to unhinge his jaw to say the words that needed saying but he couldn't. He quickly got up and hurried to the door. She'd agreed not to use that name, she'd taken it off the contract, he'd just made it clear it was off limits and still. She did it. To satisfy herself. To get her therapeutic kink met. Just like all of them in his life. She was a user. A manipulator. A *liar.*

"Sade!" she called, the sound of her steps chasing after him. She caught up to him before he could shut the door to his room. "Wait, please."

"You broke the contract, doc, it's fucking over," he grit, "it's so, very fucking over." And he was glad, fucking ready to tear something apart now.

"I'm sorry, please," she stepped in and he stepped back, repulsed by her. "I forgot."

His rage shot up and his fingers bit into the door with the need to rip it off the hinges. "I can't believe you're a fucking liar," he gasped, dizzy with the sick realization. The kind of liar he hated, one that lied to get what they selfishly wanted.

"No, you're the liar," she gasped, pointing at him.

"You need to move away from this door, doc. I didn't lie to anybody."

"That's a goddamn lie and you know it."

"What the fuck did I lie about? That everything I did, I did for you and not me, *doc*?" he yelled, slamming his hands on his chest.

"That! That's the fucking lie, that was for you too, you wanted that, you! You wanted me, you needed me, *Johnathon* needed me and my love!"

Sade's fury gripped him and he yanked her in his room by the front of her jacket and slammed the door shut then pushed his forearm into her chest. "What the fuck is wrong with you!" he roared.

She met his gaze with her wide one, panting, realizing she'd pushed him too far. "Okay, okay," she whispered. "I won't hurt you again, Sade. I promise. Session's over. I was out of line. It won't happen again, it won't happen again. I was just trying to do therapy, trying to deal with things, I'm very sorry, you have to believe me," she whispered, tears and all.

A sneer slowly twisted his mouth as he stared down at her. "You fucking bitch," he muttered, stepping back, nodding a little with his head angled at her. "You just can't stand it, can you? You just won't rest until you have your fucking way." Rage had his muscles quivering now and he knew it was only a matter of time before he lost it completely. He stared at her and all he saw was just another face from the past. Another face that wanted to use him. "Does it make your pussy hot doc, to drag all my dirty secrets out?" He angled his head the other way. "Maybe you're right, maybe you're the real sadist here, Miss Mercy. You like to hear all the dirty details?" He gradually drew closer until he stood directly in front of her. "You win," he said softly. "Would you like to finger your pussy while I tell you?"

She closed her eyes. "I'm sorry, I'm sorry, I... I didn't realize. You don't have to say it."

"Ohhhh baby," he whispered, gripping her jaw tight. "So fucking sweet of you." He slid his lips across hers, his tongue tasting. More hate filled him when her body responded. "Ah yes, you want that don't you? I know you fucking do. Because everybody likes Johnathon. You want Johnathon? You want to call me Johnathon?"

He dug his fingers harder in her jaw and gripped her pussy until she whimpered, proving him right, proving she was just about that fucking pleasure, just had to have it. He knew what that was like, and seeing it in her, overflowed him with disgust. "Look at you," he gasped. "So ready for me. So ready." He nibbled his way across her face, his breath shaking as the past trickled in and locked away his sanity. He slid his hand up her front, feeling her body beneath the soft fabric, pushing his leg between hers. "Johnathon is here, he's all yours baby. Johnathon is for everybody. He's a team player."

"Stop," she gasped, sounding panicked. "Please, I'm sorry, I'm sorry," she barely rasped.

"No, no, no," he cooed, "shhhh, don't worry about Johnathon." He stroked her lips with his fingers, licking them. "Because he likes it, see? He likes when daddy *fucks* him and calls him *his boy. His best Johnny boy.* I was sooooo fucking good, I was his favorite little pussy *fuck*."

She tried to turn away and he pushed her mouth open, kissing her with a brutal force, growling and latching his fingers in her hair. His entire body trembled now as he pulled her head back and devoured her mouth. All he could think was she wanted Johnathon. Just like they did. "I was such a precious boy," he rasped, still on her mouth. "His prize toy. I was famous," he bit softly at her lip, "a real superstar." He heard his father's laughter in his head with those words of praise. "I remember," he shuddered in her mouth, "How much I fucking loved it."

She sobbed and it was another *lie*. Just another fucking *lie*. He shoved her away then stormed back to her. "Don't you cry for Johnathon!" he roared in her face, hate boiling in his veins. "He likes it! Don't you fucking cry for that pussy face boy!" The need to smash was there, and he stormed around the room, looking for something to break, crush, shatter—just like him, just like his life. It wanted out, it wanted to scream, beg, be heard, be known.

"Don't you fucking cry for Johnny boy!" He hurled the lamp at the wall, the shatter like a drug to his ears. "He's just a pussy-face boy! Wanting daddy's attention!" He slammed the nightstand into the wall and Mercy ran to a corner. "Johnathon will do anything for daddy's little wink, daddy's pat on the head!" He grabbed blindly and smashed whatever he could. "Don't you cryyyyy for Johnny," he sang in a deep voice, mimicking his dad. "Johnny is a team player! He's a mommy's boy, Johnny is a fucking mommy's boy!"

Sade tore the room apart, roaring the words over and over, no longer seeing or hearing anything but those words. Those words his father always said to his mother. *Don't you cry for Johnathon. Don't you cry for that pussy-face boy.*

The room spun and Sade was suddenly staring at the ceiling, his vision blurry as he fought to breathe. Mercy knelt next to him, screaming and crying, calling his name while his mouth still moved to voice the madness swirling in his head. "Don't cry..." he gasped, reaching for Mercy, his hand covered in blood, "Don't you... fucking cry...for Johnathon."

****

"Dad? Dad, come in," Mercy sobbed.

Liberty took the radio from her. "Let me, sweetie. He's not dying, I told you, it's only twenty-one stitches and it missed the main hose."

"It's not that," Mercy sobbed. "I'm so stupid, I'm trying to help him and I'm killing him!"

"You're not killing him," she soothed, getting on the radio and trying other channels until she reached her dad.

Liberty handed her the mic when she got him and Mercy took it. "Go check on him, stay with him, make sure the medicine is working, make sure the bleeding has stopped. And he's comfortable," she gasped, her sobs clawing to get free.

"I got it," she assured, heading out.

"Mercy, talk to me," her father said, sounding panicked.

"Dad," she whispered into the mic, fighting not to cry. "Are you alone?"

"Yes, I'm alone, baby. Daddy's here, tell me what's wrong."

"It's Sade," she gasped. "He's not dead but he got hurt. Twenty-one stiches," she said, not wanting her dad to panic.

"Ah, honey, what happened?"

"Dad," she barely managed, putting the heel of her hand on her forehead. "You know I'm not a quitter, dad, but…"

"No, you're not a quitter."

"I can't do this. I can't keep hurting him like this."

"Hurting him how?"

"Everything I try, it-it backfires. I try to do the things you taught me with him but they're not working," she whispered.

"I want you to do something for me right now."

"What? Tell me," she cried, desperate.

"I want you to calm yourself. Remember how to do that?"

"Yes," she gasped, closing her eyes and obeying his instructions.

"Tell me when you're calm."

Mercy knew the drill, he wouldn't proceed until she was. "I'm there. I'm calm."

"Close enough," he said, knowing she wasn't entirely.

"Some things happened Dad," she whispered.

"Go on," he said.

"Well, I'm... I'm trying to retrain him the way you helped me, only he's a sadomasochist, right?"

"Right. And how is that going?"

She fought to keep her emotions in check but every word she spoke trembled. "He seems..."

"Worse?"

"Yes," she gasped.

"Not surprised."

"Why?"

"His mother came back from the dead, and with that resurrection came every demon he'd buried without realizing."

"Like what, Dad?"

"Like all his fears of losing the one he loves. It's transferring, baby."

"He's fighting me, Dad," she was back to crying. "I'm sorry, breathing. You wouldn't believe what a huge mess I am. I am such an epic failure in this, I mean you would not recognize the person that I am. All that training Dad, it's like, *poof!* Gone. And he's stuck with this driveling, cry baby bitch."

"Stop it," he ordered. "There is no amount of training on earth that equips us for being in love. And you, sweetheart, are very much there."

She stopped in her tracks, startled with his words. "I am," she whispered. "I very much am. So… are you saying this is normal for me to feel this way?"

"Yes, baby, I'm sorry, yes, it's normal. Not fun, but normal. And our boy Sade. He will fight you. He will do what it takes to keep from losing you. And not having you is the only sure way to do that."

She closed her eyes. "That's not an option."

"Baby, you have to understand something. Sade perfected his game. He found ways to maintain an impressive measure of goodness while harnessing his sexual issues. But there are some demons he has not been able to manipulate. The one's close to his heart. His mother. His father. Now you."

"His father? He hates him."

"Yes, and he loves his mother. It's the source of his sadism and masochism, I believe."

"What am I?"

"You're the new risk, it's a repeat of his mother's scenario. While she may be safe from his past, you are not. And the only way he can keep you safe from it, is to keep you out of it. And since he's trapped in it, he's doing the only thing he knows how. He's willing to give up the one thing he needs and wants more than life itself—just to protect it. And Mercy… that's love. That man loves you more than you know and more than he can voice to you. But I am here to tell you, that is the truth."

Mercy's heart swelled with love till she had to hold her chest from the pressure. "So, the more I try to get him out of his past, the harder he fights me. Oh my God," she said. "I pushed the issue, dad and he had a little slip."

He sighed and it went quiet.

"Don't worry," she wailed, remembering the horrific aftermath, "I nearly killed him for it."

"Fuck," he whispered.

She'd never heard him say that word in front of her, and it alarmed her. "Dad, you can't tell him, please, I'm confiding in you."

He mumbled something again and she waited, her heart ready to beat out of her chest. "How bad did you hurt him?"

"He says he's had worse to make me feel better, but I know he's walking around with fractures all over his body."

"Oh Jesus. I'm thinking of his mother, honey, I'm not upset with you, you didn't do anything wrong."

"Dad! You sound like him!"

"He probably hoped you killed him."

"He did," she cried, swallowing hard. "I should have not put him in that position, I should have stopped him before he went too far."

"You panicked."

"I did! I did," she sobbed, "I panicked really bad, I messed up."

"You didn't mess up, you're human." He sighed and mumbled again. "Where is Sade now?"

"Oh, well after I pushed him in a corner then half killed him for it, I drove him off the other deep end by making him talk about shit he clearly didn't need to."

"Did he try to hurt you then?"

"No! No, he destroyed everything around me though.

"Jesus, that boy's got more control than he knows."

"Dad, please," she remembered. "He's talking about talking to you, asking you for help, can you? Can you help him?" she asked. "I won't touch him again, I swear, I'm done. You can do it."

"Of course I will, baby. But you're not done in this."

"Oh God, I'm so tired of failing him."

"Listen to me. Get calm again, Mercy, I need you entirely coherent for this."

She quickly got calm, nearly making herself dizzy in the process. "I'm calm. Talk to me dad," she sniffed and wiped her eyes with the palm of her hand.

"Can you teach him a new kind of sexuality?"

"Yes," she said, nodding. "Yes, I can. I was. It was working until he lost control."

"And what would prevent that?" he asked simply.

Her mouth hung open in thought for only a second. "Restraining."

"Bingo, baby. Therapy from you is a must. I can't touch that. But Daddy will teach him how to deal with his rage. You give him that sweet light of yours and it will light his path out of that dark."

She stood there in mild shock that her dad had just suggested she restrain him for sexual therapy and the fact that she'd not thought of it first. A slow joy spread through her until she was laughing and sobbing with it. "Thank you, thank you, Dad. Oh my God, I thought I was done, I thought it was hopeless."

"Glad to help baby. But listen. I'm going to take a day or two extra before returning. I would prefer his mother not see him battered, it'll set her off.

"Oh God, agreed. Agreed." Mercy paced as far as the little mic allowed. "He looks so much better, the swelling is down, just bruises now."

"Well, you know I hate lying but if we come back and he's not entirely healed, have a story ready, will you?"

"Okay, I will. Of course."

Chapter Thirteen

Sade woke up to the sound of mumbling.

"No, this is good, thank you. Well, remember he'll be gone a couple more days." That was Mercy's voice.

Sade's head pounded when he turned it just an inch left. Fuuuuck. What happened? He lolled his head back to center, mentally feeling around his body for answers. All he got was numb and unable to feel shit. Sharp pain streaked from his shoulder to his fingertips, and almost immediately a memory hit. Mercy screaming, crying, blood on his arm. What the fuck had he done? Flashes of him losing his shit and tearing the room apart made his heart lurch. Oh fuck, Mercy! He fought to sit up, his arms dead weight along with his legs. What the fuck, was he paralyzed?

"Mercy," he called, his voice sounding like he was in a tunnel.

"Oh God, he's awake," he heard her say.

"Holler if you need." That was Liberty's voice. Where was he? When was it?

"Gooood morning," Mercy sang, hurrying next to him.

He realized he wasn't in his room. But he couldn't figure out where he was, the unfinished walls weren't ringing a bell. A basement?

"You're in the basement," she confirmed. "The storage room next to the gym as a matter of fact. With a little bit of elbow grease, I got it transformed." She looked all around, impressed.

"W-what... Why?"

She turned to him. "I just needed you someplace suitable."

Suitable. The meanings of words got bogged down in his mind. He was loopy, he realized. "Suitable for what? What happened?" He turned his head carefully. "My body feels paralyzed."

"Well, I gave you some pretty good medicine so that you could sleep. You had an accident. Got a little cut on your arm. Okay not little, you hit a pretty serious vein."

Sade finally realized it. "Why am I tied down?"

She hissed a little while lifting a huge bandage on his arm. "Weeeeelll," she said lightly, "You weren't really the most cooperative person, mister."

Sade wasn't surprised with that but there was something in her happy tone. Maybe it was the happy that was off. Why should she be? He licked dry lips, trying to organize his thoughts and speak them coherently. "Why am I in the basement? What did you mean suitable? And why are you so happy?" He realized he sounded like a little pussy. "You finally decided to give me shock treatments?"

That look on her face, the sparkle in her eyes, reminded him of something. Then he realized what it was. It was how she looked when he first met her. Before all the blood, tears and heartache. A deep hunger to have those days back, hit him. They weren't perfect but… to him they were. He remembered the plan starting out—just explore her authenticity as far as his sick life would allow him to go. He'd never imagined she would turn out to be the real deal and he'd get this far, or this deep. Nor did he once dream in a million years he'd fall so fucking hard for a woman. For her.

"Shock treatments," she laughed, flashing him the same pretty smile he'd first fallen for. "Are you hungry? I have breakfast warming for you."

He fought to gain his bearings, feeling like his brain was running on half a cylinder in the memory department. Fucking dreaded when the oblivion would pass and leave only the ugly reality.

"Made it myself?" she tempted.

Hungry. Maybe he was. But he didn't want Mercy to leave yet. "I'm good for now."

She scooted a little on the bed, stopping at his knees and angling her head while staring into his gaze. He waited for the shame that should be there after being a royal fuck up. "I'm glad to see you're calm at least."

He tried to shrug and winced. "I usually am after I let my demons run wild." She continued to stare at him like she were looking for something. "A little early for soul meshing, huh doc?" He looked away, mostly because staring too long made him want things that led to trouble.

"I'm sorry, I'm just wanting to see how you're feeling."

"And my eyes tell you that?"

"Your eyes tell me a lot of things," she said with raised brows and that pretty smile again.

He looked around and realized he was propped up on a lot of pillows. "Am I cooperative enough now to be set free?"

Her smile slowly turned into a grimace with regretful brows.

"Oh come on, Mercy. I'm not in the mood to play this."

"Wellllll," she cooed. "I'm not playing. I've given this a lot of thought."

"Holy fuck," he muttered, closing his eyes.

"Hear me out, please, Sade," she nearly mewled.

He looked at her, shaking his head for many seconds. What was up with her? She was too calm, too happy. "This is not happening. What the fuck are you thinking?"

She took a deep breath with a hopeful smile like he actually wanted to know that grand scheme cooking in her head. "I'm glad you asked that," she said seriously. She looked up at the ceiling, organizing her thoughts and wiggling her ass on the bed next to him, waking his dick up. "I was thinking," she began, "seriously."

"And stalling, because your idea sucks and you know it."

"I'm not stalling," she argued lightly, "And it doesn't suck, I'm wanting to say it right. I was thinking that… " Several seconds of open mouth silence brought her frustrated growl right to his cock before she faced him fully and leveled her pretty green gaze on him. "Listen. I'm not going to pussy foot with this. I mean, you know how you are," she said incredulous. "And how I am," she confessed, making it fair. "And well, therapy with me and you… it's downright dangerous. No offense, I love you and all, but I'd rather not have to worry about you losing your mind and doing God knows what, or worse, me maiming you, or killing you! Why are you smiling?"

He chuckled and lowered his gaze. Fuck, she was so hard to be pissed at. "You love me and all?"

"Well duh, you know that," she said so very softly with lowered gaze while brushing her hands over jeaned legs.

"And so you want me tied up for therapy," he helped. "Safety precautions."

She gave a cute eye squinty grimace. "Yes?"

Why did his body have to need her so fucking bad? And why did being tied up while she performed therapy on him suddenly seem like the magical solution dropped right out of heaven? "I think I am hungry now."

"Oh, I'll go get your breakfast."

"Not for food."

She paused, her face slowly softening with hopeful emotions and desire until he was rock fucking hard. He realized then that he was only in his underwear.

"You undressed me?"

She drew back a little at the question before pinning him with a pissed green stare. "Well, Liberty sure as hell didn't."

Jesus Christ how could he possibly need her so bad? But there he was, tied up and there she was, ready to accommodate without it risking her. "I need to brush my teeth," he said.

"Coming right up!" She hopped up like she was excited to show him how well thought out this all was, how good she'd done. Sade watched her ass wink at him as she power walked to a door on the far end of the room and opened it. She returned with a toothbrush filled with toothpaste, an empty glass, and a proud little smile as she set the items on a small table next to the bed. "Hold on, let me get you some water." She sprinted back to the room she'd just come from and returned with a bottle of water, opening it on the way. "Are you thirsty?"

He eyed her, licking his lips. "Very."

She put the bottle of water to his mouth and he drank down about half of it. "Wow you *were* thirsty." She slid her thumb over his chin, wiping the water that dripped and he fought the instinct to devour it with his mouth. Sade continued to eye her, his hunger back to ravenous at the idea of being her patient. Memories of the last time she'd taken matters into her own hands and doctored him, made his heart race and his dick sing.

She set the water down and approached with the loaded toothbrush. "Oh come on," she said at his quirked brow. "It's brushing teeth, I think I can manage."

He opened and allowed her to perform the oddly intimate task. Sade soon fought not to laugh at how she moved her mouth around to accommodate her efforts. "Spit," he finally muttered.

"Spit," she repeated softly, placing the cup at his chin, oh so seriously. She presented the water next and he rinsed twice.

"Oh," she said, hurrying to that room again and racing back with a couple of washcloths. She used one to wipe his mouth then the other to wipe his face, beginning with his forehead. Sade closed his eyes, as she took her time, slowly cleaning every inch of his face. "There we go," she sang lightly. "All fresh."

Sade stared at her, debating on how to get her closer. He decided the direct route. "Come here."

She regarded him in uncertainty and Sade felt like he needed to be more specific about it. "I missed you."

The shocked look on her face cut him. Like she'd needed to hear those words and didn't think she ever would. She snapped out of her surprise and gushed a smile that turned his insides around. "Like… here?" she asked, scooting along the bed to his chest area.

Sade's hunger grew as he stared at her.

"What?" she asked, her smile slowly fading with worry.

"Closer," he whispered.

"Closer?" she asked, breathless.

"To kiss me."

Like a virgin, her cheeks turned pink and she swallowed.

"You remember how?" he asked.

She only nodded, her eyes trained on his mouth as she slowly leaned toward him. She stopped six inches away and raised her eyes to his. "You're not going to... head-butt me, are you?"

He turned his head, busting out laughing. "I so should," he muttered, looking at her. "But no." His final words deepened with desire and she continued until her lips barely touched his. He remained still, wanting to see how she'd kiss him. At first her lips were a little firm but when she pressed a little, they softened to liquid silk, sliding barely over his. Her warm breath shot desire through him and she angled her head, pressing soft kisses on his lips.

She pulled up a little and he slowly opened his eyes. "Am I doing it wrong?" she asked, looking worried. "I'm not a very good kisser," she whispered.

He grinned at the cute absurdity. "Who told you that?"

She bit her lower lip, seeming so sure she sucked at it. "I just don't have a lot of practice with it outside of..."

He waited to get the rest of that interesting info. "Outside of?"

"Mostly you."

"Mostly?" Excitement at that news roared through him.

"I mean obviously I'm not a virgin but kissing was never... never a part of..."

"Shhh, come here," he whispered, not wanting her to ever experience any more bad memories. "Show me more of this terrible kissing."

She smiled and he was glad she knew him well enough to know he was joking. Her smile slowly faded as she leaned toward his mouth again. She went back to pressing those soft silky petals on his lips, angling this way and that. Sade only returned as much as she gave, following her lead. "You missed me?" he asked as she continued, hoping to move her to the next level he knew was right there.

"I did," she gasped.

"How much?"

"So much!" Her breath blasted in his mouth with her whimper, and he opened for it, for her hunger, devouring it with his own. "God, so much," she cried weakly, gripping his face in desperate fingers, sucking and licking as far into his mouth as she could climbing on him to straddle his chest. Her mouth left his and roamed all over his face, biting and sucking, licking and kissing with tenderness, then a passion so brutal, it rattled him.

She suddenly pulled back abruptly. "Oh my God," she gasped, hurrying off the bed.

"What?" he asked breathless, his entire body on fire.

"I'm…" she paced next to the bed. "I need to talk to you first, not… not do that."

"Why?" he asked, his heart hammering with dread.

"The idea is to actually help you," she said, facing him. "Not just tie you up and fuck you when I want to which is every waking moment of the goddamn day," she whispered, putting both hands over her face then shaking her head. "What am I doing?" she wailed lightly under her hands. She went to pacing again and answering her own questions. "What I'm doing is what I'm supposed to do," she said firmly. "And what I'm supposed to do, is do the right thing for you—at the right time" she pointed at him.

"Which is what? Keep me tied up? Starve my problems out of me?"

She faced him in all seriousness. "No, which is to force change," she said in a *duh* kind of amazement.

"Force change. Why didn't I think of that one? Just make Sade not want sadistic and masochistic sex, make him want boring vanilla sex."

"Oh there's not going to be anything *boring* about it." She paced again. "And my father agrees—"

"Your *father*?"

She paused with a blank look. "Yes," she said lightly, like it was no big deal. "He's highly trained in this kind of thing, I told you he helped me. He knows."

"Holy fuck," he gasped. "You told your *dad* about this?"

Her jaw dropped to accommodate her epic justification. "I had to! You're over here tearing the place apart, trying to kill yourself, what the hell am I supposed to do?"

"Wow," he gasped. "I'm so fucking dead. Why bother saving me, did he tell you to do this? Tie me up here? Holy fuck, he's likely planning to cut my dick off and feed it to me. Did you fucking *forget* who your father is Mercy? He's Kane Kross. Oh my fucking God, does my mom know? Jesus, of course she does, the whole world knows I like to rape asses and throw a fucking tantrum when I can't."

She stared at him aghast and confused. "I didn't *tell* him exactly *that* part Sade, and dad *loves* you, you're the son of the woman he loves, how can you even think that? And he does know I nearly killed you for it," she added like that evened the score. But there was nothing in the world that could ever remove the stain of this kind of sin against the daughter of Kane Kross, Jesus, holy Christ.

"And don't use our new and weird relation as a means of comfort. And that may be my only hope, right there. My mother."

"We are *not* related," she said in exasperation. "And I don't want to do this anymore than you do."

"Then *don't!*"

"I don't mean I don't want to, I mean I wish there was another way. I do want to do whatever it takes, make no mistake about that," she said pointing at him.

"So is this going to be like a group therapy thing, or are you going to be the main doctor working on the resident sadomasochist?"

She cocked her hip with a hand on it. "Sade, please."

"No, by all fucking means, maybe you should just call me Johnathon."

"Stop it," she gasped with wide eyes. "Don't you say that, don't you say that!"

"Or what?" he yelled. "You'll kiss me and make me want you then remind me that I'm a monster and will never be able to have something good?"

She paced before the bed now. "Shut up," she muttered before stalking over to him and getting right in his face. "You want to kiss me? You want to fuck me? You can't possibly want it more than I do but make no mistake about it, I care more about you than you give me credit. I care more about this," she poked his chest, "not this."

His breath rushed out when she grabbed his cock.

"Oh, you like that? Well, just so you know, I have a very elaborate, very therapeutic sexual schedule planned for you. You, my dearest sadomasochist, will be learning how to enjoy normal things, even if I have to keep your ass tied up for six months, spoon feeding the boring vanilla kink until you fucking *love* it!" she yelled in his face.

Sade was stunned. Speechless. And of course fucking aroused out of his sick mind with what she had in mind. Should he bother to tell her that doing anything sexual to him while tied up was a form of masochism?

Fuck no. Fuck. No.

"Then what are you waiting for doc? Let's get this party started?"

She raised her hand with her pointer finger aiming down at his arm, her brows raised. "For you to heal, for one."

"It's a little scratch."

"It's twenty-one stitches," she corrected, her pretty mouth a hard line.

"So just be careful."

"Don't worry, sexual therapy shall commence tomorrow night."

He suddenly wasn't sure what day it was. "Is he here?"

"Who?"

"Who else?! Kane!"

"They return… in a few days."

"Why'd you hesitate?"

"Because when I told him about my side of the abuse," she stressed her fairness, "he decided he didn't want your mom coming back and seeing it. Flipping out."

"Fuck," he gasped. "Definitely not."

"And that we should have a story ready in case they come back and you're not quite healed."

He eyed her. "Really. I'll just tell her the truth, I tried to get kinky with Mercy and she beat the shit out of me. She'll never believe it."

"No! No! More like you… fell from the… roof."

"While what?"

"While…" her eyes widened as she thought, "you… checked… on it."

Both his brows raised.

"We have time to come up with something, the point is, they're not coming tonight." Her rigidity lessened a bit. "So stop freaking out, you're not helping anything." She regarded his body. "Are you hungry yet?"

"What do you have in mind for my therapy? I'd like to know what's on that menu."

She crossed her arms slowly and jutted her chin a little. "I'd rather surprise you."

Fuck. His heart raced and his cock throbbed in desperation. "And how are you supposed to know when your therapy is working? Do you have some way of knowing when I'm aroused or not aroused by sadomasochistic thoughts?"

"I have you."

"Me."

She held up two fingers together. "Old fashioned honor system."

"Oh fucking brother. Letting the monsters guide the ship. Smart."

"Well I don't have a brain probe, Sade, sue me. If I did, you can be sure I'd have it installed in that hard head of yours."

"Or my hard fucking cock." He laid his head back with a growl.

"What's wrong," she asked, sounding worried. "You need more meds?"

He pulled his head forward. "I need your mouth on my dick, that's what I fucking need. I want you so bad right now, why can't you just give me that. Just don't count it as therapy yet." He watched her actually consider, his heart racing. "Do you want me to beg? I'm fucking ready to beg for it. Please, please, fucking please suck my cock. Suck it until I come so hard and long in your mouth."

"Oh Jesus," she gasped, turning away.

"And you can fuck me after," he offered, not sure his dick would cooperate but ready to try.

"Therapy starts now," she mumbled, nearly running to the door. She opened it and faced him, her finger jabbing in his direction. "First lesson—learn some restraint."

She slammed the door and he stared at it in pissed shock. "I *am fucking restrained!*" he yelled at the fucking door. God she knew how to arouse the worst of his demons. That was fine. He'd wait.

He'd wait like a good boy.

Chapter Fourteen

"Oh my God," Mercy ran into the room and to the bed. "Your mom is coming."

He jerked awake. "What? How long have I been sleeping?"

"Not long! She overheard that you were hurt and made Kane return immediately." She began unlocking his shackles. "Dad told her he wasn't sure what happened, something about an accident. So, I'm thinking Liberty and you were out and she slid off the road and hit a ditch, you flew out of the jeep," she gave him a squinty stare, "because you didn't have your seatbelt on. It's the island, who needs a seatbelt?" she nodded now, undoing the final restraint.

"And the jeep?"

"Liberty is taking care of that with a sledgehammer. Just a fender bender." She threw the restraints under the bed and looked around.

"And I'm in the basement why?"

"You're in the basement because…" she stared at him, thinking. He would help but he was having too much fun watching her create it. She focused her wide eyes on him now. "The ocean air is getting to you."

"How?"

She raised her brows and pointed at him. "Your sinuses. From all those fights," she nodded, "the passages are…" she fluttered her fingers at her face, "swollen. And the gym… is closer and… you need to use it. A lot."

"Right. To work off all the bruises."

She winced and bit her lip before snapping wide eyes at him. "Because working out helps you sleep. And you're having a hard time sleeping. Because of your injuries. And sinus issues. And you're in therapy with me—"

"She knows about therapy?"

"Only that you and I are helping each other."

"With what?"

"Stuff! Personal stuff, it's private," she exclaimed. "That's what we'll say".

"How soon will she be here?"

"They were docking the boat!"

She passed by him and it was more than he could stand. He grabbed her and pulled her into his lap, her back against him, his arms wrapping her nice and tight.

"Okay," she whispered, looking over her shoulder a little. "What are we doing?"

He buried his nose in her hair, sliding it so he could get to her skin. "Missing you."

He felt her relax a little and nibbled at her neck. "Your mother will be here."

"Mmm," he sucked on her shoulder. "Really missing you."

"Oh God," she whispered, leaning into him. "Oh my God, she's coming, somebody's coming."

"Fuck," he muttered, not moving from his position on the edge of the bed while Mercy ran to the bathroom.

The basement door flew open and his mother came rushing forward only to stop abruptly with a shocked gasp and hand over mouth. "Baaaaaaaby," she cooed, hurrying toward the bed. "Are you okay?"

"Ah yeah. You should see the ditch."

"The ditch? Liberty told me she hit a tree."

"Right," he said. "And I went…" he sailed his hand through the air, "…flying into the ditch."

"Oh my God, thank *God* you're alive!" She hugged him carefully then pulled back. "What are you doing in this awful dungeon, you've got this beautiful beach house and you're in this horrid box?"

"I just… like the air down here. Sinuses aren't used to all the salty air. And the gym is right next door. Helps me sleep."

"You have trouble sleeping?" It felt like every question was driven by her guilt, like all his problems were her fault. She leaned in closer and held his arm. "Kane mentioned you were in therapy with Mercy? I knew she was a nurse but I didn't realize she was a psychiatrist."

He chuckled. "I know right? So unbelievable that I'd end up with a psychiatrist."

"Not unbelievable at all!" his mother whispered. "I always knew you'd end up with an angel!" she said, stroking his cheek while sadness lingered in her gaze.

"I'm going to take a shower now, Mom. Muscles ache." He stood and she gave him another hug.

"Are you coming up after? I'll make some hot tea for you."

"Sure Mom," he said, walking her to the door and finally out of it after five more I'm fines and good byes.

Before Mercy could escape, he hurried to the bathroom and found the door locked. He knocked softly.

"Sade?"

"Yes," he said, smiling.

"She's gone?"

"Yes."

She opened the door with wide eyes and Sade entered the bathroom and shut the door. She stepped back with a quirked brow.

He put both hands up. "Just want a hug."

"No you don't!" she hissed. "You want to hug and put your hands on my ass and press me into that," she pointed down while keeping her eyes on his.

Sade's grin spread and he lowered his shorts over his cock. "That?"

"I'm not looking," she said lightly, aiming her gaze at the corner. "Put it up Sade, this is not fair."

"Not fair," he said, stroking his length. "What's not fair is how long I've gone without your mouth on it."

She suddenly gasped then dropped to her knees, sucking him with a ravenous hunger, shocking him. He clenched his eyes tight and braced his hands on the door and wall. "Fuck, fuck, baby, don't stop," he croaked.

Footsteps sounded on the stairs and Sade pulled her up. "Your dad," he hissed, kissing her with a hungry groan before sending her out. "I'm showering. Be out in five."

"Okay," she whispered, heading out then running back to him and kissing him. "I'll finish you later," she whispered.

"Fuck, yes," he said, leaning into the kiss as she pulled away.

She gave him a sweet smile and waved at him before shutting the door and Sade hurried into the shower, listening to Mercy's sweet voice saying hi to her dad.

Sade showered, smiling at the sound. His sweet angel had a good daddy. And God, that made him happy. So fucking relieved and happy. His stomach jerked at her final words. *I'll finish you later.*

He couldn't fucking wait for her healing lips and tongue. Bring it, Angel.

****

Sade waited for Kane in the basement, pacing, wishing he'd hurry. Maybe he should go looking for him. He wanted to see Mercy. No, he wanted her. He was ready to face the firing squad and get it over so he could.

He finally heard the dreaded steps down the flight of stairs leading to the basement. They were definitely his. Casual. Heavy. Confident.

Sade took several deep breaths, swinging his arms and tossing his head, feeling just like he did before he entered a fight. His mind knew he was about to be in the presence of possible death and his body followed suit.

The knock came finally and Sade walked over and opened the door to the legend. Dressed in khaki shorts, a button up shirt full of jungle looking plants, and flip-flops, one would never imagine the sadistic things he was so good at doing. "Mr. Kross." Sade kept his tone respectful—not too excited, not too scared shitless, while fixing his gaze about mouth level like a good little ass raping bastard should.

"Hello, Johnathon," he said softly, those gentle blue eyes inspecting him for several seconds. "Wow, you look great."

Sade felt like he should meet the man's gaze but only managed a brief connect before shaking his head a little.

"Come here, son," he said, walking up to Sade and embracing him.

The smell of his mother's perfume was on him and still, Sade's dread refused to allow him to relax, so he merely tolerated the man's hug, bracing for the blade he'd earned for what he'd done to his daughter. She said she'd not given details, and now he wasn't sure what was worse—leaving something like that to a father's imagination, or to tell it. Sade would kill, and it felt like death in this case was not only justified, it was imminent. He'd violated a highly virtuous woman, but worst of all, his precious daughter.

"Let's have a seat and talk," he said, patting him on the back and looking around. "Nice," he said. "Like a prison in here."

Sade didn't miss the humor in his light observation as they walked over to the only place for sitting in the room—the bed. Kane sat at the foot and Sade at the head, both of them facing forward, feet on the floor. Sade felt the man staring and glanced to find a half smile and look that made Sade feel like the freak he was.

A dozen ways to start the conversation had been thoroughly explored by Sade prior to Kane's visit, but none seemed right, now. "I'm no good for her, Kane," he muttered, not looking at him.

Kane didn't argue, only took a deep breath before letting it out with a mumbled, "I know that. But really, neither one of us are, son."

Sade couldn't resist looking at him. It was the last response he'd expected. "Yeah but… I think it's a little different with me."

"I know that too," he said lightly. "Listen son." Kane sounded sympathetic as he turned on the bed a little toward Sade. "I want you to understand something. But I need you to look at me for this. In the eye. Man to man."

Sade locked gazes with him until his blood raced through his veins.

"I don't want you… to ever make the mistake of thinking I won't protect you to the death. Defend you. Everything I am? Is for the good Lord. Your mother. Mercy. Now Bo. And of course you." He turned even more, getting situated with sincerity lining his forehead. "And in that same token…If you should ever…. physically harm… any one of those people in the list that I just gave you?" A smile formed then twitched a little. "Your dick is mine."

Sade's sick cock jerked with the threat and he nodded. "I do know that. I knew that before I knew the other."

"Look at me son."

Again Sade gladly did as he was told.

"You're a good man," he said softly. "And you should know something about me. I don't ever say words unless I mean them. And I don't ever say words I don't believe. And sometimes, there are some things I say because I know them to be true. And this time is one of those times."

Weird and unfamiliar energy shot through Sade. Partly because all of that felt like the final sermon before the sacrifice. But also that Kane meant what he'd said. Whether or not it was true didn't really matter to Sade. As long as he believed it, then it was true enough for him. It was Kane truth, and that was as good as God's in his book. But he only nodded. That's as much as he could give him.

He looked around. "Got anything to drink in this cell?" Before Sade could answer, he was headed toward the little fridge in the corner and returning with three bottles of water. He tossed them on the bed and offered one to Sade.

"No thank you."

He threw it in his lap anyway. "Drink it, son." It was the kind of order that meant *you had better*. Kane leaned back a little, eying Sade through drooped eyelids. "Indulge a tired father."

Sade opened the water, his heart racing at what that meant and why he wanted him to drink the water. "Not a problem," Sade muttered, drinking about half the bottle while Kane seemed momentarily content, looking around.

"Oh hey," he said in a lighter tone. "Got some good news. Package will be delivered to the neighboring island in three days."

"Package?" Kane's brows slowly rose with the spread of his smile and Sade's pulse shot up. "Abraham?"

He gave an excited low laugh. "The one and only, son."

"Holy fuck, how'd you..."

"Not your business," he said calmly before his eyes lowered to the water. "Finish up, son."

Sade did as he was told then asked, "So what will we—"

"We'll be taking a cleaning job of sorts on the island as cover work. Your mother and Mercy won't be able to know. Or Liberty. Or Bo. Nobody." He eyed him until Sade verbally agreed. "Your mother or Mercy wouldn't tolerate what we're about to go do." Even though his gaze was gentle, there was a fierceness there. "You okay with that?"

"Absolutely. But after what he did, I'm pretty sure Mercy--"

"No," he said softly, shaking his head. "Not what we're doing. She's too ethical." He gave a single nod. "I trained her to be. And Bo will be asked to watch over the women here." He picked up the second bottle of water, and Sade eyed his hands with his peripheral while trying to pay attention. "They're setting up shop for us." He fixed a smile on Sade that brought his animal out, the one he used when killing for the man, then he tossed him the next bottle of water.

"I'm good."

His smile slowly faded before he muttered, "Drink it, son." He raised his brows a little. "Indulge a patient father."

Sade bit his tongue on the need to ask, taking the water and opening it. He went ahead and downed all of it, eying Kane as he did. "Shop?" Sade finally gasped, tossing the empty water bottle.

"Kitchenette, fridge. A little cot for resting in between." Kane placed a palm on the bed and leaned back in leisure.

"In between...."

"Shifts," he said, his blue gaze like a gentle breeze as he tossed Sade the third bottle of water.

Sade lowered his eyes to the water, his jaw shifting in contemplation of how to handle that.

"Drink it, son," he ordered, his voice low and clearly warning. "Indulge a... merciful father."

Fuck. If only he had a clue what he was up to. Sade wasn't about to poke around in the dark beyond that closed door to find out, and so opened the fucking water and again drank. Halfway through, Kane finally turned his watchful eye off of him and went on like the conversation hadn't been interrupted. "I mean who knows, maybe the sick fuck will crack in the first hour, but I highly doubt it."

"So you're what… interrogating?" Sade let out a discreet belch, noting the clear humor in Kane's eyes now.

"You can call it that. But I'm just interested in one thing. The coordinates to that demented hell he calls Eden."

Sade remembered now. "So we're not just…killing him."

"He's my only hope to rescuing those kids. I need him alive for that. And cooperative. Talkative, you know what I mean?" he said, like this was run of the mill talk.

"Right." But Sade wasn't entirely sure and really wanted to be, wanted to know what he had in mind to get answers from the sick fuck.

Kane chuckled. "Finish up, son," he said.

Sade chugged the rest of the water, feeling like he was tying his own noose. When he was done, he stared at Kane, waiting for whatever was coming.

He threw his head back and laughed, like somebody who'd held it in for too long. "I know that look," he said, wagging his finger at him. "You're wondering what in the world is Kane going to do to crack that nut."

Sade wasn't sure if he meant his nut or the Abe nut. "Right."

"See, that's the interesting part of this job that I'm very anxious to teach you about." He turned a little more on the bed toward Sade. "There's really only two things you need to remember at all times when on a job of this nature." He held up his thumb and pointer finger. "One. It's never about what you do to a criminal, but *how* you do it. Two. It's never about how you do it to a criminal, but *why.*" His gaze burned with a dark passion. "And the latter… should always govern the former." He popped his brows and grinned, making Sade's insides dance in anticipation at knowing—no, seeing—exactly what the fuck he meant.

"Well," he said, his tone final as he stood. "It's been sweet having tea time with you son, but I told Mercy you were all hers at eleven. He looked around. "I also told her I'd have you ready for when she comes." He turned to Sade with inquisitive brows. "Your restraints?"

Panic slammed Sade at those words. Here it was. Dismemberment time. "Under the bed." Sade got them for him to show he had no qualms about punishments.

Kane took the restraints and held them up with a smile. "My girl," he said with soft pride before flicking his finger at Sade. "Assume the position."

Sade did, which was that annoying coffin form. "She ties the chain to the foot of the bed and the wrist chain to the feet."

"Of course," he said, impressed, glancing at Sade as he prepared the restraints. "She's special, isn't she?"

Sade's heart hammered hard. "One of a kind."

After Kane got him secure, he raked a hand through his hair, looking around. This was it. Tie him up and do God only knew. He shot his arm out and looked at his watch. "That's it for me," he said, walking off, confusing the fuck out of Sade. "Now son," he said carefully, turning at the door. "In less than an hour, your bladder will be screaming for release. You can either hold it and take the pain until Mercy gets here in two hours… or, you can piss on yourself and get relief. Both options will cost something." He angled his head at Sade. "When I see you again, I want to know which you chose, and why. And at that time, I'll share with you why you're not eating your dick right now, for hurting my daughter."

Shame and relief hit Sade at the same moment. That was all he'd planned to do? Pain he could take, but he wasn't ready to die or lose his dick, not when he needed it for Mercy.

"I'm headed to see your mother now," he said, opening the door. "She's been in a funk since we left for the island. She thinks I can't see it, but it's been stormy days for her and she's not talking about it."

Sade studied Kane, focusing on his mother now. Had she not told him about his little sick confession? He realized then why she might not. Who wanted to ever voice how they'd failed their only child? "Hey," Sade called.

Kane waited in the half open door.

"I uh. I think I know what's wrong with mom." He only responded with a blank stare and Sade hurried before he lost his nerve and puked the water up. "I had a talk with her. She... found out some things my father did that she didn't know, but I swear to fuck, I thought she knew it or I wouldn't have said it."

Kane's body sagged a little and he hung his head. "Jesus," he said softly. "I was going insane trying to figure out what I'd done wrong. Now, I wished it were me, not that. You have no idea how long it's taken me to convince her she was doing the right thing all those years. It was a daily fight. Daily," he stressed with a quiet vigor.

"I'm really fucking sorry," Sade said. "Not just about this but... about what I did to Mercy, you have to know that."

"I know, son. I know you love both of those women more than your own life," he said so very confidently. "Sometimes these things are meant to come out. Need to. But only the good Lord can help with the things that bite into the soul." He shut the door only to open it again and stick his head back in. "Oh and then there are God's little helpers in the world. And your's plans to change your bad-ass into a harmless little pumpkin." He gave a slow genuine grin with a wink like he couldn't wait for the torture to begin, then shut the door.

Chapter Fifteen

Jesus Christ, wow. Pent up anxiety slowly left, deflating Sade's body until he laid there, gasping in the aftermath. As it was, anytime Sade was in that man's presence for any length of time, he felt like he'd gotten a backstage pass to undeserved fame. But to be in that sacred space without knowing *what* the outcome would be, took him back to that first time he found Kane's red crosshairs flickering on his body in the dark. Yeah, he was rescuing him, but when he hadn't known that, it was one awe-full experience. Even now, somewhere in his mind, his guilty dirty mind, he waited for the shoe to fall. The poison in the water he just drank to kick in. The microscopic bomb he'd somehow slipped in one of the bottles to explode in his gut. Or his dick when he was pissing all that out.

Speaking of pissing, his bladder was already screaming. And salvation in the form of Mercy was still *two hours* away. Kane's words replayed in his head, his little riddle. Hold it or piss. And tell him why he chose which. He was holding it. He just needed to figure out the why part. He was sure it was some kind of test and Sade wanted to pass it.

Wow, he was actually going to be *working* with him. He should start up a training routine. And how convenient that he was now next to the gym.

Setting up shop. For days. Fuck, and what kind of cover-job were they supposed to have, and how was he supposed to keep that from the soul meshing, mind melding Mercy? And what about his *mother*? Jesus, they had better be fucking good to get past those two.

Another wave of rabid excitement rolled through him. He'd get to be in the presence of that sick motherfucker again. Wonder how ole' Abe would react to seeing him while *his* feet weren't nailed to the floor.

****

Mercy had finally done it, she'd found that center, that heavenly *center* where she once used to be, the one she had just before her father had supposedly died. The one she'd semi-regained when she'd found Sade's file outside her door and found reason to live again. Then she realized no, this center was different. Not more centered, more… deep. She'd grown, she could feel it. She was stronger. Thank fuck, she needed it. Amazing how failing epically could grow a person.

Now if only she could find the right damn outfit to express that inner kick-ass-goddess. Problem was, she'd never dressed the part, but now... now seemed important enough to, it seemed right. She yanked a black dress out of the closet and put it to her body. It brought back memories from the last bat cave they'd hid out at. The party, in particular. Hmm. Dancing would've been nice to do with Sade. Too bad he had to be restrained. Flashes of him naked with his legs open and his cock standing tall, face tight and sexy in orgasm sent heat flooding her womb and clit. Okay, not too bad.

She glanced at the clock. Shit, twenty minutes. Eleven o-clock. Felt like Cinderella in reverse. At the stroke of midnight, the spell would begin. She was to be there with... something sexual. Something non-rough, non-mean, non-violent in any way. And dammit, she *still* hadn't settled on any particular routine, she was trusting that the answer would present itself when the time came. Then she recalled her *I'll finish you later* promise. Well, she'd definitely be making good on that one.

But there *was* one thing she'd settled on after explaining to her dad what set Sade off the last time—the use of his Christian name. She recalled her father's words, *"Damn those who crush the innocent. But blessed be the ones who restore that which was stolen."*

Johnathon was his birth name. Desecrated, raped, and ruined. New beginnings were definitely important but that particular thing right there seemed to demand more. Maybe she couldn't reclaim the innocence stolen from him, but she could reclaim *him—Johnathon Lee.* Just the thought of somebody daring to strip a person of their identity and force them into another? For their *pleasure? Money?* Fucking tragic. How fucking dare they?

Well they wouldn't. Not if she had anything to do with it. She would reclaim the name. And she would create the man he was always destined to become. Life had knocked him off track for a couple of years, that's all. She'd help him get back on.

Now all she had to do is win his trust and cooperation in that one.

She suddenly had the idea of a sensual massage. Where she touched sensually next to things that make him go mmmm mmm, ohhhh, Mercy, fuck yes. She giggled, thinking she could even do it naked. Maybe even… let herself get off to it. He definitely liked that and she needed to use all her ammunition in this one. Nobody said it had to be amazing or technical, it just needed to be something different to throw off the groove gripping his ass. Mmmm, his ass… his fine, perfect ass.

Did he even realize what he did to her? Maybe she should make more of a habit of verbalizing that. Verbal stimulation. She added that to her growing list of harmless pleasures. God, she needed more.

Mercy dressed to the hilt, and made her way quietly to the basement stairs. She didn't really want to be seen—

"Hi sweetheart."

Mercy yelped and spun to see her father about to go into his bedroom. "Hi Dad," she waved.

"You look lovely, baby. Go teach our boy some manners. Oh," he said. "He'll be needing the facilities as soon as you get there." He winked and continued into his bedroom, leaving Mercy to hurry down the stairs in worry over what that meant. What had her father done? Shit shit.

She threw open the door at the basement and found him chained in bed. "Fuck baby, get the jar, quick."

"Pee?"

"Yes," he gasped.

She flew to the bathroom, fetched the jar and hurried back. "What did he do?" she gasped, pulling his shorts down while he turned his hips. "Don't talk, don't talk, just go." She slid the jar over his thick cock and he went, his body trembling in strain as he emptied his seriously over full bladder with loud groans and gasps.

"I am soooooo very sorry." She eyed the quickly filling jar, wincing. "Shit, you may need to angle more for me. "Why are you tied up?"

"Your dad," he gasped.

"What? Why? What did he do?" She carefully removed the makeshift toilet and slowly walked it to the bathroom to dump it. After washing her hands, she wet a washcloth and brought it back then proceeded to dab it on the head of his cock. "There, all clean." She raised his underwear and shorts back over it, only to find it didn't quite cover him. "Uh…" she reached in the band and poked it lower.

He groaned and rolled his hips, pushing it back out. "How about you untie me so I can stretch my legs?"

She glanced at him.

"Trust me, I'm not going anywhere after having a talk with your father," he mumbled.

She winced, not even wanting to know the details of that. "Thirty minutes?"

"Anything, my ass is fucking numb."

"Okay, okay." Mercy's heart raced at the idea of freeing him even though she didn't feel like he would do anything stupid. "Are you sure you're not going to beat me up?" she half joked, more worried about him running while she got the keys from the little drawer next to the table. She regarded him when she sat on the bed by his feet and found him brow quirking her. "What! It's a legitimate question."

"Is that what you would do?"

She thought about that for a second and half shrugged. "I… don't think so."

He snorted. "Yeah well you're stuck performing therapy on me tonight, doc. I wouldn't miss it for the world."

"I'm glad," she said, honestly, excitement making her nearly nauseous. She just hoped he thought that when she told him about using his real name. She was on his last wrist when she eyed him. "Last one," she sang.

He answered her with an angled stare.

"God, you're making me nervous," she mumbled, unlocking the final lock then stepping back from the bed. "There you go."

He rubbed his wrists and sat up, putting his feet on the floor, his back facing her. He took a deep breath and let it out, his head hanging.

"You need me to help you do anything?"

"Nah," he mumbled, sounding… depressed almost.

"Sooo," she clapped. "Thirty minutes and then it's therapy time and then after therapy, you're free to go as you please." She hoped that good news lightened his mood but she saw no real need to keep him restrained now that everybody was back.

"Good. I want to start working out," he mumbled.

He stood and stretched and Mercy's eyes devoured the bulge and flex of muscles—especially his ass in those black shorts almost as fitted as the matching briefs beneath. He tossed his head side to side and took a few steps while swinging his arms around. The tension in her body said any second he'd bolt for the door or run at her and do something.

He made his way slowly around the room, then went into the bathroom. "Think I'll shower if that's good with you, doc."

Shower? "What about your bandage?"

"I'll watch it."

She made her way closer to the bathroom. "You need help?"

She heard him either snort or laugh lightly. "I don't think that would be wise, doc."

"Okay, I'm here if you need any actual help. Nothing sexual I mean."

"Right," he said just as the shower came on.

God he was acting weird. Quiet. What had her dad talked to him about? Is that what put him in this mood or was it something else?

She sighed, hating to think he didn't want to be doing any of this. She busied herself around the room, not allowing any of the negative ideas to fester in her head. The plan was straightforward. She was helping a broken man that didn't believe he could come out of all that darkness around him.

He finally came out of the bathroom and Mercy's heart dropped as he strolled out naked and headed toward the bed where she sat, waiting. "You'll need to dress it again, it fell off."

She realized after she unglued her eyes from his engorged cock what he meant. "Oh," she cleared her throat. "Yeah, I can do that."

"You're in my spot, doc," he said as he approached.

She hopped up and gave him plenty of room, trying not to see him as he sat on the bed then laid down, plopping his thick legs open with a sigh. Again, her gaze locked on his action packed groin. At least some part of him seemed eager to start therapy. That was good. She tried to calm her fear and excitement.

He held his hands up, indicating he was ready and Mercy hurried to restrain him. Then she suddenly realized that maybe she wanted his arms up. And... his legs open. Would be easier to access the tools. Hmm. Maybe she could settle for legs untied and just have his hands bound. If things went well, she could rework the restraints to accommodate what she wanted next time.

After she secured his hands, she said, "If you don't mind, I'll leave your legs free."

He eyed her now, drawing up his leg. "Whatever you need."

She straightened and met his gaze, her stomach tensing at finding it a hundred degrees hotter. His lips remained parted as he followed her movement to the foot of the bed. As she went and stood at the front of it, facing him, she knew what personality she needed to be and what route to take tonight. The same one she'd started, before he went nuts. The naughty doctor patient role fantasy. It seemed to have been working quite well. And now that he was restrained, she could freely do as she wanted or needed without worrying about another volcanic eruption.

But first... "I need to... talk to you about renegotiating the contract." She miraculously kept her voice firm and confident.

"Talk," he ordered, softly.

"Your name," she jumped right in. "The one that you don't like me using?"

"What about it?" Caution edged his deep tone.

"Long story or short story?"

"Short."

"Okay," she said, taking a breath. "Here's the thing. It's your birth name. The name your mother chose for you. Things have happened that make you not like your name, and I get that.

"Short, doc."

She paused briefly, focusing on the point. "I think it's detrimental to my therapy that we use your Christian name… during sessions only."

He eyed her, his gaze unreadable. "Det-ri-mental." He dragged out the word.

She nodded. "Absolutely. This is your name and I think… we should reclaim it."

"Do you," he said, his eyes piercing and unusually clear.

"I do."

Chapter Sixteen

Sade's heart was hammering as he stared at his angel. Not because of her contract negotiation request, but with her *reasoning*. She wanted to fucking *reclaim* his name. Walk right into his nightmares dressed in a fuck me black dress, delicious blood red lips, green jeweled eyes framed in angelic lashes, and just take it the fuck back? God, could she get any more irresistible?

And ever since her father had been in there to talk to him, something had changed. He no longer felt driven to run in the opposite direction of her little therapy classes, but instead, headlong into it. And to hear her say she wanted to be his angel of mercy, had his cock beyond desperate for her touch, her lips, her fucking healing however she wanted to bring it. Because *if* it were possible, if anybody could do it, Mercy could. That much he knew. And he also knew that he craved to let her *try*. Try baby, try as long as your heart's content.

But how long would she last? How long before his failure translated into rejection?

"Done," he said.

"Done?"

By her surprise, she'd expected a major fight on using his name. She would be right, except that somehow the stars had realigned, maybe just for her. And he was nothing but genuinely interested in seeing what she could accomplish. Maybe even rooting for her. "Only you. Only during therapy." The special exception bought him a glow on her pretty face, and Sade considered the little gift fair payment.

He angled his head, locking attentive eyes on her body again. She was so fucking hot in that skin tight dress too. And black high heels. He wasn't sure what she had in mind, but so far, so…fucking…good. He raised his gaze to hers finally. "I'm ready. Doc. Or would you prefer I call you something else during sessions?"

She licked her lips, another unanticipated ingredient he could see. He waited, letting her think about it. "What would you like to call me?" she asked.

Sade heard the slight tremble in her firm tone, indicating she was going for strong and confident, the perfect teacher. What did he want to call her? He drew up both his knees, and held them there, watching her gaze. "I like Angel when you're being sweet."

She smiled a little. "Fair enough. How about you call me Angel when you're liking therapy, and Doc when you're not? That way I know without you telling me. And in the same token, I'll call you Johnathon when I think you're doing well, and Sade when you're not?"

Mmmm. "What if I like being bad?"

She raised her brows. "What if you like being good?"

He opened his legs, his cock so fucking hard with the near threat. "Bring it, Angel."

He waited for her to say his real name, but she didn't. She was going easy. Or maybe she was afraid to. He'd let her warm up. But all he could think about now was the last therapy she'd done and how fucking turned on it had gotten him. God, he hoped she did that again.

"First thing I'd like to do is ask you a few questions. Honesty and transparency is a must for this to work. And there are no wrong answers."

"Got it," he said, watching the profile of her ass while she paced before the bed.

Sade let his knees fall open, his hands itching to hold his cock while she talked. She paused in her pacing suddenly then walked over to the bed and covered his lower body with the blanket. Sade fought a smile. "First question," she said, getting back to her studious pacing. "Are you ticklish anywhere?"

He wasn't sure what surprised him more, the question, or the lack of answer he had for it. "I'm not sure."

She paused and looked at him. "Really?"

He shrugged. "I… don't remember if I am."

"Okay," she said. "Noted." She angled her head then. "Mind if I check?"

His brows raised. "Check?"

"If you're ticklish?"

"You're the doctor, not sure how that helps anything though." Sade watched her approach the bed and his legs opened more. "Think I'm ticklish between my legs."

She sat on the bed next to him, quirking a brow. "Very funny. But the idea is to find things that bring happiness with pleasure in some way. Any way." She eyed him while yanking the bed covers off of his feet. "Don't knock it, I'm limited in resources, I'm doing the best I can."

"Not knocking it, Angel. You're beautiful." Sade didn't know where that came from, but he was glad for the slip, with the pretty smile it got him.

She stroked her nails over the bottom of his feet and he jerked back. She looked at him. "Tickled?"

"More like startled."

"Okay now that you're ready for it." She slowly dragged her nails over his foot again and he didn't jump this time. "I'll continue up, you tell me where it starts to tickle." Sade could hardly breathe as she moved more of the blanket aside and stroked her nails over the top of his foot. She moved to his shin next then along his inner calf. "Chills," she noticed on his legs, happily. "That's at least a reaction." She pushed the covers up higher, until they were bunched up on his groin and in response, he opened his legs more. He tensed when she scratched along his inner thigh and eyed him. 'Tickled?"

"Maybe," he strained.

She scratched softly again and he pulled away. "Yes."

"It tickles?" She stroked again and smiled when he jerked.

"Yes, Angel, it tickles."

"Do you like it?"

He loved it, he was sure. "I don't not like it." Oddly enough, he was also very turned on with how she gave him a choice in the matter. No, how she cared about what he liked. That was the difference. And for reasons that were purely sweet and angelic. That fucking turned him on in ways he didn't understand. Didn't need to understand, either. Just needed it.

"Okaaaay then," she said happily. "Moving along." She jumped her hand over the covers and started on his stomach.

"You missed a very, very, large spot," he said.

"Come on," she whispered, raking her nails along his stomach. "This is serious." She traveled up his side and he jerked a little. "Oh? Another spot?" She repeated the steps, making him grunt and jerk with it. "Wow," she sang happily. "Two tickle spots. I feel like I'm finding buried treasure."

"If you say so, Angel," he muttered, eying the creamy flesh peeking out of her gaping cleavage.

She suddenly stood and his eyes lowered to her ass. 'Okay, so are you ready for the serious stuff?"

"Beyond."

"Okay. So what I think I'll do is some "soft" therapy.

He was too excited to speak now. He watched as she slowly approached the left side of the bed and sat so her ass touched his hip. "I think we should continue with my original plan. Teaching you different pleasures all while experiencing the proper emotion."

The hot burn in the depths of that pretty green gaze, stole his breath. He slowly angled his head. "What emotion is that, Angel?" he nearly whispered.

"How about you tell me," she said, making it a silky command while placing her palm on the bed between his legs.

He slid his eyes to her hand so close to his cock now, then looked at her. "Is there a God emotion?" he asked.

She gave him a quirked brow. "Let's go with the human terms."

"Then… I'm guessing that would be love."

She winked at him. "You get your first A plus."

The lethal amount of desire in his veins heated the air between them. "I usually never get good grades."

"Hm," she said. "Maybe because you never had the right teacher."

No. Fucking. Doubt. "Maybe," he muttered, the tip of his tongue peeking out and remaining between his lips. "Teach me, Angel," he whispered. "Please," he added, as if to show he was ready to be a good student.

"The first thing I'm going to do is talk to you…" before he could groan in frustration, she rolled a sexy gaze up to him, "while I kiss you. A little."

His hips rolled on their own, anticipating what that would feel like. "I'm ready."

She slowly sat next to him. "One of the things I want you to work on, is control. Your mind and your body. When you feel yourself wanting to stray from the soft, sensual, sweet course, say, 'Doc'."

Soft and sweet didn't appeal to him unless he knew it would lead to rough and hard. And if he wasn't supposed to go there…. "Doc?"

She looked at him with concerned eyes.

"Usually, if you tell me something like that, I bypass the problem of soft and sweet by thinking of the hard and rough, knowing that's where I'm headed. I don't want to be a bad student so I'm just warning you."

"Thank you for telling me," she said, sounding impressed and thrilled that he did. "How about we think of this part like a physical assessment. I have to know the exact status of your body's responses to stimulation so I can formulate a solution that you can adapt to."

God, she was gorgeous. "Got it, Angel."

"And please tell me what you like and don't like as we go."

He could manage that. "I like you talking to me the way you are. I like the way you say please. I like the softness in your voice. I like that you care about me. Care about what I like and want. Need."

She regarded his cock as though wanting to measure things from there. It wasn't a flat tire but it wasn't a raging erection either. It was ready, on standby. "And I love being soft with you," she barely whispered, stroking her fingers over his stomach. His cock jerked a little when they neared his pelvis. "I love being sensual." Her fingers continued down and bypassed his cock, gliding along his inner thigh to his knee, then slowly back up the same path. "I love teasing you too," she whispered, her fingers sweeping beneath his balls, nails softly scratching and making them tighten. "I'm going to teach you how to love it soft. Gentle." She raked her nails softly over his balls and they tightened with need. "Do you know how?"

His cock laid thick and hard on his stomach as her fingers continued to stroke too softly and so close to where he needed. "How," he whispered, looking at her pretty tongue, poised between her red lips. Again his mind envisioned them spread around the base of his cock.

"By making you."

His stomach jerked at the term.

"Doc?"

Her eyes met his but there was no concern, maybe knowing. "You get pleasure from pain…" her finger barely slipped between his ass cheeks, making his heart race. "And I'm going to teach you how to get pain… from my pleasure. Place your feet on the bed and open nice and wide for me."

His breath shot out as his mind grasped at those words. *See the pain in pleasure.* His body seemed to understand as he did what she said, opening as wide as he could.

"I'm going to get between your legs now."

The anticipation of what she'd do clenched his stomach. She sat between his legs so that everything was right at her fingertips, her mouth too if he lifted his hips off the bed. He remembered about telling her. "I like this, Angel."

"I want you to think about something for me, can you do that, Johnathon?"

He clenched his eyes shut at that name. "Doc," he whispered.

"I'm here, baby. You're mine now, all mine. And I love you," she said.

He opened his eyes at feeling her tongue on the tip of his cock, barely licking. She took a soft hold of the base and he rolled his hips, hissing with need, his body shuddering when her other fingers glided over his balls, barely touching the opening of his ass. "Angel," he gasped.

"Tell me what you like, remember." Again she glided her fingers the same way, eying him.

"I like it there," he whispered, opening more, reaching.

She took her lower lip between her teeth, focused on what she was doing now, stroking his balls. "That?" She glanced at him, her fingers going lower to his ass, making him pump for it.

"Fuck," he hissed.

She stroked over the opening, and his cock jerked. Fear of what she'd think of that kink froze him. "Oh," she said with a silky understanding. "This." She stroked again over the opening of his ass. "You like this."

"Angel," he said, still worried about what she'd think yet desperate to tell her. "I love it," he confessed. "So fucking much."

He stared at her, looking for the verdict in her gaze. When she raised it to his, his heart nearly stopped at finding a lethal amount of naughty desire. "So glad you shared that," she breathed, delivering tiny flicks of fire on the top of his cock, while looking at him. "Your body belongs to me now, baby. And I love this body, would never hurt it. Except with pleasure. Do you understand what I'm saying?"

He wasn't sure if he did he only knew that he needed her to fucking hurt him in that second. "Doc," he gasped, fighting it.

"Talk to me, Johnathon, tell me what you're feeling."

Chapter Seventeen

"I want you to fucking do it, I want you to do it hard and fast," he grit.

"Right here?"

He lifted his hips off the bed, reaching for the barely touch on his ass. "Fuck, yes, please." His body heaved as he fought for her touch.

"That's it, you're doing so very good," she whispered. "Lift higher for me. I want to use my tongue there."

He nearly had an orgasm at those words. Her tongue there. That was new for him.

"Do as I say, Johnathon," she said, her nails raking softly on his ass cheeks.

"Fuck, I like that, Angel." He had to tell her, he wanted her to know.

"I'm going to lick until it hurts baby," she whispered. "I want you to take my pleasure pain. Take it the way I give it." She licked at the opening of his ass, her tongue probing in, barely, and his hips bucked for more.

"Fuck, Angel," he growled.

"This is your pain, Johnathon—to take it the way I give it. The way I say, when I say, how I say, and especially why I say. Do you understand?"

Sade's breath shot out of him as it dawned on his dark, sadistic circuited mind. Her pleasure pain. Beautiful torment. Delicate agony. How did he miss that? "I like when you make me, Angel. Make me take it."

"I will baby." She probed her tongue inside again, pushing her nose into his balls. Her hot breath on his ass while she stroked his cock slow and with a firm grip, holy fuck.

"Angel," he strained, reaching for that agony.

"Very good, Johnathon," she whispered, her finger at the opening now. "Lower your cock for me," she ordered softly. "You're going to come for me but you'll do it the way I say to, do you understand?"

"I fucking like this Angel," was all he could think as he lowered for her.

"I'm going to put just the tip in, that's all you get. And you're going to like it that way," she ordered softly. "You're going to learn to like what I say, do you understand?"

The fire in her green gaze as she locked them to his brought Sade so close to that edge, he could hardly believe it.

"Answer me," she said, her tongue flicking along the ridge of his cock while her finger pressed at his ass, waiting for his obedience.

"Yes, Angel, fucking yes, I'll do as you say, I'll do very good."

"And you won't do it a second before, do you understand?"

"God, yes," he croaked, nodding while watching her torture him with her tongue. Fuck, he felt it. He felt the agony of her delicate will. Formidable silk biting at his mind, his body, shaping his desire. Binding him to its angelic and elegant torture. And fuck it was every bit as powerful as his volatile sadism and masochism, maybe more so since it forged a path against the grain inside him.

"I'm going to suck your cock now, Johnathon. You will not buck your hips, do you understand? If you do, I will punish you by stopping."

"Yes, Angel. I love obeying you." He needed her to know what she was doing to him, that it was working, and yes, that he fucking loved it.

She knelt between his legs, opening her own to lower her mouth where she needed. Right at the head. She placed soft kisses all over the top, her tongue licking the slit with firm but slow strokes. "Your cock tastes very good, Johnathon," she whispered. "Look at me," she ordered softly.

He did, and his heart hammered in his balls as her finger niggled its way deeper inside him, making his breath shudder out.

"I'm going to take your entire cock into my mouth," she said, still kissing at the head. "And I'm going to suck very hard as I slowly pull up. And when I get to the very top of your cock, I want you to come so very good, do you understand? And when you begin to come, I will reward you, here." She shoved her finger in deep and he choked down the sudden orgasm it brought. "And I'll reward you here." She opened her mouth and covered the head of his cock.

"Angel!" he grit then hissed, when her teeth barely raked.

His cock popped from her lips. "And one more thing," she said, her voice like commanding velvet as she soul meshed with him. "This one is very, very, important." She moved her finger in and out of him, slowly again and Sade had never been so tormented by anything. "When you're coming in my mouth, you will not buck your hips, you will hold your cock very still while I blow your beautiful mind." She sucked at the head again, eyes still locked on his while her finger pushed in, and eased out of him. "Do you understand me, Johnathon?"

"Fucking yes, Angel." He bit down hard on his lower lip when the urge to thrust slammed him.

Without another word, she began taking his cock into her mouth. She did this so fucking slowly, her lips tight, her mouth a hot suction that devoured him, inch by torturous inch. Her finger maintained a sensual push and pull in his ass, but it was the way she exited completely then worked it back in the same way. It was like getting penetrated by her over and over, each time it gave him the same thrill and hunger for more.

Sade's body heaved and his legs trembled as he watched her mouth getting close to the base of his cock. When he felt the back of her throat, he gasped then let out a vicious growl, fighting the violent urge to buck. "Doc!" he strained, losing control.

Her finger stopped moving and he looked down to find her green gaze on his, hard and threatening.

"Angel," he shuddered, trying to tell her he was okay, please don't fucking stop.

Keeping her eye on him, her finger resumed the slow push and pull while her eyes drifted shut and she groaned on him.

The vibration caused a bolt of heat to shoot all the way into his spine. "Fuck, fuck," Sade gasped as she began that slow reverse up his cock. It was suddenly not *if* he could come but if he could *wait*. "Angel, Angel, Angel," he grit. The slow, hard pull up his cock came with a change of pace with her finger now. She no longer used a shallow tease, but plunged very deep until her hand pressed against him. "I'm fucking there, baby, I'm there," he gasped, clenching his eyes and thrashing his head in effort to wait and be still like he was told.

When her mouth got to the fucking head of his cock, Sade gasped, his mouth open in astonishment at the fact his orgasm was on him and *waiting, begging*. She rolled that green gaze up and locked it on his… and slowly bit.

Sade's orgasm exploded in her mouth and he barely remembered the rules when her finger fucked him so hard and deep, her hand hitting against him. When she bit harder, the effort it took to not move brought Sade's roars straining out of him, one after another until he felt like a man gripped in an erotic seizure.

The slow down spiral of his orgasm came with a gradual release of pressure on his cock as her finger eased like silk out of him. Sade panted in the aftermath, his eyes still closed, mind swimming in shock at the *holy shit fuck* he'd just experienced.

His body trembled as she gently pushed down on his hips still poised in the air. His ass came into contact with the bed and his eyes opened. He could only stare at the ceiling in shock. Shocked in so many ways, on so many levels.

"Would you like to see me naked, Johnathon?"

His stomach jolted with the name, but Jesus fucking Christ, so did his cock. He looked at her, standing at the side of the bed now, staring at him. He'd never seen such a perfect blend of angelic naughty on a face before. "Yes, Angel," he barely croaked, his heart starting to race again. Because he could see she was not finished with him. And what other amazing tricks she'd do had his insatiable desires ready.

She began one of the sexiest strip teases he'd ever seen. Come to think of it, he didn't recall ever seeing anything remotely close to that hot.

"I love when you look at me, Johnathon," she whispered, sliding her dress over her ass, rocking her hips oh so slowly. The pace reminded him of what she'd just done and his cock jerked, ready to go again.

He considered how he felt about her using his name. It was still a mix of odd sensations but with the rest of the odd things she was doing, it wasn't enough to keep his cock from pulsating in curious expectation.

"I like to think of you when I touch myself," she said, reaching her hand behind her and sliding it between those perfect ass cheeks. She peeked over her shoulder. "Does that make your cock hard?"

"Yes," he gasped.

"Open your legs for me again."

Fuck. He pulled his knees as far open as he could, his eyes locked on that finger dipping into her pussy from behind. "Do it good, Angel, so fucking good."

"You can rock your hips on the bed while I finger my dripping pussy," she whispered, walking her legs open a little so he could see more. "Did you know I love fingering my pussy while thinking of your cock fucking me?"

She'd turned just enough to let him see her other fingers slowly rolling her nipple. Heat shot through him and he gasped. God, he needed to see her tits. He wouldn't ask. He'd let her do her beautiful thing, he'd let it do its beautiful thing to him while fire forced his hips to rock and thrust in obedience to her sweet commands.

She finally faced him and his eyes locked hard on those nipples, especially his favorite one. "Angel," he gasped, licking his lips and fisting both hands in the shackles. She slid her palms slowly up her body and over her tits, letting the nipples flutter between each finger. "Fuuuucking hot, Angel."

"You like to see me touching myself, Johnathon?"

"Yes, Angel," he shuddered as she went to the foot of the bed and slowly climbed on. Again his gaze locked on her tits. The sight of them hanging that way, jerked his cock. "Fucking beautiful," he whispered, pumping his hips so that it pulled at his balls.

"I'm going to fuck you now the way I want to. Would you like that, Johnathon?"

"Yes," he whispered. "Yes, yes. Do whatever you want to me." Do it so hard and good to me he wanted to say but wasn't sure if that was acceptable.

She straddled his hips and sat, pressing the length of his cock to his stomach while fingering the tips of both nipples and hissing softly, her wet silk hot on his length.

She twirled her hips on the pounding head and slid her hands up his body until she held on to his shoulders, her hips still grinding softly on him. "Do you mind if I make my clit hot right there?"

She lowered her mouth to his and began to tease him with her lips and tongue. "Angel. So fucking beautiful," he said in her mouth, his body back to desperate for her. She glided soft fingers along his face while licking his lips and tongue, her moans as delicate as the twirl of her hips. She moved those kisses to his cheek then forehead, putting those tits so close.

She placed her hands above his head and lowered her chest to his mouth. "I need you to suck my tits, Johnathon," she whispered, forcing her breast into his mouth. "Please, I need you to," she gasped as Sade opened so very wide and attacked it with a vicious hunger. He'd been made to perform and sometimes on occasion one of his father's whores treated him nicely and asked him to do things, but what she'd just said and done went beyond everything he'd experienced.

Nobody had ever *needed* him, *wanted* him. *Loved* him. Not one, not fucking once.

She pulled her tit from his mouth and kissed him again, holding his face, the touch of one who adored. "I love kissing you," she whispered, angling her head to get more. "You taste like heaven, and when I think of you, my heart races," she said between breathless moans, her hand between them, sliding his cock along that silk. "All I can think of is how much I need you again, did you know I can't stop needing you, I can't stop wanting you?" She was at his neck now, sucking and nibbling, her words making him dizzy. "You drive me crazy."

He couldn't speak as she lifted up and positioned his cock at her entrance before closing her eyes and slowly lowering onto it. Sade couldn't stop the urge to flick his hips when she was sitting on him, her lips parted. "Yes, Johnathon," she whispered, not rebuking him. "Make me feel good." Her eyes barely opened to soul mesh with him. "Can you? Can you fuck me until I scream?"

Fuck. "Angel," he whispered, looking down at her fingers between her shaved lips. He rolled his hips.

"Yes, yes," she moaned, placing her hands on his open knees behind her now and leaning back a little. "Pound me, Johnathon."

He grunted and bucked his hips hard, drawing her sharp cries of *yes. Yes, like that. Faster.*

Sade wished his hands were free to fucking make her take it so hard. He knew how to make her scream, that he knew well. He settled for bucking his hips until she was bouncing on his body from it, gasping in ecstasy.

"Angel," he growled, hammering her core while she held onto his knees and he yanked his restraints. "Fucking make your pussy come."

"You're going to suck me," she gasped. "I want to come on your mouth, Johnathon, do you want that?" She fell forward, kissing him with a hunger. "Would you like that? Sucking my pussy, Johnathon?" Her tongue danced all over his, her teeth biting at his lips.

"Yes, fuck yes."

She switched then to delicate tormenting kisses on his mouth while he continued flicking his hips. She placed her hands on either side of his head, filling his mouth with her tit again. "Suck it Johnathon, make my pussy tingle while you fuck me."

"Fucking Christ, Angel!" he grit, thrusting his hips and biting softly at her nipples.

"Oh God, tell me you love it, Johnathon."

"I fucking love it, Angel, I love it, I love you." Sade placed his feet on the bed and lifted his ass, ramming her harder while she kissed him and pulled his hair between shrieks.

"Did you like the way I sucked you?" she gasped in his ear. "I love your sexy ass, it makes my pussy so hot when I see it." She dove on his mouth again, sucking and biting until he growled.

"I'm begging you."

"What do you want, you want to fuck so hard?" She'd pulled off of him and moved farther up his chest on her knees. "You like to ram your cock so hard?"

Sade looked down at her pussy slowly making its way toward his face. "Fucking Angel, fuck."

She slid her finger between her pussy lips and moaned, the sound of sweet and delicate with a hint of naughty. She brought the wet tip to his lips and he leaned for it, only to have her pull it away. "Wait for my instructions, Johnathon."

He laid back, staring up at her, winded and dizzy.

"I'm going to rub your lips with my pussy juice but don't taste until I say."

"Yes, Angel," he gasped, watching her finger move in and out of her.

She brought it to his mouth and he closed his eyes in agony at smelling her. The slow slide of her finger along his lips prompted him to open with hunger while breathless with restraint.

"Taste me now," she whispered.

Sade licked his lip, groaning. "Please give me more," he begged.

"So sweet," she whispered, fingering herself again then giving him that heaven in his mouth this time. He closed his eyes and moaned, sucking slowly, savoring. She crawled further up and straddled his face with her knees, placing her feet on his shoulders. "I want you to suck my pussy the way I tell you."

"Yes, Angel, yes, tell me."

"Just lick it softly," she said, opening her pussy lips with one hand while gripping a handful of his hair with the other. "Right there, Johnathon."

He flicked the tip of his tongue on her clit and she held his head firmly to the bed, letting him know she wanted him still.

"Kiss my clit," she whispered, her voice straining.

She pressed her pussy to his mouth, and he kissed it everywhere he could reach, her fingers pulling harder in his hair, lifting his head while she moved over his mouth.

"Fuck Angel, you taste so good," he gasped. "Make me suck it, make me suck it."

"You like me to make you?"

"Yes, I fucking love it, Angel, more than I knew."

She let out a long sexy hiss and latched both hands in his hair. "Be still while I make you suck my pussy." She pressed it on his mouth and twirled her hips. "I want to feel your tongue in me. Oh God, yes, like that," she whispered when he probed as deep as he could in that dripping opening while she rubbed her clit against his nose.

"I'm going to come like this, Johnathon," she gasped, sounding close. "Would you like that?"

"Come on my fucking mouth," he said against her.

"Suck my clit, Sade," she gasped, "suck me so good!"

The slip of his other name meant she was there, losing herself. But it also meant that Sade was who she called for at the end of that rope, and the idea lit his sadistic fire. If he had been free, he would have failed her therapy in that second, failed it so very fucking good.

"Mercy," he whispered, shaking his head and lips against her clit as he yanked on his restraints. She jerked her face down, her mouth open in pleasure, brows a line of harsh need. "Yes, yes," she gasped. "Please, yes, oh my God, Sade!"

He finally managed to get her clit between his teeth and he didn't let go as she screamed and came all over his mouth, her fingers pulling his hair hard enough to make him want more, make him want more pain while she called for Sade, over and over.

Then he realized in that second that he didn't care what name she called him in climax, just so he was the one bringing it. Johnathan. Sade. Either worked in that case.

But maybe. Just maybe. He could learn to like hearing that other name. But only her. Only from her.

Chapter Eighteen

Sade laid awake in the dark, waiting for the shame to come. He'd done something with her he never wanted to but she'd touched that trigger spot on him and while she was using that fucking name that he wanted so bad to hate and loathe, it had overcome him and he suddenly needed *her* doing that to him. Fucking him. But where was the shame? Where was the dirty feeling?

Sade's heart hammered in fear and excitement as he realized. It was that magic she did. She'd been doing it from the day he met her, captivating and mesmerizing him with it. The little boy inside was holding his breath to see what she'd pull out of her hat. And this was it. Her power was being able to take the vilest parts of him, touching it with her love, and making him clean.

He turned on his side, looking at the clock next to his bed. She wanted to sleep apart. Thought it was good for therapy. To which he'd said, "Now, that's a superbly idiotic idea, Doc."

To which she busted out laughing. To which he smiled about because he was fucking wrapped around the tiniest of her fingers. No, tiniest of her toes. Could he live until the next therapy session, was the question. He'd never wanted something so much. To see what else she had for him, what tricks she could perform and make him feel like there was hope.

First he'd need to fucking fall asleep.

****

Sade jolted awake to a giggling Mercy on his bed. She'd tickled him. "Morning, sleepy head," she whispered.

The sight of the angel he was dreaming about, there in his face and on his bed, stole his mind. He didn't think twice about pulling her onto to him, arms and legs hugging her tight to his body with a groan of ecstasy.

"Ohhh did somebody miss me?" she squealed.

"Not me," he whispered with a grin, hugging her tighter with more hunger sounds, pressing her ass into his raging hard on.

She gasped at feeling it. "Nooooo, no no, remember the rules, no hanky-panky outside of therapy?"

"I hate you," he mumbled, pressing her ass and grinding her on him anyway.

"I mean it," she wailed.

"You fucking want it," he said, hearing it in her voice.

"Yes, you know I do, but what are we doing?"

He rolled his eyes and growled. "Being boring and stupid," he nibbled on her neck. "You know you came here just so I'd force the issue." He grabbed her ass and squeezed hard, again grinding her on him.

"Okay okay," she whispered, "listen to me." She held herself above him, her pretty green eyes sparkling. "You be good and I'll reward you with something special tonight."

He angled his head, so very interested. "Like what."

"Something... that you will be extremely glad you earned?"

"That doesn't tell me anything." He stroked his thumb over her lower lip and she smiled, taking it into her mouth and biting softly.

His cock jerked with that little hint and he raised his brows. "Fuck, baby."

"Within reason." She licked and sucked on his thumb, stealing his breath. "Soft, sensual, delicate reason." She ended with a small bite that stole his breath.

"Fuck." He slowly closed his eyes, the idea of her biting him anywhere was worth a day of torture. "You got a fucking deal, Angel." He took her face between his hands, showing her his appreciation *and* self-control with sensual, slow kissing.

She moaned, impressed. "So soft," she whispered.

"You know you hate soft," he mumbled, gliding his lips over hers.

"Not with you, you are so good with it," she gasped, smiling on his mouth.

"Okay, what's your real reason for being in my bed besides Mercy masochism?"

She gasped and slid her body off of his while remaining glued to his side, head propped on her fist. "I was thiiiiinking," she said, tracing her finger over his chest. "That—"

"You wanted to fuck on the beach?"

"Yeees, but no," she said, laughter in her voice.

"In the water? In the pool," he guessed. "The boat?"

Her laughter made him smile and she finally got her great plans out in an excited voice. "I want to fly kites with you!"

He drew his face away, looking at her. "Kites!"

"Yes," she squealed, "I *love* flying kites! I haven't flown one since I was fourteen."

"Really." He kissed her once on the tip of her nose. "And I haven't flown one ever," he admitted, which earned him a huge gasp and wide eyes with Mercy tugging him out of bed.

And fuck, that promised to be one long ass day.

****

Anxiety had Sade so fucking tense as they headed into the kitchen for breakfast. What was he nervous about, he was going fly a fucking kite. It was a gorgeous day, everything was exactly how he could possibly want any day to be. Except maybe one thing. His mother. He'd really hurt her and worried about her.

"There's the two love birds," Mercy's dad called from the outdoor patio next to the dining area. "Breakfast is waiting, cooked it myself."

Mercy held his hand and dragged him faster than he cared to follow. The second they stepped through the patio opening, his mother hurried to him and hugged him tight. At the slam of emotions inside him, he realized he'd been expecting her to resent him. He clutched her back just as tightly, holding her head to his chest. "Morning baby," she whispered.

The tremble in her words told him that maybe Kane had confronted her about some things. "How's my beautiful mother?" he asked.

"Not feeling so beautiful," she whispered bitterly.

Pain cut through him and stole his breath as he lowered his head. Mercy and her father were chatting lightly, giving them privacy and he put his mouth at her ear. "Hey," he said. "You were right about telling Mercy. She's kicking my ass into shape."

His mother let out a small sob and nodded in his chest. "She won't fail you, Johnny."

"Ma, ma, please," he strained at her ear. "You didn't fail me."

"I left youuuu," she barely wailed before breaking down into loud sobs. "I left you, I left you!" She gripped his shirt and pounded on him and Kane hurried over and pulled her into his arms only to have her beating him next. "You made me, why did you save me, you *bastard*! Why did you save me, I shouldn't have left him," she cried, collapsing into his embrace. "I'm sorry, I'm sorry," she wept bitterly.

"Fuck," Sade gasped, grabbing his head and turning.

"Oh my God," his mother gushed, pushing out of Kane's arms and wiping her eyes. "Look at me, I'm a mess!" she laughed. "What are we doing here? We're going to have a great day, that's what the fuck we're doing here," she said, hurrying to the table and bringing Sade a cup of coffee in trembling hands.

He took it from her and kissed her on the cheek. "Fucking right we are, Ma, we're having a great day, we've earned it."

She let out an exuberant laugh, wiping the remaining tears. "We certainly have Johnny."

"And we're flying kites!" Mercy said, excited. "It'll be Sade's first time."

His mother's face fell, twisting Sade's stomach. "I... I never... there wasn't much place to fly kites," she said to Sade, fear and regret in her silver eyes.

"Mom," Sade said firmly. "Where the fuck are we gonna fly a kite in LA, you don't, you go to circuses, remember? Now quit with the guilt. I mean it."

God, he was one to fucking preach. He glanced at Kane, not wanting to disrespect his wife and he got a slight nod from him.

"You're right, oh my God," she exclaimed, like she just realized something amazing, "I am so *blessed!* I have my *son,* a beautiful daughter, the best husband in the world! And this gorgeous day!" She busted out laughing, hugging Kane, then Mercy, then Sade again. "Let's *eat!*"

Chapter Nineteen

Sade felt a little better as they ate and his mother demonstrated she was either really feeling better or a great actress. Mercy was a great distraction, holding his hand under the table and sneaking him naughty looks that made him wish the day was over and it was time for her angelic therapy. She seemed to be enjoying tormenting him in front of her father, knowing he'd make zero retaliations in his presence. But he nodded slowly and winked at her with a threatening *wait... I'll get you.*

Before they could escape to the beach, fucking Ralph and some other jelly bean motherfucker showed up, eyes all over Mercy.

"Here for the roof repairs," Ralph said, walking toward the patio.

His mother became the gracious hostess, offering food and drinks all around while Kane took care of introductions. When it came time to shaking the new dude's hand, Sade gripped it nice and hard, meeting his sneaky beady gaze with a killer glare.

"Sis will be over later, Ms. Kross, to help start the garden."

"Oh fantastic! I cannot wait to have fresh vegetables!" his mom said while Sade strained to hear the mumblings of Tommy, the new guy. Ralph responded in another language which was really fucking rude in Sade's opinion. Anybody who talked another language in front of people for the specific purpose of hiding what they were saying, were un-trustworthy fuckers, plain and simple. And the only reason Sade halfway trusted ole Ralphy was because Kane seemed to.

But this new guy was another matter.

"Big brother?" Mercy laughed, touching Sade's arm. "He is big, but he's not my brother, he's just a good friend."

Sade was instantly stunned and pissed by her words.

"So he's your boyfriend," Jackass probed.

"Yes, he's my boyfriend," she gushed, sounding... embarrassed?

"You sure, Angel?" Sade couldn't keep from muttering.

"Well, we've got kites to fly," Mercy said, hooking her arm in Sade's.

"Yes, yes," mom cried. "Go fly your kites!" She busted out laughing, seeming to find that very funny, as did everybody else, including Tom and Jerry.

When they were finally out of earshot, Mercy gasped. "Oh my God, that was awkward. That guy gave me the creeps."

"Did he," Sade muttered.

She looked at him as they walked. "What, what's that tone for?"

"The only thing awkward was you tripping over what I was to you. He was clearly asking if you're available and you fucking said yes, I am."

She gasped and stopped walked. "What? He asked if we were brother and sister, I was saying no!"

"I think your exact words were, 'he's just a good friend.' And only when they horny bastard cornered you with the boyfriend question did you say that's what I was."

She choked on incredulity. "Sade, I'm sorry I was more thinking of the awkward brother sister thing our family has found itself in, that's all."

"Yeah sure, I got it."

"You're still pissed!"

"Yes I'm fucking pissed."

"Because you want people to know you're my boyfriend?" she asked, sounding flattered.

"Well, I thought it was pretty clear that's what I am, not sure what there is to get tripped up about."

"Oh my God," she wailed, covering her mouth while eying him with laughter in her eyes.

"This is so not fucking funny to me."

Her eyes popped, "You're so right. It's not. How can I fix this? Oh come on," she whined, holding their caterpillar and butterfly kites at her chest now. "I'm sure I can do something to make it up to you," she smiled.

"You can start by not looking at that fucker or talk to him. I don't care if you have to be rude, he had his fucking eyes all over you."

"Yes, fine, of course, I'll ignore his ugly, stinky, fat, stupid ass, easy peasy. Now let's go fly our kites!" She turned and ran toward the beach. "Last one there is a rotten egg!" she screamed.

Sade took off after her, passing her and making her laugh.

"Cheater!" she gasped, arriving right after him. "I had our kites!"

"I never asked you to start without me," he laughed, sitting on the sand, just at the edge of the surf, the salty air flooding his lungs as he watched Mercy untangle their kites.

"You ready for this awesomeness?"

"Oh yeah," he said, his eyes straining to see more of those creamy thighs than the knee-length flowing skirt allowed. The soft purple flowers against the white reminded him of the ones he'd picked for her.

"You like what you see?"

He raised his gaze and found her green eyes glowing with a breathtaking joy. Fuck, it was a scary sight to see. Powerful. The kind you didn't want to get too close to for fear of fucking it up and yet, needing to drown in it, have it all for yourself. "I love what I see." He'd meant to say the words lightly but they were anything but, and that joy in her eyes transformed into something just as potent, only sexy and raw. God, how did she imprison his soul with only a look? She smiled softly with a wink and handed him his kite, never unlocking her eyes from his.

Sade slowly stood, keeping the soul mesh tight as he took it from her. "Your butterfly kite, sir."

He grinned and lowered his mouth to hers. "Thank you, Angel," he whispered, cradling her head while he softly explored her mouth with a dire need to *fuck* her.

He pulled up and she said dreamily, "I'll help you get your kite up."

"You sure got my dick up quick." He pulled away before he took her in the sand in broad daylight.

Mercy quickly switched to her flying production, putting her kite down and handing him the stick with a roll of string attached to his butterfly contraption. "You hold this and don't let it go." She walked a ways from him and held the kite. "Now, I'm going to throw it up and you're going to run when I do. When the kite goes up, start letting more string out so it can go higher."

He nodded. "I got it, I got it."

"Okay, ready?"

"Ready to fly, Angel."

She gave him the biggest smile and Sade couldn't stop his own grin, loving the torment she always inflicted on him.

"Now!" She tossed up the kite and Sade ran with it.

"It's up," she screamed, "let the string out!"

Sade stopped and let the string out, watching the wind take the big eyed butterfly into the sky.

"Oh my God, you did it! You did it!" Mercy cried.

Sade grinned, carefully letting out more and more string. He sort of lost track of how much he'd let out and right when he wondered where the end was, it was there. And then it was gone. All of it. Snapped like a strand of hair. "Oh shit," he said, watching it fly further into the sky as Mercy readied her kite for flight. 'Uh, Angel?"

"What?" she asked, looking at him then down at the empty kite-string contraption in his hands. It took a second for it to register and she gasped, looking into the sky. "Oh nooooo!" then she busted out laughing, offering him her kite.

"No, you better fly it," he said, laughing.

Mercy got her kite up all by herself and Sade sat on the beach, watching her, his cock set to ever-hard. When she got her caterpillar high in the sky, she suddenly tossed her hands up and let it go. "Go find your boyfriend!" she called, waving her arm at it then running over and falling into his lap, laughing.

Sade caught her in his embrace and held her. "You're fucking something, you know that?"

She wrapped her arms around his neck and smiled. "I know," she sighed, making him laugh.

"You do know, don't you?"

She squinted up at him. "Yeah," she said, like she was sorry to say it. "I do."

"How many hours till therapy, Angel?" he asked, his body aching.

"Hmmm, is my patient in need?"

His cock jerked and his breath shuddered out. "You have no idea."

"Welllll, they don't call me Mercy for nothing, you know."

He grinned at her, kissing the tip of her nose. "Is that right."

"I *wonder* if maybe we should have class early?"

"Depends on how much earlier," Sade said, his stomach tense with excitement.

"Liiiiiike," she looked at an invisible watch on her arm. "Now?"

"You fucking serious? Don't fucking joke about that."

She leaned up and kissed him. Really kissed him until he was ready to combust. "Does that feel like a joke to you?"

"Fuck no," he gasped, winded.

"We'll both need to shower for this."

"Oh fuck, yes," he whispered, helping her up now and running with her back to the house, making her squeal in laughter when he threw her over his shoulders for being too slow.

Sade hauled Mercy into the house and ran into a woman, literally. Had to be Ralph's sister. "Damn, I'm sorry," Sade said, putting Mercy down.

"What?" Mercy turned and Sade eyed her reaction to the native looking island beauty.

"You must be Ralph's sister?" Sade asked the girl when Mercy stood with her jaw stuck on open.

"I am, yes." She nodded or maybe bowed and looked at Mercy. "You must be Mr. Kross's daughter?" she asked, holding her hand out to Mercy.

"Yes, I am." Mercy snapped out of whatever had her and shook her hand. "This is Sade, Mrs. Kross's son. But we're not related," Mercy added.

The irony struck Sade at the turned tables and he couldn't help himself. "Mercy and I are good friends," he said, holding a hand out to the girl who shook it.

He'd meant it as a joke but one look at Mercy said that the joke would cost him big. "Okay, nice meeting you," Sade said, ending that and dragging a silent Mercy off and down the basement stairs.

Three steps down and she jerked her hand out of his. Sade held both his up in slow surrender. "It was a joke, Mercy. I was just—"

"Fuck you," she hissed, storming ahead of him into the room.

Chapter Twenty

"No, no, no," he said, following her. "We're not fighting, not now." He shut the door and locked it.

"Why? Because you're worried you won't get your fuck in? Why don't you go see little Miss Lolita about that? I'm sure she will be verrrry obliging with the way she ogled you!"

Sade lowered his head and shook it, mostly to hide his grin.

"You think this is so funny?"

"No," he said, unable to keep from laughing.

"It wasn't funny when it was you though, was it," she spat.

"Mercy!" he cried, holding his arms out. "Why are you *so* pissed? You *know* I was joking! Unlike you, who genuinely stumbled over our relationship status!"

She actually squinted her eyes at him and Sade had to turn away to keep from laughing at how fucking much he loved that she was *this* jealous. "Well, it's not like we're *married!*" she said.

Sade paused, eying her now in disbelief. "You really just said that?"

"That we're not married? Is this news to you?"

"So what, we're free to fuck other people? Is that how you think it goes for people not married? For us?"

"You're the slut here. You tell me Mr. Fuck-a-thoner. How *does* that work?!"

"It doesn't work that way for me and you, I know that."

"Oh it doesn't?" she said, eyes wide. "Does this mean you want to marry me?" she laughed.

But Sade didn't laugh. He stared at her, thinking about that. Marrying her. Living for the rest of his life with her or whatever was left of it. "What if I said yes?"

The slow shock and awe dawning on her face made his stomach flip around. "Wait…" she whispered. "You're serious?"

He thought about it again, carefully, and the answers were all the same, more emphatic. "Dead serious," he whispered.

She covered her mouth with both hands, eyes filling with tears as she shook her head.

Fear struck him. He'd not considered that she might not want that.

She ran at him and threw her arms around him. "You're serious?" she gasped. "Oh my God, I can't believe you'd want to marry me." She pulled back and looked up at him. "Are you serious?" she whispered heatedly.

"What the fuck do you mean, you?" he said, confused, stroking the tears from her cheeks. "Who else in my life means the world to me?"

She covered her mouth again, nodding now. "So what, are you asking me?"

"Asking?"

"Me to marry you?"

Sade's mouth hung open, not sure how to answer that, not sure what the answer was. "I'm not sure."

"What? You just said you wanted—"

"I do, I just don't know how… I'm supposed to do that… I mean you don't just go up to the person in the middle of a fight and, 'say you wanna marry me?'" Jesus, what the fuck did he know? "Right?"

She wiped her eyes and seemed to think about it, then shrugged. "I don't see why not."

"Well I'm not positive but something in me says this should be more special than just an, oh by the way deal."

She smiled at him, tears filling her eyes again. "You want to make it special?"

"Fuck yes, I do," he said at seeing how happy that made her. "I want it to be something we never forget."

She lowered her gaze, her cheeks pink before she hesitantly said, "A… beach wedding would be… amazing." She bit her lip, excitement dancing in her green gaze.

"With kites?" he asked, pulling her into his embrace.

She bit her lip and gave him a squinty eye. "Sooooo," she began. "How will you propose?"

He laughed, sliding his hands all over her. "That's a surprise."

She squealed and danced in his arms a little. "I love surprises! And hate them!" She gasped, pushing out of his arms. "Can you at least tell me when you will? So I can plan to plan to tell everybody?"

Fuck, her joy was beautiful. And to think he was responsible for that in any kind of way was… unimaginable.

He stood there, enraptured as she went on in non-stop wedding plan chatter. It was like watching his very own Cinderella getting her fairytale dream come true.

Sade made his way to the bed and sat. He was suddenly the bum little kid, looking into a window from the dirty alley. Witnessing the royal princess. She'd received the announcement, she'd be marrying her true love, a handsome and noble prince. Sade smiled, so fucking happy for her.

Then it hit him, slammed him so hard until he couldn't breathe. He was the one. He was the handsome prince she'd picked. The dirty alley kid, the thief, the boy prostitute with a legacy of sadistic blood and ghosts that never passed on, demons that devoured without stop.

"What's wrong?"

Sade looked up to find Mercy staring at him.

The fear in her eyes made him sick. She wouldn't be able to handle that he wasn't the right one for her, that he had nothing but never-ending sexual issues to give. What kind of husband could he possibly make? What had he been thinking? Fuck, he hadn't been, not past his nose. God, what if she wanted a family? How could he possibly be a father when he hated his own and had no idea how to be one? He didn't know how to be a fucking man, how would he be a *father?* A *husband?*

He put his hands over his face and leaned forward, unable to face her.

She hurried and sat down next to him, putting her arm around him. "Whaaaat," she said softly. "Talk to me, don't hide from me. Are you nervous? Scared? It's okay if you are, that's normal," she cooed.

It took several seconds for him to even organize his scattered thoughts.

"I don't know what I was thinking, Mercy," he said.

"What do you mean?" she whispered, rubbing his back.

He shook his head slowly. "Marrying you. I mean, I go from committing to leaving to committing to staying forever."

"What… do you mean you… wait, you committed to leaving?"

Panic hit Sade at realizing what he'd just said. He gave a huge sigh, looking right. "I mean just what I said, I committed to leaving," he admitted quietly.

"When?"

"When I saw that I was just going to end up hurting you, Mercy," he said, looking at her. "Ever since we've gotten here, I've been insane and I don't know why. I wanted to hurt you, I did hurt you!" he said. "And I still want to sometimes, what the fuck kind of person would I be to let that happen to the one woman I love more than anything in the fucking world," he strained.

Tears filled her eyes and she looked forward, wiping them. "And now look at you," she whispered.

"Yeah, now look at me. I have one good day and I can suddenly have the world? No, Mercy, that's stupid!"

"No," she cried back softly. "Not one good day, many good days. You have to be fair in this, to me to you."

"I have to be honest and realistic," he said, standing.

"Yes, you do," she agreed, "but you're not!"

"You like to see the bright side of things," he said to her, "I get that, I understand why you do that, there's nothing wrong with it. But you can't ignore the other side."

She stared at him shaking her head, perplexed. "Who do you think you're talking to here, Sade? Royalty? You don't think I have a dark past? You don't think I have demons that would love to have me back? You don't think I know how to look both ways before I cross the street, how to see both sides of the coin?" she said incredulous. "How can you be with me all this time, know the fucking shit I've survived, in my past – my present, really know me, and act like I'm a fucking air head?" she whispered heatedly.

Sade took a deep breath, looking down. "I know that you love me, baby," he whispered. "And you want to be with me more than anything in the world."

"No!" she said, pushing him. "This isn't just about what *Mercy* wants! This isn't about what *Mercy* needs, that's the thing about relationships, there's *two* people in them and you are that other half of this equation. You talk about not seeing the other side, and you," she pointed at him, "are the one who isn't looking both ways crossing the road, *you* are the one not seeing both sides of the coin, *you,* Sade. Not me. I see clearly. And what about our therapy?"

"What about it?" he asked, his anger kicking in.

She crossed her arms over her chest. "Tell me about it, tell me what it's done for you."

He paced now, feeling like there wasn't enough air in the room suddenly. "So I had a couple of good experiences, Mercy, do you think that means I'm healed? Demons are gone, slate is clean?"

"No, I don't," she said casually. "Anything of this magnitude takes time. A long time. I should know, remember?"

He paced now. "And what happens if I slip again? Huh? Are you going to kill me next time? Am I going to decide not to let you kill me and kill you? Huh?"

She stood there, nodding her head for many seconds. "So that's it? Do you realize with a mentality like that, there's no point of even trying? Why are you wasting my time? My body, even?"

"Because you demanded it, you had to have it, you made me sign a fucking contract, remember?" he roared.

She jerked back a little with a gasp then finally said, "Well, you know what?" she walked over and stood just before him. "Look at me."

Sade met her gaze, feeling like the dirtiest loser.

"I am so tired of begging your sorry ass, chasing your sorry ass down, tying your sorry ass up. Somewhere inside you, there is a good, and beautiful man. You can believe me, or you can not believe me, but if I were you, I would fucking believe me because I am a pretty smart chic," she gasped, her words shuddering. "And if you so happen to find this good, beautiful man inside you," she whispered, wiping her tears. "Come looking for me. But until you resurrect that man. We are done."

Sade could hardly breathe as she walked out, leaving him standing there in a swirling mass of chaos, pain, fear, and confusion.

Chapter Twenty-One

"I need you to look at his file, son," he'd said in a near regretful tone. "All of it. Don't skip anything, not one thing, do you understand?"

Sade's gut was already in knots as he sat next to Kane on their way to the neighboring island forty-five minutes away. He took the folder from him, thinking he'd be looking at stuff that would help him know how to engage the monster in a professional manner. But the fucked up shit in the file was more a visual diary of a mad man, extremely graphic pictures of children he'd abused, what he did, how he did it, why he did it, when. Just not where. Which was the missing ingredient Kane planned to get.

Sade fought nausea as Kane rattled on loudly over the surf and screaming motor of the tough fishing boat he'd borrowed. The mid-sized iron giant was made to weather storms with a solid, large holding tank in the belly for tending to their "catch" properly. "I know it's not easy to see, son, but I can't have you getting soft on me and forgetting the *why's* when I have my way with him, you understand?"

Kane was right, too. There would be no forgetting, no unseeing these images of children from the age of three to early teens, body parts cut off, maimed, eyes gouged, and sexual orifices burned shut with the sick fuck's soldering iron. There was no way Sade could ever fully appreciate what was coming to him without seeing the *whys* as Kane called them.

All the pent up terror they'd endured at Abraham's hands started to seem like fun times compared to what he was seeing. He just couldn't fucking imagine what it was like for these kids to have to endure anything like this. What made him the most sick were that these horrific deaths he was looking at had not come quickly or easily.

By the time Sade had finished looking through that file, he knew it marked him deep. Felt like he'd lived a thousand nightmares. The suffering in his life suddenly felt like child's play next to this deranged shit.

He thought about Mercy again. He'd intended to leave without saying goodbye but she met them at the dock. He assumed she'd done it for her father, except it was Sade she'd made a beeline for and embraced tightly. "Be careful," she mumbled. "I may be pissed at you, but I love you and I don't want you to be confused about that."

Then she left, not even giving him a chance to say anything back. Not that he'd have known what to say. That he loved her too, was about the only thing he wasn't confused about.

And every one of them seemed to buy the "job" story. Going help Larry the fisherman whose crew was shorthanded. The family had to eat and Larry was too proud to take money, so it was find a way to work the nets or they'd all starve. His mother thought it was noble of the man and of Kane to help, while Sade found it stupid, even if it was fabricated. He couldn't see feeding a family with pride. Seemed like you would use whatever the store accepted in exchange for food—fuck pride. Sade would let them take it out of his ass if he had to feed Mercy and...

Sade shook his head. It never failed. Every goddamn thought he had always led him back to that. Marrying Mercy. Being a husband, possibly a father, even though she was sure she'd never have kids. There was adoption. There was having animals, there was all sorts of responsibilities. To her, her wellbeing, her existence. Where she lived, how she lived, *that* she lived, and the quality of all that.

Just the idea made him nauseated. And it wasn't the unknowns he feared, it was the knowns, inside him. *There's a beautiful, good man inside you. And when you resurrect him, come looking for me.* Fuck, he was going to lose her. He could feel it. He was on a timer now. She'd taken that hourglass and set it on the table before him. Time was definitely slipping away. He could feel it. He was going to slowly lose Mercy, minute by minute, day by day.

And part of him said good, let it be.

And another part of him—maybe that little boy at the magic show—said, just close your eyes. And believe.

If only he knew how to do that.

"So let's go over the plan," Kane yelled.

Sade gladly turned his attention to him.

"I'm going to use the Three Tears technique with this fuck. It's a pretty basic torture routine that involves breaking the human down at three levels. Body, mind, emotions. Only I'm replacing his emotions with a wild card—the spiritual. Every sick thing he's ever done is rooted in the spirit realm. He thinks I'm his rival, and in a sense, I am, just not to the extent he imagines. Unless God has kept this information top secret from me, then I'm just an average Joe who decided he's not going to put up with shit. Anywho," he said casually, keeping his eyes on the endless span of water before them, "I'll break his body, break his mind, and use that spiritual wild card to get what I need. We leave every morning at dawn, and return to the beach house at dusk. I have a babysitter arranged for a night shift. Any questions?"

Sade shook his head and yelled, "Not yet."

"Good," he yelled back before looking his way with a smile. "Enjoying the ride so far?"

Sade nodded, unable to keep his grin from spreading. "So far."

****

"Help me get the fat fucker in the chair, will you?" Kane huffed, sounding both annoyed and excited as he dragged an unconscious Abraham in a grain sack to the middle of the room. He dropped one end and straightened. "God, would it be too much to get these people to bleach their hulls at least once a goddamn year?" He looked down at the package, shaking his head before muttering, "Smells like fifty thousand generations of fish guts." He looked all around, wiping his face on the sleeve of his black t-shirt. Sade couldn't help but to be amazed again with his physique. In the black cargo pants and matching boots, he was nothing but sleek terror, carved by the blade of sadistic heroism. "He'll be coming around in a couple of hours. I want to be ready when that happens. We'll work him until around seven and head home in time for dinner. Faith is frying fish, but after smelling this place, I'm not sure I can handle it."

Sade wasn't sure he'd be able to eat after seeing that file. Ever. Or sleep. "So where's he staying," Sade gestured to Abe. "When we leave."

"Here," Kane said. "We had boat troubles with this one and had to borrow another to get back," he said simply." He kicked at the sack with his foot. "I'll cut this thing off so I can see what the hell we're touching." He eyed Sade now, sweat dripping off his nose, "Telling you now," he muttered softly, "I'm not touching that with my bare hands if I can help it."

Sade wasn't sure why he didn't want to, but he definitely understood. They got the sack removed from Abraham and Sade's heart hammered in his sick gut at seeing him again. He laid on his side, duct taped. Mouth, wrists, and ankles. He wore a black suit and whoever delivered him hadn't been very careful with the package. He looked like he'd been in a human blender with dull blades.

"Jesus," Kane muttered, staring down at him. "He ain't fresh, that's for sure. I'll have to make do with scraps." He smiled up at Sade. "But don't you worry Son, I can make a mean stew with leftovers."

Nervous excitement ran through Sade at what was coming. To see the legend at work with his own eyes gave him more anticipation than all his fights put together, but to *work* with him in any sadistic capacity was just off the charts exhilarating. "What's first?" Sade asked.

"Well," Kane said lightly. "We'll get him nice and secure and then we'll talk about that over coffee." He flashed a smile. "Brought one of those nifty campfire ones with the hand pump? Been itching for a reason to use it and a good strong cup of coffee sounds like a great way to kick this off, what do you say?" He shrugged then. "We've got soda too, your mom packed all sorts of goodies. Up to you."

"Coffee sounds perfect," Sade said, grinning at his boyish enthusiasm.

"Great," Kane said smiling back, eying him. "Are you excited?" he muttered. "Because I sure am. Sort of feels like our first fishing trip together in a way." The sincerity of his words gave Sade a happy rush.

"It does. And I'm really honored too, just so you know."

"Glad to hear it, Son." He looked down at Abraham. "Well. This sick fucker ain't torturing himself." He leaned and grabbed Abe by the front of his suit jacket. "Get ready to help me get his fat ass *on* the chair, I might miss."

Before Sade could offer to help, Kane yanked him off the floor in one jerk and plopped him in the chair. Sade saw what he meant as his body fell to the right, so he hurried over to hold him up. Feeling the dead weight of that monster gave him the sudden need to kill.

"Damn," Kane gasped, his boot in the center of Abe's chest as he looked around. "We should've brought the duct tape for this step. Go fetch it, will you, it's in that duffle bag stuffed under the bed in the cabin. Just bring the whole bag in fact. I'll go ahead and prep him for surgery."

Surgery? Sade hurried out, not sure if he meant that literally or figuratively. Once outside the metal room, he pulled in a lung full of clean air then located the bag. On his way back, he glanced around at the trees surrounding the isolated inlet they'd parked the boat in.

"Check that end pocket," Kane said when Sade set the bag down. Sade found it and Kane instructed him to tape his lower torso to the chair then his upper. "Then we'll work from there."

While Sade finished taping his upper torso, Kane took all the items out of the duffle bag and laid them a few feet away on the floor. Sade eyed them, curious over nearly all of them. The only thing that he recognized was a scalpel. Maybe he did plan to perform literally surgery. A lobotomy?

A queasy feeling hit him at what might be coming. He knew it wouldn't be anything pretty or fun and despite the fact that Abraham was the perfect criminal for this production, he wasn't into watching gore. His thing was killing with brutality. Slow brutality for Sade didn't mean soft or easy, it meant spread out and delivered, at a pace like a drawn out orgasm.

"Come here, Son." Sade knelt next to Kane who held up a wicked looking knife with a red ruby cross on the handle. "First order of business? His dick is gone. But I can't have him bleeding out," he said softly, "so we're going to use this." He held up a tool that looked familiar. "I think it's only fair to burn the evil hole shut, don't you?"

Sade's junk jerked at the idea even though he knew this was Kane's signature way of doing things and that this dude, out of any dude, deserved it. "Agreed."

"Good," Kane said with a light joy. "And I'll need to install a tube so his bladder doesn't rupture and kill him before I'm done so I brought this." He held it up. "Recognize it?"

Sade studied the odd looking tube.

"It goes to a stethoscope," he said with tickled-to-death snickers. "I don't know…" he mumbled, shaking his head, "…there's something about borrowing from one genius tool and substituting it for another." He looked at Sade. "Like an artistic challenge for me."

"So," Kane said, getting back to showing off his toy collection. "After we cut his dick off, we'll use these mega-pliers to extract his teeth." He gave a toothy grin. "In between each tooth extraction, we'll offer him an opportunity to sing of course." He lifted a long tube sock next. "And this. Because I really don't have the patience for bellowing in my ear while I work." He looked around at his items. "Oh, and then," he snatched up the scalpel. "Guess what I'm using this baby for? I'll give you a hint," he said, not waiting. "You'll wish you'd… *listened* when I'm done."

Sade raised his brows, not sure what the fuck that meant.

"His ears," he squealed lightly before getting serious. "Did you know you can cut those off with no real consequence other than a lot of pain? And I do mean a lot of pain—if you do it slowly as I plan." He leaned in with a smile and said, "I plan to yell, *'are you hearing me, Father?'* during that one." He laughed quietly before looking back down at his supplies, shaking his head. "You can't forget your humor in all of this, Son, or it'll get to you. Okay, so, by this point, I predict our father to feel pretty chatty. And this is where I'll bring in the big guns, the spiritual warfare." He leaned in closer to Sade. "I've heard that he thinks I'm the Angel of Death." He grinned and wagged his brows then got super serious. "And hey. I'm not going to argue with him if he wants to think that. I'll be whatever or whoever if it gets me what I need, you know what I'm saying, son?"

"I get it, yeah." And he did, but Sade's mind seemed stuck on the soldering part after they cut his dick off. Would Kane require his help with that? The idea had him a little sick. Then teeth pulling and ear removal right after.

"You know what?" Kane said, leaning back on his haunches. "I just had the *best* idea." He stared at Sade with that light bulb moment look. "Since this is your first time, how about I let you decide how we do all of this. Yeah!" He nodded, gesturing to all the supplies. "You orchestrate this, you lay it out, you tell me how we're going to exact vengeance on this monster. I got other supplies if you need, just tell me what you'd like to do and it's done."

Sade's brain underwent a slow train wreck as he glanced from Kane to all the sick shit on the floor.

"I'm giving you run of the insanity, man," Kane whispered eagerly. "This is your chance to let it out, let your animal go, let your demons dance. And it's all oookaaaay," he sang softly.

Sade couldn't speak as Kane rattled off more torture tools, in an effort to inspire ideas. "I can get anything you want pretty much, just name your sadistic kink."

Fuck. "This…" Sade shook his head. "Look, I'll kill anybody but…" he shook his head and leveled his gaze on Kane. "This isn't my thing."

Silence stretched as Kane stared at him. "I thought you wanted to hurt this guy, I thought you wanted him dead?"

"I do," Sade looked at him. "I just... I mean I'll kill him right now if you want, but all that other stuff?" Sade looked at the supplies, shaking his head. "I mean, maybe I could, but fuck, I'm not wanting to. I'll be honest with you, I don't get off on the idea of doing it."

More awkward silence stretched before Kane finally said, "Get off?" Kane's gaze narrowed on him. "Is that what you think this is about? Getting off? Don't you see the cause here, son? The why?" He shook his head slowly. "Listen to me. Your dick... isn't supposed to be tied to every pain and doesn't have to be. In here?" He tapped his finger on Sade's chest. "And here?" He tapped his forehead. "That's where what we're doing needs to happen. That's where the whys are forged. Keep your dick out of it, that's not the same shit that we're dealing with here. Compartmentalize, Son. Organize your lusts and put them in their rightful place. We're not here to have an orgy, this is business. Our dicks are for fucking, not fighting, not killing. Your dick isn't a staff of destruction and awe." He angled his head at Sade. "You feeling me, son?"

"I am," Sade said. "I just... it's hard to separate sometimes."

"Who told you that?" Kane said lightly. "Not hard at all. It all starts right here." Kane tapped his own head now. "With you saying this is the deal. This is how it works. This is the way. The truth. You do that steady Son, and your body will catch on." He spread his arms wide now. "But that doesn't help me right now, does it? Because I need answers from that sick fuck!" he pointed behind him.

"I know," Sade agreed, feeling like a fucking wimp and a failure. "How about you tell me what to do, I'm not into orchestrating this shit, just tell me where to cut and I'll fucking do it."

Another span of silence came before Kane said, "Don't you see it?"

Sade made himself look at Kane, feeling like nothing about him would ever be right. "See what? That I can't even be fucked up right? Can't even do that right? Yeah, I see it," Sade muttered, looking down.

"Holy fuck, man," Kane whispered. "No. No, not how you suck at being fucked up. At how fucked up you're actually not."

Sade looked at him, confused.

"I mean, here I am needing to torture answers out of this sick fuck and I've got a sudden humanitarian crisis, and all you can see is how you don't quite make the cut for the job. Don't you *see* what it takes to not lust for this man's torture? Don't you? It takes having a heart that isn't black as death. And you, son, don't have that." He gripped his shoulder and smiled. "That's a *good* thing!" he whispered. "You feeling what I'm saying to you, son? You're more of a good man than you give yourself credit for, remember that. Preferably when Mercy wants to do her little therapy sessions with you," he said.

Sade let out a gasp of confused shock. He really hadn't seen that coming, not that.

"Can you imagine that?" Kane mused softly. "Sade the sadist doesn't like to torture people."

"Not like that," Sade admitted. "I can give pain, but I don't... I have to be..."

"Angry?"

Sade thought about it. "Yeah."

"So if this sick fuck had done that shit to Mercy, that shit you saw in those photos, do you think you could... you know?" he said lightly.

The pictures flashed in his mind and his brain put Mercy in them, making him scrub his face. "I'd kill him, yes. I would beat him to death with my bare hands, I don't know, yes, fuck, I'm not sure now."

"See that's the key right there. It's putting those you love in those pictures, those close to you. That's the *key*," he hissed. "Those kids are all little Mercys before I had a chance to save her."

"I know, I know," Sade muttered, not just feeling like a pussy, but a stupid one. "Like I said just… tell me what to do, I'll do it. Not a problem."

"Compartmentalize, Son." He tapped his temple again. "Organize your passions and your lusts. Give them the right purpose and with that comes the courage to do the right thing at the right time. No matter what it looks like, feels like, seems like. But…" Kane patted his back roughly. "That does take more time than we have to give right now."

Sade spun at the sound of a moan behind him.

"Looks like I won't be getting my damn coffee," Kane muttered with a low eagerness, turning and standing. "Good morning, Father Abraham," he boomed loudly, his voice bouncing off the metal walls.

Chapter Twenty-Two

The bound man's head hung and Sade was a little surprised at how much smaller he looked tied up. He slowly lifted his head and Sade held his breath at how the man would react. He blinked several times, seeming to focus his eyes on Kane who stood before him with both arms crossed over his chest, waiting.

"Mmph," was all Abraham said, until he saw Sade. That ice blue gaze slowly softened, maybe in memory of the purpose for his trip. Either way, seeing those nasty eyes on him niggled at Sade's sadistic side, the one he was familiar with. Abraham's softened gaze narrowed, then with more grunting sounds.

"I hope the trip here was pleasant," Kane said. "Because we have some exciting business, the three of us." Kane leaned and ripped the gray tape off his mouth with a hiss. "Sorry, better to yank it like a Band-Aid."

"W-what…what business?" Abraham fumbled the words before looking at Sade. His stare turned immediately lusty, turning his stomach.

"Well… you know, I was going to go with a fun and artistic three day ceremony, but… it doesn't really suit my son's tastes. And since this is his first ride with me, I'll expedite the end game. You good with that Father?" Kane nodded, not waiting for his answer, "Good," he said happily, straightening then glancing back at Sade. "You think I should go ahead and tell him? I don't see why we need to wait at this point."

Sade wasn't sure what he meant, but felt he was supposed to say, "I don't see why either."

Kane leaned forward, just to the left of the man, his mouth near his ear. Sade realized he was talking to him, whispering.

Sade strained to hear what he was saying but only got mumbling. He watched Abraham's countenance slowly change until he was gasping in shock. Kane continued talking quietly, placing a gentle hand on Abe's shoulder nearest him, patting softly as the man's face slowly hardened into a mask of fury.

Kane finally stood before him and opened his arms wide and said, "Do you think maybe they don't know who they fucked with, Abraham? You think, maybe this is a classic case of kindness being taken for stupidity? I mean, even I know who you are, the question is, how is it that they don't?"

"They. Have. No. Clue what I am capable of!" Abraham roared, his face shaking with rage.

Kane paced before him as he nodded, then angled his head at him. "I'm very sure they don't. Which is why I spoke to God about it. Pulled some strings." Kane stopped before the furious man. "And I think what I obtained for you will be worth so much more than the measly years you'll spend on this filthy planet."

Abraham's face slowly morphed from fury to burning rapture. "What do you mean?"

"In a nutshell," Kane said, walking to his supplies and picking up the ruby cross blade, "God gave me a gift." He straightened and turned, aiming the blade at Abe. "Don't think he hasn't noticed your faithfulness… brother," Kane said. "To the darkness-to the light," Kane gestured with either-or. "Faithfulness is faithfulness. Hot is hot, cold is cold."

"I'm more faithful than any before me," Abraham hissed, his cheeks trembling.

"Indeed," Kane said lightly, fingering the blade of the knife now. "And that's why when you leave this world… you will enter the underworld as Vicar of the flesh demons."

Abraham gasped as a hungry light burned in his eyes. "Vicar?" His shock said the position was one he'd only dreamed of ever getting.

"All that is required of you…" Kane held his arms out at his sides. "Is to give that which your brother, and the good Father Assford, have sworn you would never give. Have sworn you would never have the guts to give. The very thing both used to steal your rightful place in Hell." Kane knelt on one knee before him now, putting his gaze even with the monsters. "Give…. Me…. Eden."

Sade realized he was holding his breath as he watched Abraham. As though sensing Sade's eyes on him, he looked his way. "What do you think of this, Johnny? Do you think this is a good deal?"

Sade nodded slowly, not knowing what the fuck any of that was or meant. "I think… you've worked hard for the position. If anybody deserves it, it's you."

"I have! I do!" he cried, as though wanting to convince him. "Johnny, I've worked looooong and so very hard." He said it with an erotic lilt.

"Then take it," Sade whispered, his gut twisted with disgust. "Take what's rightfully yours."

Abraham looked at Kane now, angling his head. "How do I know you're not just another liar?!"

Kane gave a low laugh. "Who am I, Abraham?"

He seemed to slowly consider, or remember. "I know who you are," he snarled. "I won't say it."

Kane nodded slowly. "Knowing is enough."

He looked at Sade again. "Is he lying Johnny? You would tell me. I know you would," he said sincerely.

Sade's heart pounded as he mustered as much convincing authority as he could. "He's a man of his word."

The excited light in Abe's eyes said he believed him. He looked at Kane now, a slow grin filling his face before whispering, "Eden is under the Vatican." He gave a gleeful laugh, looking from Kane to Sade, then back to Kane. "Who would ever guess?! Who would ever guess," he said lustily, looking at Sade. "That was my idea. All of it was my idea, I'm the one who thought it up. I'm the one who made it happen! Me!" he yelled to Kane now.

Kane put his left hand behind Abe's neck. "Brother," he whispered, making Sade strain to hear. "The voices of the tortured innocent sing to me. Vengeance, they cry. Vengeance." He plunged the blade into the man's heart and Abraham's eyes flew open with choked gasps. "But the Lord said… vengeance is mine... deliver him to me." Kane stared serenely into his face before he twisted the knife in his chest then slowly pulled it out. "Go," he whispered softly, wiping the blade on the man's suit. "Eternal wrath awaits you."

****

The boat ride back to the house was full of screaming internal reflection. At least it was for Sade. He wasn't sure where Kane's mind was but judging by the light whistling, his head was someplace Sade's longed to be. At fucking peace.

To do what they just did, and were about to finish doing, took more restraint than Sade could fathom. Somewhere between here and yonder, they'd dump the body strapped with every manner of weight they could find, into the deep blue, and then head home for a nice dinner with the family. That wasn't unusually fucked up in the least. *Compartmentalize* Sade reminded himself. The whys. Fix the whys and he was good to go. They'd just taken out the source of countless children's nightmares. That was a good thing. Not a bad thing. Killing to protect was not sadistic if that was the last option. It was humane. It was just. It was good. And with an insane individual like Abe, the qualifications applied.

"You know," Kane yelled to Sade who sat in the passenger seat next to him. "I wasn't really planning to do all that shit to him."

Sade looked at him with a mix of surprise and skepticism at his words. Mostly skepticism.

Kane laughed, scanning the ocean before them. "I'm not kidding," he said. "I knew you weren't the torture type son, I just needed you to realize that about yourself and see it for what that was. A positive, not a negative."

Sade continued to stare at him, the burn of being schooled in such a way slowly taking him. "You're shitting me," he said.

Kane busted out laughing and shook his head. "Not at all."

"So plan B was…"

"Always plan A," he finished with a sly glance his way, hand gliding over the steering wheel with a contented grin.

"You're shitting me!" Sade said again, dumbfounded.

Kane laughed even more. "I'm not! Do I look like a man that likes to torture?" he said, looking offended. "Vengeance is mine, saith the Lord," Kane said loudly.

Sade turned his chair at those words and faced him, incredulous. "You cut their dicks off and shove them up their asses."

Kane stared out at the ocean, nodding a little before giving him an apologetic look. "I'm a work in progress Son, nobody's perfect. And compared to what I used to do, it's really just…" he turned to Sade, "cute."

"Cute?" Sade gasped, unable to hold back his laughter. "No, cute is you tying me up for hours while my bladder is full."

Kane laughed with him on that. "You're so right, that was so *cute!* And it reminds me," he said, angling a stare at Sade.

Sade nodded, looking out at the water grinning. "Right, what did I do and why. I held it of course."

"Duh," Kane said. "Aaaaand why?"

"Because I wasn't going to piss on myself. That's..." he shrugged.

"Shows a lack of self-control?"

"Was thinking more it showed I was a pussy."

"Of course," Kane muttered. "So give me the why, impress me."

Sade looked out at the water again. "Honestly I didn't have a why yet."

"*You* didn't have a why?"

"Right," he muttered, grinning at the fun Kane poked at him. "But now..." he stroked his finger along the vinyl armrest with a shrug. "I think I realize that... when I thought I couldn't control something—and yes there was a point when my bladder said I couldn't," he laughed. "I realized I could in fact control it." He looked at Kane then. "I didn't know why I decided to do it at the time, I was hoping an impressive answer would come to me."

"And I see it has," Kane said with raised brows. "I'm officially impressed."

Sade couldn't keep his grin back at the compliment. It felt so damn good coming from him.

"Alright," Kane said, standing and shutting off the engine. "This is as good a place as any."

Sade's stomach jerked at that final business they had left to do. He followed Kane to the holding room and helped drag the body out. Once at the side of the boat, Kane and Sade panted, staring down at Abraham wrapped entirely in duct tape, weights taped to him as well.

Before Sade could wonder how they were going to do it, Kane scooped the body up into his arms and chunked it over. "There," he huffed, leaning over the edge to see. Sade looked too and watched as Abraham sank into the blue sapphire. The odd sight was surreal as the source of their own nightmare descended into the darkness beyond the deep. A cold shiver rode his spine at the ominous sight of it and that it was over. And the insanity known as Abraham, was gone.

Chapter Twenty Three

"Surprise in basement," Kane muttered, reading the note on the door. "I told her not to do anything for my birthday."

"It's your birthday?" Sade asked, peering in the window, hoping to see Mercy. His heart raced hard, feeling like he'd been away from her for days instead of twelve hours.

"No," he said, angling a lying glare. "It's not my birthday."

Opening the door and looking around, Sade headed to the stairs only to stop when Kane clapped a firm hand on his shoulder. "Oh no you don't," he muttered. "You're coming with me. I'm sure your lovely Mercy is in on this."

"I'm sure too and was thinking I should shower," Sade said, following him.

"Well, that can be our get out of the party card."

Heading down the stairs, Kane paused at the bottom and put a finger to his lips. "I think they're trying to surprise us," he whispered. He opened the door and called extra loudly, "Well, I wonder where everybody is."

Sade grinned as he followed him in, only to run into his backside a second later.

"Welcome home!"

The familiar male voice jerked Sade's heart. His father.

****

There it was, the nightmare, standing behind his mom with a gun to her head. Two masked men rushed Sade and Kane from either side with guns as Sade stared into his mother's wide eyes, filled with *I'm sorry, I'm sorry.* Sickness hit his stomach at seeing her face bloodied and bruised, hands and legs duct taped to the chair.

"Come in and shut the fucking door or I blow her fucking brains out. And Johnny!" he yelled as Sade and Kane were shoved into empty chairs. That's when he saw Mercy, across from his mother, head hanging. The blood on the front of her white summer dress, the matted knots in her hair, stole his sanity. "Get your sorry ass in here before I have my way with your girlfriend's brains. Damn," he said, laughing, "I thought you sorry bastards would never get here! Come in, come join the party, as you can see, we've been enjoying ourselves here!"

Sade's heart hammered as he barely held on to his reflexes that screamed *rampage*. The gun at his mother's head wasn't the problem, it was the man behind it. He'd use it on her, Mercy, and all of them, without blinking an eye about it.

Mercy slowly lifted her head, showing what they'd done, what they'd fucking done. Sade roared at seeing both her eyes black, her lower lip split wide open, nose bleeding. Her cheek, eyes and half of her forehead swollen.

Sade's dad laughed. "Ohhhh, Johnny's mad at daddy!" he mocked. "What did you think would happen Johnny when you betrayed your flesh and blood?" he yelled, storming over and slapping him across the face with his fist. Sade jerked back to him, glaring with a burning hate.

"Ohhhh," his father said, eyes wide at seeing it. "You want to fuck with me Johnny boy? You want me to remind you what daddy can do? Huh?" He went in reverse to his mother and grabbed her hair, jerking it back. He yanked the gray tape off of her mouth and aimed her face at Sade. "Tell your boy what he needs to do momma, tell your pussy face boy what he needs to do!"

She screamed and rammed her head into his face.

"Fucking whore!" he cocked back and punched her in the forehead, rocking her entire chair back.

"Stop it!" Sade begged.

"Fucking dick is mine!" Kane roared, lunging at him with his chair and hitting the floor. "Your dick is mine, you hear me! I'm going to kill you so fucking slowly!"

"Work that motherfucker over will you?" his dad muttered. "Teach him some fucking manners. Jesus you people are so unhospitable around here." He kicked Kane in the face. "Teach him what happens when he *steals* another man's wife!"

His mom and Mercy screamed as he kicked Kane's face repeatedly.

"I never loved you, I never loved you," his mom screamed! "I loved him, he was the best fucking thing that ever happened to me you piece of shit!"

Mercy jerked and lunged with her chair at the men beating her dad, hitting the floor while his father stormed to his mom.

"Dad!" Sade roared, diving with all he had toward the men kicking Mercy now.

"I'm coming Johnny!" he yelled. "But first I want your momma to show us all what she can do! Come on guys, come get some dirty pussy, come and get it!" he roared.

Sade gasped, fighting to see Mercy while wondering where Liberty and Bo were.

"Sade," Mercy whispered from the floor, her face toward him. "I'm okay baby," she sobbed through swollen lips. "They had a gun on your mom, I'm sorry, I'm sorry Dad, he was going to shoot her. Answer me," she cried.

Kane grunted. "Daddy... daddy's here."

"Do me, do me, Dad, I'm your fuck," Sade roared at hearing him hitting his mother. "I'm your fuck, goddamn you! Leave my mother, leave her, I'm begging you dad," he sobbed. "Don't' hurt her, don't!"

"Awwww, Johnny," he rasped, pointing at him. "Don't you worry, daddy's coming for you, just wait your turn like a good pussy face boy. Keep that gun on her head," he said to the two men. "If she does anything stupid, put a fucking bullet in it," he grit. The sound of him cutting the duct tape came and Sade fought until he turned his body and chair. "Now tie her hands to the chair, I want her on her knees so we can all access that dirty cunt." He grabbed her hair and jerked her head back. "You like it from behind, right baby? Right!" he yelled before slamming her face into the chair.

"Daaaaaad!" Sade screamed, yanking with all his might against the restraints. "Do me!"

His mother screamed and Mercy managed to flip over and push her chair into the legs of the guy near her, knocking him off balance. He fell and Sade eyed the gun in his hand, panic hitting him at what he might do.

His mom let out a scream of fury and panic hit Sade, knowing she was fighting, knowing what his dad would do.

"Goddamn *bitch*!" his dad yelled. "Get her fucking hands!"

She screamed again and sick thuds followed. Sade fought his way toward them in the chair, finally seeing his mother. She had something in her hands, the fat part of a chair leg. She swung it like a bat into the man's face next to her. His head snapped back sending blood flying.

His dad ran for her and she spun with a scream, swinging the make-shift club. It slammed into the side of his head and she followed with another swing in the opposite direction, dropping him to his knees.

"Mooooom!" Mercy screamed behind him.

His mother spun to Mercy, her eyes wide and frantic. She let out a screech and ran forward, club raised over her head. She brought it down on the dude's face and the crunch of bone followed as she clobbered continuously, her face gripped in a mix of terror, and insane fury.

She let out another roar then turned. "No, no," his dad whimpered.

She answered him with scream after scream of pent up agony and pain, slamming the club down. Sade fought his way along the floor, working to his knees, watching her raise the club high above her head and slam it down as hard as she could, over and over and over, screaming and sobbing.

Sade's eyes zeroed in on where she aimed. He only knew it was his dad's face by the hair above the mangled bone, blood, and skin. One eyeball dangled, staring his way, unseeing.

His mother didn't stop. She didn't stop. She hammered him with that thing over and over, screaming, screaming until she was hoarse. Something snapped in Sade, something deep. Maybe that hidden place where the idea of having a father's love refused to ever fucking die. "Moooooom!" he sobbed, unable to take it. "Mooooom please! Stop mom, fucking stop!" he roared. "He's dead! Dad's dead, he's dead, he's fucking dead!" he gasped, his heart breaking inside him to see her so insane, to see his dad on the floor, dead, so dead. "Daaaaad! Dad, dad! You bastard! You fucking bastard! How could you do this," he sobbed. "Daaaaaaaaad!" Sade fell forward and hit the floor with his face.

The door behind him banged open. "Oh Jesus fucking Christ!"

Pain gripped Sade at hearing Bo's broken voice, bringing with it all his childhood longing and pain in to suffocate him. "You never said it," Sade cried, his chest exploding with the agony of what should have been. "You never said sorry! You never said you were sorry," he roared into the floor, sobs tearing through him. "You never said your sorrys! I tried, I tried so hard for you dad! You never said your sorrys! You never said your sorrys," he wept hoarsely.

His legs and arms were suddenly free and Mercy was there, sobbing, pulling at him. His body came alive and he latched on to her. "Mercy!" he wailed loudly, brokenly. "Mercy! I'm sorry, I'm sorry. I'll be good I'll be good, I'll find the good man, I'll find the good man, help me find him!"

Epilogue
Three Weeks Later

Sade stood next to Mercy on the beach. He turned to her as she looked up into his face before the minister. "You may kiss the bride."

Mercy gave him this huge smile with tears in her eyes as Sade took her face carefully between his hands and gave her the kiss he'd rehearsed in his mind. With the utmost gentleness, he kissed his bride, commanding his lips to be silk for her. To be gentleness for her. To adore, to impart the immaculate respect he had for her, for the love of his existence.

She grabbed his face suddenly and devoured him, stealing his breath and bringing a round of raucous applause around them and his mother's get him Mercy!

Sade smiled and wrapped his arms tightly around her, lifting her off the ground. "To the honeymoon suite?" he whispered in her ear.

She answered with a sultry giggle that set him on fire. But Sade had plans. Big plans he'd been practicing for several weeks. And he was ready.

"Good," he mumbled. "Because I have a wedding present there for you."

****

Mercy felt like she might throw up as she waited for Sade. Biting down on her lower lip, she smiled, looking around the bedroom, unseeing. He'd tied lavender satin over her eyes after she'd gotten into her honeymoon ensemble—a few scraps of sheer material that made his job very easy but sensually alluring and sexy. And white.

Sade had worn black. God, she loved him in black. That was just his color. And just what was this surprise of his? She hoped it was a dance. She'd been lusting to have him dance for her again.

Her stomach and heart jolted when the bathroom door opened. She bit her lip to keep from laughing in joy and excitement. God, the first thing she noticed was the way he smelled. What was that? Some kind of kinky oil?

"No touching," he whispered, next to her ear, making her jump a little. "Keep your hands on the bed unless I tell you otherwise."

Oh God. She'd been playing the therapist for the past month and to have him in command made her body go wild.

She tried to figure out what he was doing then it happened. That song came on. The one he'd first danced to for her. Oh God, she wanted to see. She felt the soft stroke of his fingers along her left arm and gasped at the slow silky glide all the way to her hand. He cradled her arm in both hands and lifted it, kissing softly all along before wrapping the wrist in something soft. He tied the material to something that held her arm up in the air before repeating the sensual steps to her right arm.

Mercy was panting with need when he was done, sitting on the bed with both arms stretched up and out at her sides. She felt like that woman on King Kong, waiting to be sacrificed to the beast. She knew that she'd been working with Sade, or Johnathon rather, teaching him how to love soft pain, but she couldn't deny it. She missed the rough, bad boy side of Sade.

He suddenly removed her blindfold and her breath caught in her chest at seeing him in only the black slacks and that collared tuxedo tie. But that wasn't all. He had on his body jewelry. Rings in both nipples and his navel. Her heart hammered as she followed a chain beneath the waistband of his slacks as his hips gyrated perfectly to the music. She jerked her head up and he locked gazes with her, his lips parted, those silver eyes burning with things that should have made her nervous. His tongue slowly licked over his full lower lip, showing the silver stud there before he bit his lower lip, drawing close enough that she could smell him, taste him if he asked.

His rippled abs in her face, she waited, breathless for his command, hoping he saw it in her gaze, the need to be commanded. "Angel," he whispered, stroking his finger under her chin. "Tonight I'm going to be the teacher. And you're going to learn some things."

She gasped in excitement, licking her lips. "I'm ready, Johnathon."

He shook his head and stroked his fingers along her jaw with one hand and her neck with the other, leaning so his mouth was just over hers. "Tonight... I'm Sade." His fingers turned hard on her jaw and he kissed her with that brutal passion she realized she'd missed so much. "Do you understand, Angel?"

Her gasp shot out. "Yes, yes," she nodded.

His other hand slowly tightened in her hair and he pulled gently, tilting her head back, his tongue licking firmly and slowly along her lips and inside them. "Yes what?"

"Sade!" she cried weakly.

"Very good, Angel." He gripped her hair tighter and angled her face so he could devour it, licking the entire side of her face with hungry sounds, biting at the skin, sucking every part of her, his hot breaths making her dizzy. He straightened finally and held her head to his torso. "Taste me, Angel. Start right here."

Her pussy throbbed at the sound of his zipper lowering. She licked and sucked with a hunger now.

"Are you ready to take my cock into your mouth, Angel?"

"Yes, Sade."

"You know how I want it, don't you? You know how Sade likes it."

She whimpered her answer, angling her head to get more of him, sucking at the silky muscles hard, letting him know she knew, she knew very well what he wanted and that she'd give it. "I want you, Sade."

"You missed me, baby, I know you did." He stroked her face with one hand and pulled her hair hard with the other. "I fucking missed you too." He slid his thumb in and out of her mouth, then it was there, the silky head of his cock. "Look at my bad cock, baby."

She stared at it, gasping for air. The jewelry in it looked painful and yet she knew that was a part of who he was. She looked up at him, biting her lip, letting him see it in her eyes. Acceptance. "You like my cock when it's bad, Angel?"

"I love everything about you," she gasped, needing him to remember that's what it was about. Them loving each other enough to be what it took, to be what they needed to be.

He moved the tip along her lips. "Just kiss it baby. My cock wants to be very bad tonight. Kiss it like a sweet Angel."

Mercy was dizzy with need, pulling at her restraints, so desperate for his bad cock.

"Lick the tip where I'm dripping for you. I need to see your tongue on me."

He kept tight hold of her hair, controlling everything. God, she missed his control. So much.

"Look at me, Angel," he whispered.

She looked up at him as he stroked his wet cock on her lips.

He removed the jewelry from his cock with a hiss. "Keep looking at me while I push my cock into that pretty mouth of yours."

Oh God, yes. He worked his delicious cock slowly into her mouth and she whimpered on the verge of orgasm. But it was that look in his silver eyes. Lethal. Lethal and something she might've once been scared of, but not now. Not in this moment.

His mouth opened and his breath shuddered out as he pushed his head against the back of her throat. "Fffffuck," he grit, his handsome face twisting in harsh desire. "You fucking know what to do, Angel," he gasped, slowly pulling out, his gaze burning into hers. "Set my world on fire."

Mercy gradually bit down on his extremely hard cock as he very slowly withdrew. Her heart hammered, knowing this was a crossroad for him, a breaking point. He held her gaze, hissing then clenching his eyes tight.

When he was at the end, he pulled out entirely, leaving them both gasping. He lowered his mouth to hers and kissed her. Softly. His fingers still bit in her hair, his other hand on her jaw, holding her still while he made passionate love to her tongue and lips, his grunts and growls low and eager. Promising that it was just the beginning.

"My Angel has been so very good, hasn't she?"

"Yes," she gasped in his mouth, giving herself entirely to his command, silently begging him to take it. Take her.

"What does my Angel want?"

He pulled off of her mouth, stroking her lips with a hungry thumb, waiting for her answer.

"I want Sade."

His breath shuddered out on her lips. "And I want my Angel," he gasped in return, devouring her mouth again, his fingers pulling hard in her hair, digging into her jaw. But his lips and tongue were still careful, exactly measured. The combination between reckless and restrained was dizzying, and yet had her breathless and begging for more of the same.

She understood in that second what he was doing, what he wanted. Her submission. No, her trust. "I'm yours, Sade. Take me. Take me so very hard."

"My cock wants to be so bad, Angel," he whispered on her mouth, as though warning her.

Butterflies zapped through her. "Do it. I want your bad cock so much."

"I know you do, Angel. I can feel it in your sweet body. How it begs for it. Longs for it. He removed his pants and stood naked except that delicious black collar and his body jewelry. He stepped back and looked at her on the bed, his chest heaving. "You're all mine, aren't you?" he whispered, as though needing to hear it out loud.

"Entirely. Always."

He held his balls tight while stroking his cock, gazing between her legs before raising it to soul mesh with hers. "Open wide for me Angel. So very fucking wide," he gasped, drawing closer. "I need to pound into you. Over and over. I need to hear you scream with it. Feel you break for me. Just for me."

Mercy whimpered, drawing her legs back for him.

He looked right and retrieved another lavender tie. She saw these were made of a stretchy material as he draped it around her knee then pulled it back and up. She watched him as he got another tie just like it and did the same to her other leg. When he was done, he inspected his work, gliding his fingers and hungry gaze along the underside of her thighs, stroking just next to where she throbbed with a savage need.

"Sade," she gasped, swallowing.

He knelt on the floor before the bed, closing his eyes and sliding his face along the same path his fingers had just been. He did it again, this time his mouth on her, his tongue sliding along the muscle then stopping right at the juncture of her thigh until she quivered and mewled for more.

"Angel," he whispered, looking up at her, nudging his nose against her open folds. "I'll give you one wish," he said, sliding his nose exactly up the center of her opening, stopping at her throbbing clit. "Tell me what you want."

"Sade," she gasped, undulating her hips. "Your tongue on it," she cried softly. "I want your tongue on my clit, please. Make me come like that, make me come so many times baby."

He growled and slid the broad side of his tongue slowly and firmly up her pussy, his thick dark brows drawn hard. "Sade," she gasped, squirming against the stud pressing into her clit.

His hands gripped her ass and his fingernails dug in as he lost control on her pussy, his mouth, lips, teeth and tongue a vicious storm on every part of her, pressing, sliding, plunging, biting, sucking, growling. "Oh God, Sade!" she shrieked as he made her come hard. He drew her clit into his mouth and sucked with a milking motion, not letting up as she shuddered and bucked on his mouth.

"Fucking beautiful, Angel," he whispered right on her pussy as he leisurely lapped softly at it while she recovered in breathless moans.

He stood before her and she looked up, feeling drunk. He leaned and kissed her, his lips and tongue a delicate touch, unlike his fingers that bit in her hair and on her jaw again. "My fucking Angel," he whispered in her mouth. "All mine. You taste your pussy?"

Shame filled her and his fingers bit harder in her hair as he licked along her mouth.

"Your pussy belongs on my lips."

"Yes," she gasped, wanting it there, liking it there.

"Just like my cock belongs on yours." He pushed his thumb into her mouth, licking at her lips while she sucked it with a hunger. "I have to fuck you now. I have to, Angel."

"Yes, God, please, yes."

He grabbed hold of her waist and looked down, his hands lowering to her hips.

"Yes, fuck me," she whimpered as he lifted her off the bed and placed her onto the head of his cock. "Fuck me so good Sade."

"Look at me Angel," he barely managed.

She stared at him, panting with need, locking her gaze onto his darkened one. "I have to see you when I break you," he shuddered.

Her mouth opened and her pussy clenched when his fingers dug into her hips, getting ready. His lips went tight with that lethal intent, then he jerked her so very hard and utterly onto his cock. She gave him what he wanted, that scream of surrender, of devastation and his mouth was there, hungry on hers as he ground and twirled his hips, eating up her every cry and breathless moan. "That's what I've missed, Angel. Your fucking beautiful screams in my mouth." He grunted and bucked hard, making her shriek. "That's what I need," he said with a long hiss, pulling her on and off of him, slamming deep on each stroke. "That," he strained, "that right there. Do it for me, Angel." He moved her faster on him, lowering his gaze. "Fuck, yes," he whispered, sounding awed. "My Angel's pussy all over my bad cock." He looked up at her, his mouth hard. "I'm going to fucking come like this but I'm not fucking done with you, Angel. Not fucking done!" The final words growled as he worked her relentlessly, throwing her into a hot, mindless oblivion where all she knew was his cock fucking her so good. So good like she'd needed.

He didn't hold back when his orgasm took him. His fingers latched hard on her face as he kissed her, his own roars mixing with her shrieks as his tongue and lips consumed everything.

The second he was done, he untied her legs. She watched breathless as he untied her arms next. When she was free, he pulled her into his embrace, hugging her tight to his heaving body, making her gasp in surprise. "I fucking love you," he said, laying her down on the bed. "I need to see you," he whispered, kneeling next to her as she lay there, still, and waiting.

"My Angel," he whispered, stroking soft fingers over her. "All mine. My wife." He looked at her, his gaze raw. "My wife," he gasped, shaking his head in disbelief.

She sat up and looked at him, caressing his face. "My husband," she said softly, smiling as tears came to her eyes. "You're the best thing that's ever happened to me, do you know that?" she asked, her voice trembling.

He pushed her down with his kiss, his hands soft as silk on her now. "I'm going to make love to you, Angel. Would you like that?"

"Yes," she gasped, tears pouring now. "Make love to me, Johnathon."

He shook his head, covering her body with his. "Sade wants to make love to you," he whispered, kissing her lips softly.

She gasped and ran her fingers in his hair. "Is this your gift baby? Oh my God, is this your gift?"

"You finally figured it out?"

"Oh my God," she gasped. "You… right! You were soft and hard, you were…"

"In control?" he nipped her neck now, nibbling. "I'm learning Angel." He sucked hard at her neck, making her cry out before licking over it, his fingers between her legs, silk on her clit. "Learning how to control. And do you know what?"

"What?" she gasped, when his finger plundered her core with a dominance while his lips remained sensual over hers.

"I learned that it fucking turns me on playing both sides."

"Oh God, me too," she whispered.

"Doc," he gasped, smiling on her lips. "I especially love when you take all control from me. This world you've given me, Angel. Is unlike anything I could have dreamed." The words trembled out and he gathered her in his embrace, burying his face in her neck. "More than I ever dreamed, Angel," he whispered heatedly.

"And I learned some things too," she whispered.

He kissed her softly, smiling on her lips. "Tell me what you learned, Angel."

"Well, I learned I really like being in control," she said, embarrassed even though she was sure he knew that.

"Thank you *God,* for that."

She laughed. "You like it?"

"You know I do. Jesus fuck, you're making me want it."

"Mmm, well, I did have my own wedding present in mind for you."

He pulled his head up, looking down at her. "What?" he finally asked making her laugh at his utter little boy curiosity.

"Well… I was thinking… how much fun it would be to… play the bad teacher."

"Bad?"

She felt his cock jerk and she moaned. "How about you tell me what you think that means… Sade."

"Fuck, you'd do this while I'm Sade?"

"I'd do it to you however you want. Or I want, in this case."

"Oh fuck," he whispered, kissing at her lips again, still being silky and sensual. "What kind of bad?"

She widened her eyes. "The really bad kind of bad!"

He erupted in snickers and put his head on her shoulder.

"What!" she said, offended.

"You? Bad? Come on, Angel," he whispered, nibbling at her neck.

She got up on her elbows now. "Ohhhh you want to test me? Have you even seen Grease? Where his sweet Sandy gets kick ass and dresses in black at the end? That's me!"

He howled in laughter and she smacked his shoulder. "Baby," he finally said, pushing her back down on the bed and kissing her. This time his kiss wasn't sweet, it was so very sexy.

Mercy got sexy back and grabbed his tongue-ring between her teeth. He groaned and froze in her mouth and she released it with a naughty look. "Put your cock jewelry back on Mr. Sade. I bet I can get creative."

"I'm yours to command, baby."

Mercy scrambled off the bed and pointed at him. "I'll need to tie you up."

"How do you want me?" he asked, laying on his side, staring at her tits.

She thought about that a moment then said, "On your back." She raised her brows at the sudden heat that darkened his gaze. "Legs spread. Arms together over your head." Yes, that was it, judging by the raw lust on his face.

She quickly ran to the bathroom and got dressed in her black leather cat woman looking out fit with the matching riding crop and thigh high leather boots. When she walked out, he lifted his head and stared at her. "Jesus, I've died and gone to heaven, thank you God," he whispered.

She had to smile, despite her intention to go in with her domme guns blazing. "You like it?" she couldn't help asking, doing a little spin for him only to trip a little. "Eeek," she muttered, shame burning her cheeks. The smile on his face was worth the humiliation. "You look like a man awestruck and in love," she said, walking toward him now.

"Oh I fucking am," he said, grinning. "Come make me sorry for laughing."

"I will," she assured, climbing on the bed and straddling him.

"Fuck, I'm tormented already, Angel," he whispered.

She smiled and lowered to his mouth. He held her face softly and let her have rule of the kiss until he moaned in growing appreciation. "I was thinking I'd make love to you," she whispered, feeling like she really needed to get his approval for that.

He smiled. "That might be too sadistic," he teased.

"I meeeean," she cooed, kissing his chin, "I was going to do you. The way you like? In sessions? Only with a… you know?"

He paused. "How about you surprise me," he whispered, stroking his hands over her butt, pressing her to his cock.

"Are you sure?"

"Very."

"Oookay," she warned lightly. "Be right back."

"Again?"

"I have to get it."

He didn't say another word and when she returned with her little member strapped on, he got up on his elbows and stared. She was waiting for him to laugh until his eyes met hers. The hunger in his gaze made her stomach flip. She made her way to the bed, ready to play. "Hands above your head," she ordered firmly.

He was ready too and raised them above his head, even opening his legs until his cock stood tall. Mercy used the same restraints on him, rather liking him in lavender. She'd stashed the tiny tube of recommended lubrication in her leather bra and pulled it out, getting ready.

"Fuck," he gasped, watching her. "Angel, you're really doing this?"

The heat in his gaze answered that one. "I'm going to make love to you," she whispered. "So very good. Do you want that?" And just like that, Mercy slipped into her role. A role she found she was very comfortable in it.

"Yes, Angel, I want that. So. Fucking. Bad," he croaked.

Her heart raced as she slowly crawled her way over his body until her face was above his and she was between his legs. She smiled at him, stroking his face and kissing him softly. "Who loves you, baby?"

"Mercy loves me," he whispered, stroking her ass now while pumping his cock against her stomach.

She reached between them and stroked her member along his ass softly, watching his brows crimp hard in need, his mouth open with sharp gasps.

"You ready for me, baby?"

"Fuck yes, Mercy. So ready for you."

She pushed the tip inside him and he strained out a deep groan. Mercy laid on him, kissing him with a sudden hunger, holding his jaw the way he did, gripping tight. "Feels good, baby?" She pushed in more.

"Oh fuck, Mercy," he strained.

The sound of his pleasure drove her and she pushed the cock all the way in, making him bow off the bed in harsh groans.

She pressed her body against his, then began pumping her hips, keeping penetration nice and deep. She'd never been so turned on than watching him thrash in ecstasy that way. "I love making love to you," she whispered, pumping faster and faster, her stomach masturbating his cock. "You look so good while I fuck you," she gasped, holding his arms and pressing them into the bed. "I want you to come just like this, Sade. Come while I make love to you."

The words set him off and he let out a roar. "Kiss me," she ordered, driving her tongue in his mouth. She reached under his shoulders and latched her hands, fucking him fast and hard, her body stroking against his cock.

"Mercy!" He roared again, thrashing beneath her and it was suddenly like riding a bull, his body solid muscle, bucking in return. Mercy kissed him as he came, her breaths lusty and hungry for every little drop he gave, every sound, every sweet breath from him. From her husband.

Mercy kissed him softly, smiling and snuggling in his neck. "Wasn't that fun?" she whispered.

"Fun?" he gasped. "That's… definitely a new fucking term for that."

"Why shouldn't it be fun?" She pulled out of him and he wrapped his legs around her, burying his face in her neck.

"I don't' know," he gasped.

At hearing the emotion straining the whispered words, she froze. "Everything is new, remember? I'm your Angel?" She stroked his back. "Nothing I do will ever hurt you. Because I love you so very much," she whispered.

He gripped her tighter and rocked with her, the force he held her with bringing tears to her eyes. Then he let out a sob, and she fought to embrace him back.

"All new," she hurried, stroking his head.

"All new, Angel? Always?"

"All of it, always," she assured, tears pouring now.

"I need to thank you," he wept. "I don't think I ever fucking did, not straight out."

"I know you're thankful," she whispered, fighting to hold her emotions back now.

"Thank you for loving me, Mercy," he whispered, kissing all over her face now. "Thank you for coming into my life baby. Coming into that fucking darkness," he gasped. "And taking my hand and walking me the fuck out," he cried. "Thank you Mercy. Thank you for loving me. Thank you for loving me."

Three More Weeks Later

Bo's laughter rang out over the multitude of voices at the table and the happy sound made Sade grin. "I'm a turkey? No, you're the fucking turkey here." He shoved Liberty with his shoulder who howled next to him.

"Language!" his mother scolded. "Watch it."

Sade eyed Mercy next to him, leaning over and whispering," I love you."

She turned and winked at him then leaned and kissed his cheek.

"How about somebody say the blessing before we eat like pigs," Sade's mom suggested. "I do think we have so so very much to be thankful for," she sang lightly. "Who will do the honors?"

Sade's heart skipped a beat and he raised his hand when nobody else did.

His mom gasped, putting her hand over her chest, tears coming to her eyes. "Really?"

He grinned and shook his head, standing at the table and glancing around. He was the last person qualified to say blessings but fuck, he felt like he really owed it. He lowered his head, hoping that was right. "Fuck—" he looked and caught his mom's glare, "I mean... heck."

Laughter erupted around the table and Sade nodded and grinned. "Alright, alright," he said. "I'm not good at this."

"Shhhhh!" Mercy ordered, "Before he changes his mind!" She looked up at him and grabbed his hand, smiling him on.

"Okay," he began again. "Uh… I'd like to thank God… for my family. For um.. giving me… everything I could ever want," he said quietly, pushing back the sudden rush of emotions. He cleared his throat. "Thank you for my beautiful mother." He winked at her and looked at Bo. "My brother." Bo winked at him, making his smile. "And thank you for his future wife, Liberty." Sade laughed at the eruption of racket that brought. "Soon," Sade warned, smiling at the love birds. "And… I'd like to thank God for my new dad." He looked at Kane, nodding. "You were worth the wait."

At seeing tears come to Kane's eyes, Sade quickly looked down, unable to take seeing him cry. "And most of all," he hurried while he still could. "I'd like to thank God for my beautiful wife, Mercy." Despite his effort to not get emotional, her name gushed out of his fucking mouth and she squeezed his hand. "Thank you God," he whispered. "Thank you for my angel of mercy. Amen."

He sat and everybody said their loud, happy amens and the clatter of dishes ensued.

"And thank you for miracles," Mercy yelled over the noise, looking all around. "Especially the one growing inside me."

Everything went suddenly quiet at the table with all eyes on Mercy, especially Sade's.

"Yeah," she gasped, tears pouring down her face, hugging Sade's neck. "Especially the one inside me," she whispered in his ear. "Daddy."

THE GREAT, AWESOME, HAPPY END!

THE LUCIAN BANE BOOM TEAM:

Alicia Reitz Huckleby
Amalina Basri
Amanda Craig
Amanda Reiter
Amy N Eric Abendroth
Andrea Logan
Angela Hester
Angela Peters
Ann-Marie Morency
Antonella Ciarico
April Alvey
Babel Td
Barb McCarty
Barbara Danks
Barbara McCarty
Becky Rios
Booklover Joy
Brandi Reeves-Pearson
Briar Rose Elliot
Cahty Schisel Knuth
CarlaJane Christian
Carmen Ferrer-Torres
Carol Ann Sonnet-McCall
Carolina Mamos
Catherine Byerly Coffman
Cathy Passwaters Brown
Chasiti Forster
Chrissy McMillan
Christi Lynne
Christina Princess Tatt
Christine VanBruggen
Clare Roden

CW Nightly
Cynthia Loki Graves
Danielle Wittenberg Fulton
Dawn Murphey
Debbe Teresinski
Deborah Bean
Debra Novak Frazier
Des Yearning
Donna McManus
Dorene Selg
Doris Hires Collins
Dorisa Lynne Homes Curry
Edith Dubielak
Elaine Kelly
Elena Cruz
Ellie Masters
Fran Brisland
Fran Jones
Frida Friberg Pederson
Geneva Vaughn
Genoveva Hill
Gina Terribile Enge
Hazel Elliot
Heather Holland
Heather Young
Gerianne Slavinsky
Hilary Suppes
Holli Gronas Annamaia Folkerts
Hope Elser
Jack B. Daniel
Jackie Lemay
Jami Tamblyn
Jamie Buchanan
Jan Kinder
Jan Wade
Janna Crowley
Jellie Gillispie

Jen O'Brien
Jennifer Conken Capizola
Jennifer White
Jenny McKinney Shepherd
Jessica Gallagher
Jessie Baldwin
Jessie Mora Llewellyn
Joey Ross
Julie Hanna Kolt
Karen Shortridge
Katherine DiLauro
Keanna Porter
Kee Ke Martin
Kelly Mallett
Kim Poe
Kim Urichuck
Kimmy Johnson
Komal Chandwani
Kristi Widner Collins
Kristin Hoard
LaGina Keisha Hagerman Reese
Lauren Danielle
Lauretta Gomes
Laurie Johnson
Leslie Twitchell
Lianne Heaps
Lilli Collier
Linda Baldwin Martin
Linda Kidwell
Linda Romer-Como
Lisa Campbell Dean
Lisa Dillon
Lisa James-Loyd
Lissette De La Hoz
Liz Stephenson
LJ Knox
Lori Garside

Lorraine Campbell Darcy
Louisa Gray
Louise "Loppy Lou" Bailey
Margarita Hyromania VegaPrice
Maria Ria Alexander
Maria S. Brownfield
Martha Rodriquez
Mary Forster
MiChelle Brown Fortress
Michelle Louise
Misty Chapman
Nan Lindsey
Nanci LopezBryan
Nanette Magers Stewart
Natasha Weir
Nathalie Pinette
Nichole Vincent
Nikki Moses Brant
Nina Stevenson
Pamela Chase Carlson
Pamela Shorkey
Patti Cortez-Bell
QuiMo Monica
Rebecca Kummel
Renee Marquis
Renee Mills Henson
Rhiannon King
Robin Cornelius
Ronda Bearden
Ruby Hinkleberry
Samantha Ann Marie Achaia
Sara Prevendoski
Sarah McKenna Ferguson
Sheila C.Lawrence
Stacy Treadway West
Stella Martin
Suzanne Gangarosa

Tammy Sammervold
Tammy Sngleton Buch
Tamra Simons
Teresa Jorgensen Winter
Teresa Travnichek
Terrie Meerschaert
Tina Eastridge Henry
Tina McClay
Valerie Spearman
Veronica LaRoche
Vicky Darnold
Wendy James Kelley
Wendy Tucker Wignall
Yulando Bolton
Yvette Grines
Yvette Mathews-Lowe
Zarah Chan

Printed in Poland
by Amazon Fulfillment
Poland Sp. z o.o., Wrocław